Dating Santa's Son

Nicole A. Mullaney

Published by Pen It Publications in the U.S.A.
713-526-3989
www.penitpublications.com

ISBN: 978-1-63984-456-2
Edited by Ashlee Wyzard
Illustration by Korey Woods
Cover design by Donna Cook

DEDICATION

To my good friend, Candy Cain. Thank you for asking me where to begin. Without, I don't know if I ever would have written this story.

OTHER BOOKS BY NICOLE MULLANEY

Ivy & Mistletoe
Deck the Heart
The Maltese Holiday
Magic in Mount Holly
Joy & Hope by Ethan Dulane
Ethan Dulane is a character created by Candy
Cain & Nicole Mullaney for Joy & Hope

Watch the Books You've Read
Movies by Writer/Director Candy Cain
Ivy & Mistletoe
The Maltese Holiday
Deck the Heart
Joy & Hope
Magic in Mount Holly

CONTENTS

CHAPTER 1
Jack

Tapping my phone screen, I see a text from my mom glaring up at me. "How was your date last night?" I grimace, knowing I don't want to have this conversation with anyone, especially not my mother! She doesn't understand why I haven't found someone to settle down with, but she knows it's not easy, especially for me. She tends to ignore the obvious when it comes to my dating life, ready for me to move on to the next part of my life.

"She was nice, but she's not for me," I text back, hoping that's enough of an answer. Frustrated, I drop my phone on my desk, not waiting for her response, which is bound to be more like an interrogation. I run my hand over my face, scraping over my dark stubble as I look out the window of my New York City office, my blue eyes taking in the view of rooftops and skyscrapers like the one I'm standing in.

Sometimes I can't help but wonder why I couldn't be one of the millions of people in this city with a normal life. Honestly, I don't really know what normal would look like, but my life isn't even in the same universe. I know I shouldn't complain when so many people out there really have it tough. My heart truly goes out to them, and I will always do what I can to help those in need, but sometimes being happy with your life can be difficult, even for someone like me who seems to have it all. But I know better than anyone that perceptions are not necessarily based on reality.

I drop my hands against the windowsill, thinking about my disaster of a date last night. She was beautiful with red hair, light gray eyes, and a petite package at only five feet two. She's smart and has a successful business. Walking in, I thought she was exactly what I have been looking for, but when I asked her about what she did for the holidays, she admitted she wasn't a big fan of Christmas. She thinks it's all just a big hoax to get people to spend money. Believing in Christmas is a must for me. I couldn't get out of there fast enough when she added if she didn't have to work over the holidays, she would do everything she could to escape the chaos of Christmas, hopefully by going to a tropical island for a winter vacation. That kind of escape for Christmas is definitely not an option for me or for my future Mrs. Claus. Maybe for the New Year, but that's not the point.

With a heavy sigh, I turn around as the click of heels echoes against the hardwood floors, stopping just outside my door. I sit back down, leaning back in my black leather desk chair as my assistant Allie walks into my office, her long, blonde hair tied up in a neat ponytail with a red ribbon. She's wearing a black pantsuit paired with red high-heeled shoes. She has a notepad in her hand and pulls a pencil out from behind her ear as she steps up to my large cherry desk with a bright smile. "Good morning, Allie," I murmur with a sigh.

"Good morning, Jack!" she exclaims with too much cheer for me this morning.

"Why couldn't I be a normal businessman who goes home at the end of a long day to his wife? A wife with a normal job as a teacher, or a doctor, or maybe even a police officer?" I complain. It's the same complaint Allie has heard from me for the past two years. Sometimes I wonder how she keeps a smile on her face hearing me grumble so much lately. "I never meet anyone I can bring home to meet my family. I take a woman out a couple of times, and then it's time to break it off with my typical, 'It's not you, it's me' speech, afraid to take it any further," I mumble sarcastically. "I'm sick of dating women who aren't right for me, knowing it can never go anywhere. I want to find someone I will be able to spend my life with. I'm ready!"

She gives me a look filled with empathy, insisting, "You just haven't found the right woman yet. You need someone who will not only mesh with you and your life, but someone you know you can trust to bring them home to your parents as well as live the legacy by your side," she reminds me. "Meeting that special someone is not an easy task for anyone, especially not you."

"I know. That's the problem, Allie! At this rate, when it's time to take over the family business for my dad, I'll be the first single Santa Claus in history!" I groan in frustration as I lean forward, dropping my hands heavily on my desk with a thud.

"A world without a Mrs. Claus?" Allie questions doubtfully, her eyes going wide.

I huff a humorless laugh and shake my head in defeat. "You may think I'm exaggerating or being dramatic, but at this rate, that's the road I'm headed down. I don't see how it can work with myself and a normal woman. And without a family to pass the family business onto as well as all our traditions, Christmas would never be the same. It would be a complete travesty to children and families everywhere."

She sighs and rolls her eyes at my dramatics and jokes, "You're starting to sound more and more like a teenage girl."

I groan again and cross my arms over my chest in exasperation, trying to get her to understand the seriousness of my complaint. "If I don't find someone for me, what am I supposed to do short of giving up my legacy?" I prompt seriously, arching my eyebrows in challenge.

Her mouth drops open, and her eyes widen in shock. "That can't happen, Jack. The business would fall back to your uncle. You know as well as I do that he would ruin Christmas!" Allie exclaims with obvious duress as she begins frantically pacing the room.

I raise my eyebrows and sardonically state, "Obviously. He's too selfish to remember the people he doesn't want to impress."

"And his family..." she mutters, shaking her head. She pinches her lips tightly together in annoyance before taking a deep breath, her nostrils flaring slightly as she exhales. "We have to do something to find you a good match," she mumbles under her breath. Then, her eyes suddenly widen as she blurts out, "That's it! What about one of those online dating sites or dating apps?"

My head falls back as I burst out laughing. "And what would I put on my profile? I plan on taking over the family business based at the North Pole. I work for my father, Santa Claus. I travel the world once a year on Christmas Eve." I ponder the ridiculousness of the situation. "Or maybe I should put, must believe in Christmas magic?" I shake my head in denial. "Wait, how about I say I believe I'm going to be the first Santa Claus named Jack? That will bring them in droves." I chuckle, amused. "If I put anything real on there, everyone will think I'm crazy!"

"Dedicating your life to help make Christmas special for kids and families everywhere is a little bit crazy." She arches her eyebrows, daring me to deny it. I chuckle and shake my head, unable to refute. She squares her shoulders, letting me know there's no point in doing anything but waiting for what she wants to say to me. "Your name is Nicholas, just like your father. Your middle name is Jack," she adds with a shrug as if I don't know my own name.

"I'm well aware. And?" I prod, dragging out the word as I raise my eyebrows, looking at her like she's lost her mind.

She shrugs in response. "Your parents thought it was funny, and so do I," she smirks. "You know, Baby Christmas, Jack Frost, and of course with how much your dad loves golf, he mentioned the famous golfer, Jack Nicklaus, to your mom. That's when they agreed, you would be Nicholas Jack," she chirps, her eyes alight with amusement.

"Allie," I groan, glaring at her in warning.

She continues her explanation as if I've never heard it before. "Besides, it was a lot less confusing to call you Jack at home. Anytime anyone hears any form of Nicholas, their heads turn, looking for your dad, unless he is the one saying it."

"I know," I grumble.

With a wave of her hand, she insists, "You shouldn't be worried about all of that anyway. You're a great catch! You're handsome and funny when you're not being cynical. You're kind, generous, and successful. What single woman wouldn't want to date you?" She takes my silence as an invitation to continue. "You run the East Coast Toys and Electronics division like no one I've ever seen either. You're going to be an amazing Santa someday, Jack!" she encourages with enthusiasm like no one else.

"I'm only the best you've seen on the east coast because you didn't work on this coast until you worked for me."

She shakes her head in denial and swiftly waves off my comment. Giving me a pointed look, she reminds me, "I've worked with your family for over a hundred years. I know what I'm talking about. Plus, I've seen all the worldwide reports with the various divisions around the world. You are fantastic at your job."

Heaving a sigh, I run my hand through my dark brown hair before I drop my hands onto my desk. "Thanks, Allie. I appreciate your vote of confidence, but it doesn't matter. I'm done talking about this," I tell her with a shake of my head. "Speaking of jobs, I need to get back to mine."

"But..." she attempts.

Immediately, I interrupt, insisting, "No more. It's not happening. There is no way I'm putting a profile on any dating app or site."

She winces and nods in defeat, relenting, "Okay, fine." Then she straightens her shoulders and mumbles inaudibly, "But you never said anything about me doing it for you, or maybe..."

"What was that?" My eyes narrow on her, assessing that familiar look. I wish I could read her mind because the look on her face tells me she's up to something, and I want to know what it is.

"Nothing," she declares innocently, giving me a sweet smile.

"I mean it, Allie," I warn, needing her to know there's no wiggle room. "I just needed to complain about my dating life for a few minutes. I'll figure it out sooner or later." I grimace, not believing my own statement.

She grins wider and nods emphatically, agreeing too easily for my liking. "Okay, I understand."

Slowly, I huff out a breath as my stomach twists, feeling slightly uneasy with her complete turn around. Then I sit up straight and attempt to focus on the work on my desk . "If I want to keep being good at my job, I need to get back to work, and so do you," I remind her, nodding toward the door.

"Got it." She grins in response, spinning on her heel and striding for the door.

"Wait, Allie, what does my schedule look like this morning?" I ask warily.

Halting in the doorway, she glances at me over her shoulder. "You have a meeting at ten with the Southeast shipping department," she reminds me. Without giving me a chance to respond, she swiftly exits, disappearing around the corner.

I breathe a sigh of relief, knowing I can forget about dating for now and put all my energy into our business, where I'm confident I will thrive. I easily get lost in the new toy safety reports in preparation for my morning meeting.

A chime alerts me to a new message, pulling my attention. I click on my mail, spotting a message from Allie sitting at the top with my name as the subject. I quickly open it, assuming it's something I need for the upcoming meeting, but what I see glares back at me as if it's a neon sign in a neighborhood I don't want to be in. My jaw drops open, and my eyes widen in shock as I stare at my computer screen. "This has to be a joke," I mumble under my breath. I blink hard and open my eyes slowly, hoping to see something different, but nothing changes. I'm staring at my own dark brown hair and blue-gray eyes. I grit my teeth and glance at the dating website profile again.

Jack C – 28

I love hiking, creating new and familiar things, storytelling, and great food, especially a good dessert, although it's much better when I'm not the one making it. I'm wonderful with kids, and animals and I have a great sense of humor. I enjoy traveling to places all over the world and would love someone to share the sites with, but I also always look forward to coming home. I love what I do and work hard as CEO of a toy and tech company, working alongside other divisions all around the world. I'm also active in the communities I work in, enjoying getting to know people and hearing their stories.

I'm looking for someone who enjoys meeting new people and trying new things but who's also ready to settle down. I want a woman who loves Christmas and family as much as I do, as well as someone who wants a family of her own. I want love, a partner, and a best friend, not just a date, and if you're a good cook, that's a bonus for both of us.

I run my hand over my face in frustration. Taking a deep breath, I exhale slowly, trying to calm myself down before I open my mouth. "Allie," I call without using the intercom.

She pops her head in my door with a bright smile. "Yes, Jack?"

I grimace and stand as I cross my arms over my chest. "You put me on a dating website," I declare the obvious.

"Yes," she agrees, nodding in confirmation as she steps into my office. "It only took me a few minutes," she states proudly. "You're welcome."

"I didn't say thank you." I grit my teeth and remind her, "I said no dating websites."

She shakes her head in denial. "No. Actually, you didn't. You said," she pauses to make air quotes and imitate the sound of my voice, "There is no way I'm putting a profile on any dating app or site." She stops, dropping her hands as she smiles smugly at me.

I close my eyes and exhale slowly, trying to get my annoyance under control, so I don't take it out on her, or anyone else for that matter. Slowly, I open my eyes and stare at her intently. "Allie, you know me. You know, when I said that, I meant I didn't want *anyone* putting me on a dating app or site."

She tilts her head to the side and gives me a crooked smile. "No, you just wanted me to think that's what you wanted."

"Allie," I whisper in irritation as I shake my head, reminding myself she's family. "As your boss, you have to delete my profile," I insist, figuring that's the only way she'll listen.

"Actually, no, I don't." She shrugs. "I just hung up with your mom a few minutes ago, and she agrees with me. You need to start dating for real."

My spine straightens at the mention of my mom. "What do you mean my mom agrees with you?"

"After you and I talked, and you said you were done talking about it, I called her," she informs me. I drop my head into my hands, knowing how the rest of this conversation is going to play out and wondering if I can do anything to stop it. "You should've heard what she wanted me to put on your profile," she pauses, giggling, "but that would just make you sound desperate."

"What?" My eyes widen in disbelief.

She waves her hands, dismissing my anxiety as if it's no big deal. "Anyway, she agreed with me, so here's the plan."

I laugh humorlessly and shake my head. "The plan," I grumble, my sarcasm thick on my tongue as I drop down into my chair.

She nods. "Yes, I can do all the work for you. First, I can go through the profiles and narrow down the field for you, and then I will set up the dates for you. After all, I am the one with your schedule. The only thing you will have to do is show up where and when I tell you," she proclaims happily, clapping her hands in excitement.

"I don't want to be set up," I remind her again, knowing I have already lost.

She rolls her eyes, refusing to listen. "Yes, you do. All you ever do is complain about your dates, and these are women you find and ask out. You're obviously terrible at judging first impressions. This way, I can sort through potential dates before you go on them. I can find a woman for you that's trustworthy, and you can go on a date to see if you click."

"I don't know, Allie," I hesitate, trying to come up with a way out of this.

"Please! If you don't let me do it, your mother may set you up with an arranged marriage," she threatens. "Then, who knows what kind of woman you'll end up marrying."

I groan, knowing that's a possibility with my mother. There's no way she would let the family business fall to my uncle or his family. I drop my head back against my chair and stare at the ceiling as I sigh in defeat. Swallowing hard, I gulp down the lump in my throat and ask, without looking at her, "Do you promise you'll do all the work?"

She shrieks in excitement, jumping up and down. "Yes! Yes, I promise!" I listen to the sound of her walking away.

Silence follows without my door clicking shut. I lift my head and meet Allie's satisfied gaze as she stands in the doorway. "Yes, Allie?" I prompt, wondering what else she could have to say.

"I'll let you know when I have your first date set up," she chirps. I moan in frustration. "Don't worry, Jack, you won't regret this!"

"I already do," I mumble under my breath.

CHAPTER 2
Jessica

I step out of my car onto the blacktop driveway of my childhood home, ignoring the chill in the air. Pausing, I glance up at the yellow ranch covered with a dark green roof and matching shutters, grateful I no longer feel the pain of loss every day when I walk in the door. I stride up the walkway, between the grassy areas barely covered with snow, to the large oak front door and walk inside, pushing the door closed behind me. Then, I hang my purse and coat on the wall hooks behind the door, where I finally exhale, letting my whole body relax after a long day working at the bakery.

Taking a deep breath, I trudge through our living room toward our blue and white country-style kitchen to find the top of my sister Holly's head tilted down toward the white and gray granite countertop. As I step closer, I realize she's sitting on one of the stools, eating a bowl of cereal. "Hi, Holly," I greet her. "How was school today?"

She flips her straight light brown hair back as she glances up at me. Holding her pointer finger up, she gestures for me to wait as she finishes chewing before she finally answers, "Hey, Jess. School was the same as always. How about you? How was work? Did you bring me home anything good to eat today?" she smirks, wiggling her eyebrows.

I smile fondly over at her and chuckle. "Yes, I did." I hold up the loaf of bread in my hands. "It's the last day we're making pumpkin bread."

"Yum!" She licks her lips and reaches for the loaf.

Giving her a look in warning, I quickly pull it away before she has a chance to wrap her fingers around it. "Let's save it for breakfast."

She narrows her eyes at me but quickly gives in with a heavy sigh. "Fine," she grumbles as she drops her hand back to the counter.

"Sometimes I wonder if you're really happy to see me when I come home or if you just want to know what I brought home for you to eat," I tease.

"Can't it be both?" she jokes innocently, shrugging, the corners of her lips tugging up in amusement.

I laugh and shake my head. Changing the subject, I prompt, "Do you have a lot of homework tonight?"

"It's Friday," she reminds me, arching her eyebrows. "I'm going over to Jen's to help her get ready for her Christmas party tomorrow night." I grimace. "You forgot, didn't you?" she accuses.

"I didn't forget," I claim, avoiding her gaze. But I can't look her in the eye when I'm not exactly telling the truth. My transparent green eyes will tell you anything you want to know, just like hers.

She chuckles and shakes her head. "Sure, you didn't. So, what are you doing this weekend?"

"I'm going to clean up around the house and maybe try out a new recipe for the bakery. I have to go in for a few hours tomorrow morning, but I'm not working the whole day," I tell her.

"Ugh," she groans in annoyance. "That's not what you're doing," she states with a disapproving gaze.

"I thought I was the big sister?" I tease, arching my eyebrows.

Holly walks over to the sink, shaking her head as she rinses her dishes and puts them in the white dishwasher, matching the rest of the appliances. Then she spins back around to face me with her arms crossed over her chest as she leans her hip against the counter. "Jess, I'm serious. You're always doing so much for me or the house or the bakery, which means you're always doing something for me and never for yourself," she claims.

"I love working at the bakery, and you're my sister," I state the obvious. "I want to do things for you."

Heaving a sigh, she elaborates, "Yeah, and I appreciate that, but after mom and dad died, you stopped doing *anything* for yourself. You don't even date anymore," she reminds me, making me wince. "What are you going to do when I go away to college in a few years, and you're here by yourself? Spend all your time off watching the romance movie channel and reading romance novels?"

I shake my head in denial. "No, but I like romance books and movies."

"That's not the point," Holly grumbles, narrowing her eyes.

"Holly, I don't need to date. I'm just fine on my own."

She grimaces and stares at me, mumbling sarcastically, "Yeah, *fine.*" I glare at her, but she ignores me and continues to push me. "Just because you're fine on your own doesn't mean you shouldn't find someone you enjoy spending time with. I thought you were supposed to be a romantic."

"Just because I like romance?"

She shrugs and rolls her eyes. Then, her eyes suddenly widen as if she just had a fantastic idea pop into her head, making me weary. "What about a dating website?" she proposes watching me closely.

I laugh humorlessly and shake my head, declaring, "No, definitely not."

"Come on, Jess," she pleads, slapping her hands against the counter for emphasis. "How are you supposed to meet anyone if you're either at the bakery, at home, or taking me somewhere? A dating website is perfect for someone like you," she encourages, a smile tugging at her lips.

I shake my head in refusal and narrow my eyes. "Someone like me? What do you mean by that, Holly?"

Groaning in frustration, she rolls her eyes and ignores my question. "There's nothing wrong with dating sites. Lots of people use them and find the person of their dreams. Why can't that be you?" she challenges.

"Sure." I laugh again, knowing I would never be that fortunate.

"Please, Jess? Do it for me?" she whines, continuing to beg. "It can be my Christmas present. You don't even have to buy me anything this year!" she exclaims, becoming more animated as she continues talking. "I could help you with your profile and everything."

Hearing the growing determination in her voice makes me curious. "Why is this so important to you?"

Holly steps toward me and takes my right hand in hers. "Like I said, Jess, you always do so much for me. You have done even more since mom and dad died. You've completely put your life and your dreams on hold to make sure I 'heal and thrive,'" she says, holding up her fingers with her free hand like air quotes causing me to smile.

"And look at you now," I state, gesturing toward her with pride in my voice.

She narrows her eyes at me, telling me to stop interrupting. I pinch my lips tightly together as she continues. "You stayed here instead of moving away. You're working at the local bakery instead of building your own bakery or a business like it with your own recipes. You barely see your friends anymore, and you completely stopped dating. When was the last time you went on a date?" she challenges, not expecting an answer.

"It's my turn to help you heal and thrive, as you like to say. I'm doing great because of you. I honestly don't know what I would've done if you hadn't done all of that for me, but I am doing great, Jess," she emphasizes, reaching for my hand. "I promise it's okay to let me just be your sister. And you need to move on with your life and do something for yourself," she insists, giving my hand a light squeeze.

I attempt to gulp down the growing lump in my throat, overwhelmed with love for my little sister. I sniffle and wipe the tears off my cheeks with my free hand. "When did you grow up so much and get so smart?" She smiles softly and shrugs. "How did you turn out so great?" I ask reverently.

Her smile broadens, and she sarcastically questions, "Now you're fishing for compliments?" We both chuckle, knowing that's the last thing I'm looking for. Then, she dramatically emphasizes, "I just told you how, *you*." We both burst out laughing.

As we get our laughter under control, I pull my sister into my arms, and she wraps her arms around my waist, hugging me back. "I'm so proud of you, Holly. Mom and dad would be too," I whisper, my voice choked with emotion. "I love you so much."

Reluctantly, I let go as she releases me and whispers, "I love you too, Jess." She steps back and grins mischievously. "If you really love me, though, you'd let me put you on a dating website and find you a date." I groan in response. "What are a couple of dates going to hurt?" she prods, assessing my reaction. She tries to hide her smirk behind her hand, knowing I would do anything for her, and I'm about to give in.

I grimace and reluctantly agree. "I can't believe I'm going to do this, but fine!"

"Yay!" she shrieks as she jumps up and down in excitement. "This is going to be so much fun!" she declares. I laugh, her exuberance already feeling contagious. "Go shower, do your hair and makeup and change into a cocktail dress that looks fabulous on you," she instructs.

"What?" I question laughing and shaking my head. "I'm not going on a date right now."

Dramatically rolling her eyes again, she reminds me, "I know, but we need to put a decent picture on your profile. I don't have a normal picture of you without me in it since..." she trails off, both of us knowing how that sentence ends.

I flinch and nod in agreement. "Okay."

"Put on your green dress," she advises, grinning. "You look great in green. It really brightens your eyes." Sighing in disbelief, I begin trudging down the hallway to clean myself up. "I'm going to work on your profile while you get ready. I'll call Jen and let her know I'm going to be late," she yells down the hall before I reach the bathroom.

I continue down the hall, knowing I'm not going to change her mind at this point. "It will be fine," I mumble to myself unconvincingly.

As I walk into our gray and white tiled bathroom, I look in the mirror. I heave a sigh at the sight of the mess looking back at me. My sandy blonde hair is sticking out of my ponytail in all directions from working all day. I have flour and something red and sticky in my hair. My clothes are covered in flour, sugar, and something else I'm not quite sure of. I even have a streak of chocolate frosting near my ear. "I'm a complete disaster," I complain to my reflection. Groaning, I immediately get to work on looking and feeling a little more like a woman.

It doesn't take me long before I'm out of the shower, and my hair is dried straight and curled under. I quickly apply a small amount of makeup, maintaining natural tones. The whole process only makes me realize I haven't done this since I went to Holly's spring concert to listen to her play the flute. As for an actual date...my thoughts trail off, coming up empty. "Wow," I mumble to myself. It really has been a long time.

I stride to my closet and search for my emerald green dress. As I look it over, I smile, gently tugging it off its hanger and slipping it over my head. Walking across my room, I stand in front of the full-length mirror hanging on the outside of my closet door to assess myself and audibly gasp in shock. I haven't looked this human in a long time. The dress is sleeveless, folding like a scarf at the top, angling down my chest, and crossing over. It narrows at the waist and falls to just above my knees, hanging just a little loose around my curves.

"Wow," Holly's voice rings out from behind me.

I meet her eyes in the mirror, feeling slightly self-conscious. "Do I look okay?"

"You look amazing!" She grins in admiration as she looks me over from head to toe.

I feel myself blush at her compliment and whisper, "Thank you." Swiftly clearing my throat, I spin on my heel, facing her. "Where should we take the picture?" I ask nervously as I repeatedly smooth down my dress with my hands.

"How about by the fireplace in the living room?" Holly suggests.

Nodding, I follow her down the hall and stand in front of the brick fireplace. I turn toward her and take a deep breath, attempting to relax while she takes a couple of pictures of me with her phone. Holly pauses and glances at her screen. She scrunches up her face in distaste, making me uneasy. "What's wrong?"

"Nothing's wrong. Loosen up, Jess, these aren't mug shots," she warns. I laugh, and she quickly snaps a couple more pictures with her phone. "Perfect," she mumbles, smiling in satisfaction at her screen. "That should be the final touch. I created your profile while you were in the shower."

"You're done?" She nods her head as she continues typing on her phone. "Can I go change out of this dress then?" I ask.

Holly's head snaps up. "No! You look too good to let it go to waste. I'm going to go change, and we are treating ourselves to dinner tonight!"

"What about Jen?" I ask in amusement.

Holly shrugs. "I'll go to her house tomorrow morning. She doesn't really need me tonight. We're just adding to her Christmas decorations. She already bought all the food, plates, and stuff for the party anyway."

"Are you sure? We don't have to go out for dinner. I don't want you to miss out on anything," I tell her sincerely. It's one of my biggest worries since we lost mom and dad. I'm always afraid of holding her back.

She smiles. "I won't be. The party is tomorrow, and besides, Jen won't care," she insists with a wave of her hand. "I don't remember the last time we got dressed up and went out to dinner together. It will be fun!" She shrugs. "Besides, we can look through some of the men on the website while we eat. I want to see if I can find someone I like for you."

"I didn't say you could pick out my dates." I laugh.

"Sure, you did," she grins wickedly. "Besides, if I wait until you pick out your dates, you may never go." I shake my head but drop the subject, knowing she's right. I am doing this for her, after all, and she would never pick someone I won't get along with, at least, I hope not. After all, she knows me better than anyone. "Give me a few minutes to change so I can look half as good as you."

"You always look good."

"Now you sound exactly like mom." I laugh as she takes off toward her bedroom. When she reaches her bedroom door, she turns back toward me and sweetly asks, "Can I drive?"

My nerves twist my stomach into knots as I grumble, "I can't believe you have your learner's permit."

She laughs giddily and begs, "Please?"

"Ugh, fine," I groan, reluctantly agreeing, "I can't believe I'm agreeing to this, but I guess you have to practice."

"Yes!" she yells and fist pumps the air making me laugh.

"What do I get myself into with her?" I mumble under my breath.

"Oh, and I just sent you your profile for you to look at it, but I already have it uploaded, so there's no going back now."

"Oh, boy," I mumble under my breath as I make my way to the couch and pull out my phone. I think I need to sit for this. Taking a deep breath, I open her message and begin reading.

Jessica M – 26

I'm passionate about baking, creating new recipes as well as returning to the familiar ones I have repeatedly tried and adored. Making treats for others to enjoy brings a smile to my face. Baking is not only something I like to do for fun, but I also do it for a living. I work hard, but I love what I do. I'm wonderful with kids of all ages and family is extremely important to me. I love watching movies and reading books, especially romance. I love meeting new people, and I enjoy being involved in my community. Although I haven't had the opportunity to travel much, I would love the chance to someday and be able to try different treats from around the world in their homeland.

I'm looking for someone who enjoys spending time with people and trying new things but who's also ready to settle down and focus on a family; mine, his, and ours. I need a man who is good with kids and wants to have a family of his own. I want a man who loves family and the holidays, especially Christmas, as much as I do. I want to find love, a partner, and a best friend.

I laugh out loud, amused that she put loving Christmas as a priority. She sounds like mom and dad. I grin, the thought squeezing my heart.

CHAPTER 3
Jack

"Here's your date schedule for the weekend," Allie announces as she strides into my office without knocking.

I look up at her from behind my computer with my mouth hanging open. "Excuse me, my what?" I question, sure I misheard her.

"Your date schedule," she repeats slowly.

"I don't need a whole schedule!" I insist, shaking my head. "And what do you mean for the weekend? You don't mean this weekend, do you?"

"Of course, I mean this weekend," she declares dismissively. She nods in satisfaction, causing me to groan.

"I just agreed to this," I complain, believing I had more time.

"You know I work fast," she reminds me, standing up a little straighter. She steps up to my desk and hands me a small stack of papers with the schedule she mentioned taunting me on the very top of the pile.

I grimace, glaring at the schedule, and flip through the rest of the papers, noticing a picture and profile on each one of the dates she set me up with, except one. "What is all this?" I grumble, already exhausted, just thinking about what she has in store for me.

She steps beside me and cheerfully explains, "Each woman I set up a date with has something that you're looking for." She pulls out the first picture of a beautiful woman with auburn red hair and green eyes, informing me, "You have a date with Josie tonight. She's a family girl and absolutely loves Christmas. You're going to meet her for drinks at Evan's near Rockefeller Center. After that, you could go see the Christmas tree and go to dinner if you guys hit it off."

"And if we don't?" I prod, arching my eyebrows in challenge.

She returns my gaze, tilting her head down and looking at me like I'm the child everyone always assumes she is with her youthful, elfin features. "I'm sure you can figure it out." She pulls out the next picture of another beautiful woman with flawless skin, straight black hair, and hazel eyes and continues. "Then tomorrow, you're meeting Taylor for breakfast at a bakery in a small town upstate. It's only about twenty minutes from the ranch. She runs a successful dating blog."

She pulls out a third picture of a beautiful woman with wavy black hair, olive skin, and dark brown eyes. "Then Saturday night, you're meeting Sasha for drinks, and of course, you could also have dinner if you want to continue your date. She's very ambitious. She owns her own business. Then on Sunday, you have a date with Jessica at a Christmas festival. I'll get you more information about her; I just haven't printed it out yet," she rambles mindlessly, shuffling the papers. "The festival is in the same area upstate as your dates on Saturday, so you can just stay at the ranch for the night," she rambles quickly, trying not to give me time to object.

"This is crazy, Allie! I can't go out on four dates in one weekend!" I declare, shell-shocked by her announcement. "You set up two dates in one day! One in a weekend already feels like more than enough. There's no way I can handle four in three days!"

"Yes, you can," she states matter-of-factly. "I planned it all out for you right here," she informs me smugly, pointing to the papers again.

"That's not what I meant," I grumble, glaring at her as I feel my blood pressure rising. As I close my eyes, I take a deep breath, trying to keep myself calm. After a moment, I open my eyes and remind her, "I have other things I have to do besides go out on dates, especially this time of year. Besides, what if my dad needs me this weekend?" I question trying to reason with her business side.

She waves me off dismissively. "There's a whole staff of elves that can help take care of him, including me. Your only job this weekend is to go out, have fun and find the woman of your dreams whether you want to or not!" she declares.

"Allie," I repeat in annoyance, trying to come up with a way to get out of this. I pinch my nose, hoping to alleviate an on-coming headache. "It's not that simple."

Nodding, she pauses to really look at me. She obviously must sense my anxiety because she suddenly makes me an offer. "How about this," she bites her lip nervously before continuing, "You go on *all four* of these dates this weekend, really putting yourself out there with each of them and I won't make you go on another date with anyone until after the New Year."

"You're not making me do anything," I begin defensively. She raises her eyebrows in challenge. Heaving a sigh, I shake my head, knowing she's right, especially if my mother is involved. "Okay, okay. I will go on all four of the dates you set up this weekend. Then I don't have to go on any other dates until after the New Year," I restate the proposal. I don't want there to be any misunderstandings.

"Deal," she nods in agreement, a victorious smile lighting up her face. "Have fun, Jack!" she encourages. She spins on her heel and waves over her shoulder as she strides out of the room as if she's afraid I'll change my mind. Then again, she does know me well. "It's time for you to go if you don't want to be late for your date with Josie," she yells just before she disappears around the corner.

I chuckle and shake my head in disbelief. "Why do I let you talk me into these things?" I mumble to myself. Sometimes I wonder if she works for my mom instead of me.

She sticks her head back in the door and grins broadly. "Because you know what's good for you," she teases, having overheard me.

I chuckle and shake my head in disbelief as I shut down my computer and slip the papers I was working on back into the file. Standing, I slip on my long black coat and grab the papers Allie just handed to me to read on my way. "Go home, Allie, before I change my mind and work all weekend," I tease.

"Goodbye, Jack," she calls as she turns and walks away from my office for the second time. "Don't forget to call with updates. I want to know how everything is going."

"I will."

"Have a good weekend! You promised!" she reiterates, calling over her shoulder as she waves.

I'm barely able to look over the first profile on my way as I fight the work and tourist holiday foot traffic to get there, the crowds growing thicker the closer I get to the restaurant. By the time I arrive, I'm nearly ten minutes late, making me feel bad for leaving her waiting.

The moment I walk through the door at Evan's, I immediately spot Josie at a small table near the window to my right. Her auburn red hair cascades in waves down her back. Quickly, I take her in before she notices me. She's wearing a button-down gold dress with a thick black ribbon belt at the waist and black high-heeled shoes. She reminds me of a beautifully wrapped Christmas present in that outfit, bringing a smile to my face. Taking a deep breath, I step up to her with a grin and hold out my hand. "Hi, you must be Josie," I greet her politely.

Leaning back, she swiftly looks me over from head to toe and exhales with evident relief, reminding me of some of the creeps in online dating. She smiles brightly and reaches out, shaking my hand. "Yes, that's me, and you must be Jack."

I nod and apologize as I take the seat across from her, "Yeah, I'm so sorry I'm late. I walked over from my office, but even the foot traffic is crazy right now."

She shakes her head in amusement. "It's okay. I know it can get really crowded this time of year, especially near the Christmas tree, but I love it anyway. This is absolutely my favorite time of year!" I nod in agreement. "So," she begins propping her elbows on the table and leaning toward me with interest. "I believe your profile said you like Christmas?" she prompts, wanting clarification.

I nod and smirk, knowing that's an understatement. "Yes, you could definitely say that."

Her whole face lights up, and she leans across the table as she begins talking fast, her hands flying all over for emphasis. "So do I! I absolutely love Christmas! Do you want to go see the Christmas tree after this? We have to go see the tree after this! Ooh! And I love watching the light show on the Sax building from the tree! Don't you? Have you seen it yet this year? I only have three times." She grimaces.

"Not yet," I mumble, shaking my head.

Without acknowledging me, she continues rambling, "I think they got this year's tree from Vermont. Have you seen any of the window decorations yet? Of course, you have," she states laughing at herself as if the question were absurd. "You do have an office here. I love looking at all of them, whether they do the same thing every year or try to come up with something different!"

Nodding, I open my mouth to respond, but she takes a breath and keeps going, not giving me a chance. "Oh, we should go by the Plaza too. It's absolutely beautiful this time of year. Plus, the Plaza always makes me think of Christmas because of Home Alone 2. I love the Home Alone movies." She places her hands on her cheeks, and her mouth forms a perfect O. She giggles at herself and continues to ramble, "That was one of my favorite movies growing up. What's your favorite Christmas movie?"

"I think…"

She continues without waiting for an answer. "Do you want to go to places where scenes from different Christmas movies happened? We could go to 34th Street, or we could go caroling in Central Park like in Elf." She pauses, her eyebrows drawing down deep in thought, "I guess they weren't really caroling, but close enough. You know, 'the best way to spread Christmas cheer is singing loud for all to hear," she explains. "Do you like to sing?" she questions with wide eyes.

She pauses and takes a sip of her drink, making me realize I haven't even ordered anything yet. "Yeah," I mumble, thinking about what I want to drink.

"So, what are you looking for in a woman?" she prompts, changing direction and focusing on me.

"Well," I begin when I realize she asked me a question and might be waiting for an answer this time. "I want a woman who…"

She doesn't wait for my response; instead, she immediately interrupts me, "Oh!" I sigh in resignation and let her continue. "The perfect man for me is Santa Claus," she proclaims proudly. She laughs like she just said the funniest thing in the world, but that statement, even as a joke, causes my stomach to turn. This date already wasn't going smoothly, but that comment just pushed me over the edge, causing me to instantly check out of this date. The only one who should ever say that is my mother. "I'm kidding, of course, but who wouldn't love a man like Santa?"

A lump forms in my throat as my stomach roils faster. I don't think I could speak at this point, even if I had to. She cocks her head to the side, and her eyes narrow as she assesses me. "Are you okay?" she prompts, pointing toward my face. "You look a little green all of a sudden."

I shake my head and barely rasp, "Actually, I'm not feeling too well all of a sudden. I think I need to go home," I inform her, taking my chance. "I'm so sorry."

She shakes her head and waves off my apology, her eyes full of concern. "It's okay. We can reschedule for another time when you're feeling better."

I barely nod, not wanting her to think I agree to another date, but I don't want to offend her either. "I'm sorry," I repeat, desperate to escape.

"Don't worry about it. You don't want to be sick this time of year, especially for Christmas," she mumbles sincerely, making me feel a little bad about bailing.

I nod. "You're right, and I wouldn't want you to get sick, either."

"Thanks, that's very kind of you."

I pull a twenty dollar bill out of my wallet and lay it on the table between us. "Thank you, Josie."

"You didn't even have anything," she reminds me as she points to the money, shaking her head.

I nod and tell her, "I know, but I would've taken care of it had I been able to stay. It was nice meeting you, Josie."

"You too. Feel better, Jack." She smiles up at me as I stand.

"Thank you," I mumble as she offers me a small wave with a tight smile. I force a smile, hoping it doesn't look too awkward, and wave back, quickly heading for the door.

The moment I walk outside, I take a couple of deep breaths. The fresh air and distance begin to calm my anxiety with every step I take. I finally pull out my phone and immediately send Allie a simple text. "What were you thinking?"

"Your date with Josie is over already? Did she stand you up or something?"

"No, she was there."

"Do you know what you're supposed to do on dates? Maybe that's why none of your dates ever work out," she taunts.

I grind my teeth in annoyance and ignore her jab. Instead, I simply respond, "She was in love with my dad."

"Oh...sorry."

"That's it? Why am I picturing you laughing?"

"Because it's funny picturing your reaction."

I laugh because she's right. "Are the next three dates going to be more of the same?" I probe anxiously. If they are all similar, I don't know if I can do this.

The dancing dots appear, and her message soon comes through. "Tomorrow will be better. I promise you will like one of them."

"It better be if I'm going to get through this weekend," I grumble to myself. "You can't promise me that unless there's something you know that I don't," I text. The dancing bubbles appear and then quickly disappear. I grimace, knowing she either doesn't know how to respond or doesn't want to respond to my comment. That doesn't make me feel any better. Sighing, I send one more text to Allie, informing her, "I'm not staying in the city. I'm leaving for the ranch tonight."

"Good idea! Much easier if you travel tonight. Have a good weekend," she encourages. "Remember to relax and enjoy your dates! Let me know how they go!"

"Got it," I reply, done with this conversation.

Tapping my Uber app, I swiftly request a car. I walk one more block before I meet a black Chevy Traverse at the next corner and slide in, pulling the door shut behind me. "Thanks," I mumble as I drop my head back against the seat with an exhausted sigh. The driver mumbles his own greeting as he pulls away from the curb and drives toward my home upstate. Hopefully, I can at least relax a little bit once I'm there, even if all my dates are a bust. If that's the case, I'll be free, at least until after the New Year. Makes me wonder how I really want this weekend to go.

CHAPTER 4
Jack

As I stroll down the sidewalk dressed in dark jeans, a navy pullover, and my brown loafers, I take in the bright shades of red, yellow, and orange streaks across the pale blue sky. The sun is now shining brightly just over the horizon. This appears to be a quaint little town. It almost feels like you're out in the country even when you're on Main Street. I notice a town center and all locally owned mom-and-pop shops like a grocery store, pharmacy, bakery, gift shop, hair salon, gas station, bank, and a diner. Everyone I pass offers me a friendly wave and smile, making me feel at home. It reminds me of the North Pole in that respect; I like it.

As I step up to the bakery, the brick front is adorned with a large picture window with a light green and white striped awning with Bakery written across it in dark green cursive writing. I glance at my watch, realizing I'm early. I step inside and take a deep breath in, loving the smell of coffee and pastries, letting out an involuntary moan. My feet tap on the white tile floor as I make my way up to the glass display cabinets with dark green cabinets and a white countertop underneath as a small smile tugs at the corners of my lips. I love desserts, especially Christmas treats. I definitely get that from my dad.

A petite woman steps out from the back wearing a candy cane-striped apron over black pants and a white button-down shirt, causing me to smile wider. She has golden blonde hair, pulled up into a high ponytail, and splotches of flour on her ivory velvet looking skin. Her green eyes sparkle as she smiles brightly at me, making my heart skip a beat. She licks her full lips as she opens her mouth and, with a sweet voice, asks, "Hi, may I help you?"

I give myself a light shake before I respond. "Yeah, one of everything," I tease. "I love dessert." Her eyes widen, thinking I'm serious, making me chuckle in response. "Could I just have a large coffee with sugar and cream for now? I think I'm meeting someone, so I should probably wait for them before I order food."

She smirks, arching her eyebrows in question. "You think you're meeting someone?"

Shrugging, I admit, "My assistant set me up on a date. I don't exactly know the woman I'm meeting."

Her eyes widen in surprise at my admission. "Oh." She nods. "I'll get you that coffee."

I continue browsing the cases of pastries as I wait. When she returns and hands me my coffee, I smile and nod, murmuring my appreciation, "Thank you."

"You're welcome," she responds with a beautiful smile that makes her whole face light up and completely takes my breath away.

I clear my throat to pull myself out of my head. Wanting to keep her attention, I inquire, "So, what would you recommend?"

"Everything," she echoes my earlier response, grinning and making me chuckle again.

"How about if I can only pick one?" I prompt instead, curious about what her favorite might be.

She purses her lips adorably and answers, "That's a tough question. But I think the chocolate filled croissants melt in your mouth, but if you like gingerbread, you might want to try the gingerbread cookies as well. They're the best, but you could always take a couple of cookies home with you for later," she suggests, arching her eyebrows.

"That sounds like my kind of plan!" I grin. As I glimpse over my shoulder, I notice a woman I believe is my date, Taylor. She's standing outside the front door of the bakery, posing for a selfie, making me grimace. I'm not really one for attention. It may be fine for others, but it's just not me. "Excuse me," I murmur, glancing toward the woman behind the counter with a warm smile.

I stride toward the door, reaching for it just as Taylor enters. She's tall and thin with silky, long, black hair, just like her picture, wearing black jeans with short black leather boots and an oversized dark gray sweater. "Taylor?" I prompt.

She holds her hand out toward me as if I might kiss it without even looking in my direction. "You must be Jack. Nice to meet you," she mumbles in greeting, her voice flat.

I grimace and barely shake her fingertips, already feeling uncomfortable. Shouldn't you look at someone you're meeting for the first time, let alone anytime, at least once? Then again, we're supposed to be on a date. Does that make it worse that she hasn't even glimpsed in my direction? "Um, would you like something to eat?"

"Just coffee, black," she replies, still staring at her phone.

I turn back toward the counter, feeling helpless. The woman behind the counter is staring at me with wide eyes and her hand over her mouth, her eyes alight with what appears to be laughter. Leaning over the counter closer to her, I whisper, "Are you laughing at me?" The corners of my mouth twitch up in amusement watching her reaction to my date.

She shrugs and hands me the coffee I hadn't even ordered yet. I chuckle softly, mumbling, "Thanks."

"It's the least I can do," she claims, nodding.

I huff a laugh and request, "Can I have one of those chocolate croissants for right now and a half dozen of the gingerbread cookies to take home with me?"

"Excellent choice," she praises.

She hands me the croissant, and I take a bite while waiting for the box of gingerbread cookies, not able to wait another second. "Oh, my goodness, this is fabulous," I moan with satisfaction.

"Thank you." The woman smiles, a faint blush flooding her cheeks.

"Did you make them?" I ask curiously, holding up the pastry.

"Yes, I did." She pauses. "I made the gingerbread cookies too," she informs me as she hands me a small white box tied neatly with red and white string.

"Now I'm really looking forward to trying them." I grin. Turning back toward Taylor, my eyes widen as I watch her now taking pictures of some of the cookies behind the glass display with her phone. I sigh as I walk toward her, offering her the coffee. "Here."

"Thanks! These are beautiful, aren't they?" she prods, without even a glance in my direction. "I want to take pictures of everything!" She pauses, pondering, "Or maybe I should do a video showing some of them. I want to suggest some of these treats as a gift to a special someone," she tells me, a small smile pulling at her lips.

I arch my eyebrows in surprise, thinking maybe I misjudged her. "Why don't you try a couple of them, so you know what you're recommending," I suggest. "My treat," I add playfully.

She makes a face, scrunching up her nose. "Ewe, no! I don't do desserts or pastries or anything gross like that." She glances at my croissant and back at the case of treats mumbling, "No offense."

I chuckle humorlessly and shake my head. I didn't misjudge her at all.

I leave the bakery less than twenty minutes later, giving one more glance to the woman behind the counter, wishing she was my date instead. Well, at least I'm halfway done with keeping my promise. I'm barely a few feet away from the door when I pull out my phone to text Allie. "She doesn't like dessert," I inform her, still flummoxed about how I ended up on a date with a woman at a bakery who doesn't like dessert.

"More for you?" she sends back. I laugh, knowing she made it a question in hopes that it's not a deal breaker. She knows me better than that.

"I don't even know what color her eyes are...she was too busy with her blog to make eye contact," I type into my phone and press send.

Her only reply is, "Oops."

As I drop my phone into my pocket, I groan in annoyance. I really can't believe I'm doing this. Remembering the bag in my hand, I open it, savoring the smell of the sweet and spicy gingerbread cookies, causing me to think about the woman who made them. Now, she was absolutely stunning, even with flour splattered everywhere. I smile, thinking about how I enjoyed talking to her so much more than my supposed date. I can't help but think I'd rather take her out, but for now, I need to keep my promise to Allie. Maybe when all this is over, I will come back to ask her out, but I need to get through this weekend first. If I survive, then I can consider it.

Lifting my hand, I glance at my wrist, grimacing at the time. Now I have eight hours to kill before my next date. I stop on the sidewalk, noticing a man and a woman, both with graying hair, painting a sign looking for Christmas donations. The list includes toys, sports equipment, decorations, lights, clothes, food, coats, hats, gloves, and much more. Smiling to myself, I walk over to see what I can do to help. "That's quite a list you have there," I state in greeting as I nod toward the sign.

"It is," she confirms, nodding. "We help a lot of people. We have a list of most of the organizations here," she advises, pointing to a pamphlet on the table. "But we work with several community groups and churches that all have different needs, especially over the holidays," the woman informs me with a warm smile.

"That's fantastic. It can be a lot of work, but I know every one of them appreciates what you do for them."

"Thank you. We try to do what we can to help," the woman replies, nodding.

"Well, you inspire me. I would like to help. Do you have information on where you want the different items to be delivered?"

"We're accepting donations right here," the man reveals, gesturing to the boxes behind them. Each box is labeled with a handwritten white sign for different types of items: clothing, food, toys, home goods, decorations, sports equipment, and other.

I grimace. "It might be easier for all of us if I can deliver it to a location where everything is separated for the families. I run a toy and tech company, and I'm part of a larger network with many other businesses as well. I want to bring more than one or two boxes from my company and I'll reach out to some of my other contacts. I'm sure we can help find all the items on your lists."

Both of their eyes widen as bright smiles encompass their faces. "That would be wonderful! Thank you so much," the woman praises.

"Here," the man offers, handing me a flyer. "Call this number and tell them Bill sent you. They'll take good care of you." He grins and sticks his hand out to shake mine. "And thank you. We really appreciate your support."

I clasp his hand and shake it firmly. "Like you, I'm happy to do what I can to help." I grin, enjoying the opportunity to be able to do something like this for a new community. Reaching into my pocket, I grab my cell phone and work on coordinating the donations for the next couple of hours before I return home to change for my next date.

CHAPTER 5
Jack

A few hours later, I walk in to meet Sasha on the bar side of the restaurant wearing black pants and a light blue button-down shirt. I glance around the dimly lit room. The modern lights hanging from the ceiling from brushed bronze poles don't give it much light. A thick, smooth long mahogany bar runs along the back wall. Small tables with curved back chairs that match the bar's wood are scattered throughout. There's a swirl of deep red carpet near the bar, but it fans out to slate tiles around the back of the bar and underneath the tables. A large mirror extends behind the length of the bar, covered with clear shelves for all the bottles of liquor.

I take a deep breath, wondering if this date will be any better than the others and if there's even a chance we'll make it to dinner, but I'm trying not to be so cynical. Just because the first two dates didn't go well doesn't mean this one won't. As I step toward the bar to look for my date, a small hand grabs my elbow firmly from behind. I turn around to find Sasha standing in front of me, no shorter than me, with her three-inch black stilettos on her feet. Like her picture, she has long, black wavy hair and beautiful olive skin. Her eyes appear so dark they're almost black, making them very difficult to read, especially in this low lighting.

Carefully, she runs her hands over the front and sides of her fitted dress, smoothing it down as she looks me over from head to toe, not bothering to hide her assessment. "Jack?" she questions, arching her eyebrows.

I smile warmly and nod my head. "That's me. You must be Sasha." I reach out to shake her hand, and she places her hand in mine, her long fingers wrapping around mine as she gives my hand a firm shake, dropping it almost immediately.

She pushes her shoulders back, returning my smile, but something about it feels cold, and I can't quite figure out why. "Why don't we grab a drink," she suggests as if that wasn't the plan, gesturing toward the bar.

"Sounds good," I murmur as I turn, letting her step in front of me and follow her to the bar. She has her order already placed with the twenty-something male bartender, grinning at my date before I even step up next to her. "I'll just have a whiskey, neat," I tell him with a nod as he drags his eyes back to his work. The bartender soon hands her a martini and slides a low-ball glass with my drink over to me. I toss some bills down on the bar, paying for the drinks before turning all my attention toward my date, hoping for the best.

"So, you're a businessman," she states, seeming to already know the answer. "I own my own company," she tells me something I already know from her profile.

"What kind of company do you own?" I question, regretting my words almost the moment they leave my lips. As I sip my drink, she launches into the history of how she got started, followed by a proposal to support the expansion of her company. After about fifteen minutes of my silence, she pauses in her presentation and bites her lip nervously as she looks at me expectantly, inquiring, "So, what do you think?"

"I thought this was a date, not a business meeting," I tell her honestly. I chuckle lightly, shaking my head, hoping she's not offended by my remark.

"It is," she agrees, nodding her head. "I just thought it was also a great opportunity to talk business as well," she admits with complete confidence.

I shift uneasily, wondering if she knows more about me than I thought. Maybe Allie shouldn't have said I was a CEO. "What do you know about me and my business?" I prompt, arching my eyebrows.

"Well," she begins, trailing off as she takes a sip of her drink.

"I know it wasn't on my dating profile, but do you know my last name?" I question, her eyes widening. "Do you know who I am?" I clarify, my stomach twisting anxiously.

Her face burns as red as my father's suit as she fidgets nervously for the first time, giving herself away. "Well, um, yeah. When I ah, saw your profile picture, I um, knew," she stutters. "I mean, who, um, who doesn't know you? You're kind of well-known in our area. You run an incredible company and have locations worldwide," she informs me as if I didn't know. "I'm sure that doesn't make it easy to date," she concedes, scrunching her nose up uncomfortably as she looks away.

As I close my eyes, I exhale slowly, trying to rid my body of its sudden tension. I should've known dating sites would be trouble for me. I'm lucky she's the only one who has recognized me so far. "I'm sorry, but I think it's time for me to go. Thanks for meeting me, Sasha. Good luck with your business," I tell her sincerely. Then I take one more sip of my drink and set the glass on the bar, nodding toward the bartender in appreciation as I stand.

"Wait!" she exclaims, grabbing onto my arm to stop me. I pause, arching my eyebrows in question and waiting for her to speak. "Can I call your office on Monday to set up a meeting with you?" she asks, her confidence returning. "Just because we're not a match doesn't mean we couldn't be really good together in business."

My mouth drops open, but I quickly snap it shut. Her intentions only prove how difficult dating can be for someone like me, and that's without bringing my famous father into the picture. Standing up a little straighter, I politely retort, "I really do wish you the best of luck, Sasha, but I don't think that's a good idea. Thanks again for meeting me. Have a good night."

"Jerk," she mutters. I heave a sigh but don't respond to her insult. What's the point? She had her mind made up before she even got here. Instead, I shake my head in disappointment, spin on my heel, and stalk out of the bar feeling defeated.

Pulling my phone out of my pocket, I unlock the screen and tap Allie's cell number as I walk out of the restaurant. "Hi, Jack!" she answers her phone cheerfully. "Aren't you supposed to be on a date?"

Licking my lips, I start with a joke, trying to keep my mood lighter than what it really is, "Did you check the naughty and nice list before you set up these dates for me?"

"What?" she asks, taken aback.

I huff a humorless laugh and sigh. "This one just wanted my money. She recognized my profile picture. Besides, you probably gave too much away in the profile. That profile has to come down." I shake my head, still in shock about my disaster dates. I don't know how she thought any of these women would be good matches for me. "And you claim you know me," I tease. "You are not good at this matchmaking thing. Don't quit your day job, Allie."

"Why would I ever want to?" I hear her long, heavy sigh through the phone. "I'm sorry none of your dates have gone well, Jack, but you have one more left with Jessica tomorrow. I promise you will like her!"

"I don't know. I think I'm done, Allie. I just can't do this anymore," I grumble, shaking my head, my hand falling to the back of my neck, squeezing out the tension.

"You have to go, Jack, or your mom and I will be forced to keep this up! One more date, and then I won't even mention the word date again until after the New Year!" she pleads, sounding desperate.

"Forced?" I challenge. As I groan in annoyance, I run my free hand through my hair, dropping it at my side. "If tomorrow turns out as terrible as the rest of these dates have been, you aren't allowed to set me up for a full year!" I inform her, increasing the stakes. I really don't want to go on another date. This weekend feels like it's dragging as I go from one bad date to the next. I pinch my lips tightly together, knowing I'm relenting and putting my love life in her hands for one more date.

She gasps loudly into the phone. "What? No! You can't do that! We already made our agreement, Jack."

"You heard me, Allie; you and my mom stay out of my dating life for one full year," I insist, my voice firm.

It sounds like she's fumbling with the phone as she stammers, "But, but, what if, ugh!"

"I never said that would mean I wouldn't date for a year, just that you and my mom are no longer allowed to set me up. After I've endured these last three dates, and if I'm still talking to you," I taunt playfully, "the least you can do is make the adjustment."

"Ugh, fine," she huffs, grumpily agreeing. "Your mom is not going to be happy with me," she grumbles under her breath.

"You should've worked a little harder on your shortlist," I tease.

"Fine, I agree with your changes," she reiterates. "So that means you're going on this date tomorrow, right?" she questions, needing to hear me say it.

"Yeah, I'll go on this date with Jessica tomorrow," I grumble, hoping it's not so bad. "Why do I always give in to you," I mutter, laughing.

She squeals, "Because you love me!"

"One more date tomorrow," I vehemently reiterate. "This is the last one, no matter what!"

"Okay, okay! I get it."

I think about the information she gave me on Jessica, realizing I don't have what I need. "Wait, you didn't send me the same profile info like you did with the other women. There's no picture attached, and there's nothing but her name and where I'm meeting her. I don't have any information about this woman at all."

"Oh, no?" she asks innocently.

The corners of my lips quirk upwards at the sound of her voice. She's up to something, but I know better than to ask; it's not like she will tell me what it is. I should've known. "Well, how will I know who she is?" I prod, sighing.

"You'll meet just outside the entrance of the festival. She'll be wearing a dark green coat, and she'll be carrying an Amaryllis. You need to bring an Amaryllis too, so she can find you," she enlightens me.

"She didn't see my picture either?" I question, confused, how that would be possible using the dating site. I thought the dates were set up through the profiles, making me wonder again if this is really a good idea.

"No, her sister set up the date for her," Allie informs me sounding giddy.

Closing my eyes in disbelief, I sigh heavily in resignation. "I don't know why I'm doing this, but I'm going to trust you."

"Of course you are!" she exclaims gleefully. "Have fun tomorrow, Jack! And don't forget the Amaryllis," she reminds me.

"Goodnight, Allie," I mumble just before I hit disconnect, slipping my phone back into my pocket. "One more day. One more date. I can do this," I mumble to myself. I need to do this because I don't want to be stuck going on more bad dates again next weekend. I can only imagine what Allie and my mom would have in store for me next. I shake my head, wishing I were already back at the ranch and ready for bed. I want this night to be over.

CHAPTER 6
Jessica

"I'm so nervous, Holly," I admit. "I don't even remember the last time I went on a date," I tell her, my hands shaking.

"Yes, you do. It was your first year of college," she reminds me, not wanting to ruin the moment by bringing up our parents. I smile appreciatively at her.

Taking a deep breath, I glance critically at my outfit again, assessing my black pants, stylish black winter boots lined with faux fur, so I'm comfortable walking but also warm, my emerald green cashmere turtleneck sweater, and my dark green tweed wool coat. I can't help but wonder if I look okay. Maybe I'm wearing too much green. I could change into the white sweater, but I looked flushed in that when it's cold.

Holly laughs loudly, pulling me out of my thoughts. "Stop! I know exactly what you're doing," she claims, attempting to give me a stern look. "But I'm not letting you change. You look absolutely beautiful, Jess."

I feel myself relax as I glance up at her appreciatively. "Thank you. Sometimes I think you can read my mind," I tell her with a loving smile.

"Oh, wait!" she exclaims and twists around to grab a single Amaryllis off the table. "Here," she offers, handing me the long-stemmed flower I used to think was a lily, but my mom taught me otherwise. The center of the flower has a burst of white, almost like a star. The white bleeds into the red as it moves to the outside of the flower petals, a favorite at Christmas time.

I bring the flower to my nose and inhale, enjoying the sweet, floral scent. "These were mom's favorite flowers," I inform her fondly.

"Really?' she asks, surprised. "I never knew that."

"Yeah." I nod, a small smile tugging at my lips. "Probably because she loved Christmas so much," I add, shrugging my shoulders. I gulp over the lump in my throat, attempting to tamp down my emotions as I murmur, "Anyway, I should probably go."

Holly nods in agreement as she smiles at me, waving me toward the door. "Yes, you should. Have fun tonight, Jess. Don't worry about me. I'll be fine. I have homework to catch up on, so I'm not going anywhere," she reminds me.

I nod. "Okay, I'll see you later. Call me if you need anything," I add, widening my eyes for emphasis.

"Don't worry, I won't!" she jokes and laughs as she practically shoves me out the front door. "Bye!"

As I shake my head in amusement, I turn toward town, needing to walk the three blocks, hoping the cool air will help me calm down by the time I get there. I can't believe I'm actually going on a date. Will I even know what to do or say?

I smirk, thinking of the gorgeous guy from the other day on that horrible date. Hopefully, this date will go much better than his. Honestly, I can't believe that woman. How could anyone not pay attention to a man like him? I don't even think she noticed when he wished her good luck with her blog, said goodbye, and left. I sure did, though. I wish I could've stopped him from walking away, but from me, not her.

I shake my head and take a deep breath, trying to change the direction of my thoughts. I shouldn't be thinking about some guy I don't even know when I'm about to go out on a date for the first time in years. I can at least put my focus into hoping my date is a man like him. There's nothing wrong with that. I don't think. I giggle at my thoughts.

I lift my head as I enter the town. The atmosphere brightens all around me. Although the main festival is held at the center of town, everyone celebrates it throughout the community, with all the stores and businesses participating. Even though I don't attend anymore, I made my gingerbread cookies to be sold with hot chocolate at the stand for our bakery, and I participated in a few of the projects with other community groups to prepare for the event. Near every entrance, there's a Christmas tree with an evergreen metal bench sitting at its base. I'm supposed to meet Jack at that exact spot at the northeast entrance, which is closest to me.

As I round the corner, I turn toward the bench and gasp, my heart skipping a beat at the sight in front of me. The man from the bakery the other day is sitting on the bench looking toward the festival with an Amaryllis in his hand. I blink, wondering if I'm dreaming, but he's still there. Slowly, I begin walking toward him, my heart beating faster with every step. Just before I reach him, his head swings toward me, and his eyes widen in shock, recognizing me. He stands slowly, his smile lighting up his handsome face. The same kind of smile that I'm sure is on mine.

"You," we say in unison, both seeming happily surprised. We both laugh and stare at one another for a moment before he takes a step toward me.

"You look beautiful," he rasps.

Butterflies erupt in my stomach as I feel my face redden. "Thank you," I whisper, grinning at him, my brain trying to catch up with reality.

"So, it's Jessica?" he prods curiously.

I nod. "Yes, or Jess is fine too."

"Well, I'm very happy to meet you, Jessica. I'm Jack," he introduces himself, his cheeks rosy as he grins. "And I believe this is for you," he murmurs, handing me his flower."

"Thank you. I'm glad to meet you too, and hopefully, you'll have a lot more fun today than it seemed you did yesterday," I can't help but tease him.

His head falls back as he laughs, the deep, joyful sound sending chills down my spine. "You have no idea," he mumbles, shaking his head.

"Tell me," I encourage, curious.

"For now, let's just say I've wished more than once since yesterday morning that I was on a date with a certain beautiful baker, never knowing that wish would come true so quickly," he reveals, sounding sincere. My whole body heats with his confession, and I glance toward the ground nervously. "Should we take a stroll and see what all the talk is about?" he prompts, gesturing with his arm toward the festival behind us.

I smile and nod as I breathe a sigh of relief at the subject change. "That sounds great!"

We walk under an evergreen archway covered in hundreds of white twinkle lights. I close my eyes and take a deep breath in, savoring the smell of pine, a small smile tugging at my lips. "You like Christmas?" he prompts.

I open my eyes and blush when I notice him staring at me. Ignoring his question, I explain my actions. "I was smelling the pine. I haven't been to this festival in a very long time, and I always remember the strong scent of pine when you first walk in. It's everywhere but so intense when you first walk under the arches. I always loved that smell. It reminds me of Christmas with my family when I was younger," I enlighten him. I'm already opening more than I expected on a first date, giving him a little piece of me.

"How come you haven't come here in a long time?"

My eyebrows draw together in confusion prompting him to explain, "You just said you haven't been to this festival in a very long time. Why not?"

"Oh!" I exclaim, surprised, my eyes going wide. I didn't even realize I had admitted that to him. I purse my lips, not quite sure what to say without a long explanation, but I'm not ready to go into that with someone I just met, no matter how easy he already seems to be to talk to. I take a deep breath and settle on a simpler answer. "I guess I grew up, and life got too busy."

"Too busy for Christmas?" he asks, probing. His friendly smile lets me know he's not judging me, just curious.

I shake my head and mumble, "No, not too busy for Christmas. We always celebrate Christmas, no matter what."

I turn my head toward the welcome table, needing to move on from this conversation with my chest feeling tight as I'm flooded with memories. The last thing I want to do is cry on a first date, especially with someone I wouldn't mind seeing again. The table is covered with a kelly-green tablecloth with a white sign draping over the front adorned with red lettering in large cursive writing stating, "Welcome to Mistletoe Haven's Christmas Festival!"

I step up to the table and smile. "Hi. Do you have a map and brochure for this year's activities?"

A woman with short dark hair, rosy cheeks, and kind, warm brown eyes, smiles up at me. "Of course, dear!" She reaches for a brochure sitting on the table right in front of me and hands it to me, causing me to blush. She leans back and runs her hands down the red Santa sweater she's wearing, straightening it out.

"Thank you," I murmur, feeling slightly self-conscious.

Jack echoes, "Thanks," with a smile that makes my heart skip a beat. He places his hand on my elbow and escorts me to the side. His gentle touch giving me chills even through my thick winter coat and sweater. "Are you cold?"

I shake my head but answer, "I guess maybe a little."

He laughs, the joyful sound sending another chill down my spine. "How about we find some hot chocolate? They must have hot chocolate at a Christmas festival, right? We can enjoy it while we walk around, and it will help warm you up."

I cock my head to the side and smile up at him. "That sounds wonderful," I admit, nodding. I point with the flowers in my hand behind him. "There's a cart right over there."

"Let's go." We walk up to a small wooden cedar cart with a small red and white canopy overhead. A white sign with fancy red lettering lists the short menu, including water, hot chocolate, tea, and coffee. "Could we have two large hot chocolates, please?" Jack orders smiling at the small, balding man with round cheeks and a polite smile.

"Of course! Would you like a peppermint stick in either of them?" he offers, with a crooked smile.

Jack licks his lips, making me bite mine to hold back a groan. "That sounds delicious," he mumbles. Turning toward me, he prods, "Would you like one?"

I release my lip, noticing his eyes widen with my movement. "Um, sure," I murmur, not quite sure what I just agreed to.

He slowly releases his breath and gives me a nod before turning back to the man and confirming, "Make that one with each of them. Thank you."

I busy myself by opening the brochure as he pays for our hot chocolate. A moment later, he's holding a red and white cup out for me. I look up at him and smile appreciatively as I reach for the cup. His fingers brush mine as I grasp it, making me gasp at his light touch. My eyes widen, and I meet his warm gaze, his blue eyes sparkling, taking my breath away. "Thank you," I rasp, forcing the words from my lips.

"You're welcome," he whispers, his eyes never leaving mine.

I clear my throat and rip myself away from his gaze and touch, trying to pull myself together. I take a small sip of the hot chocolate and release a soft moan in satisfaction. "This is delicious," I mumble under my breath. "Thank you."

He chuckles softly. "You already said that." I glance at him in confusion, and he elaborates, "You already thanked me."

I blush and glance toward my feet, mumbling, "Well, it's good hot chocolate."

His light chuckle gives me another chill. This man seems to muddle my brain with his presence. "It is really good, but I've had better." He smirks.

"You seem confident."

"I am. My mom makes the best hot chocolate. She has a recipe that's been in our family for years, and there really is nothing better."

"Sounds like something I'd love to try."

"I'd like that," he admits looking down at me. Butterflies erupt in my stomach and fly to every inch of my body as I feel myself turn a deep shade of red. Oh, this man is going to be trouble for me. Taking a deep breath, I shake it off and continue walking.

CHAPTER 7
Jessica

"I wonder what the Christmas tree theme is this year," I contemplate looking around for a Christmas tree as we finish our hot chocolate.

"What do you mean?" he questions, his eyes wide with curiosity.

I smile, feeling the excitement building inside me at sharing this with him. "Every year, the festival has a different theme for all the Christmas trees here. Every business or community group that wants to participate decorates a tree. The themes started the second year of the festival to add something a little different for people to see every year as a way to continue bringing them back, besides the normal traditions. After all, sometimes it seems there are Christmas festivals in every other town."

"True," he nods, "but some are better than others."

"Exactly! So, they started the Christmas tree themes here. For example, one year was sports, and every tree had decorations depicting a different one, like basketball, softball, or even dance. Some of the other themes have been foods, colors, art, gifts, and the North Pole. I think my favorite one was Christmases of the past," I admit, smiling at the memory.

"What a fantastic idea!" He grins, his eyes sparkling. "How do they not have two trees with the same thing, though? Like two with basketball when it's sports or elves when it's the North Pole?"

"There's a sign-up list, and you put your top three choices in order. Then a committee will confirm with you what one you got, and if, for some reason, none of them work, they give you some suggestions to choose from," I explain as we both toss our now empty cups of hot chocolate into the nearby recycle bin.

As he nods in understanding, he begins turning slowly in a circle and freezes when he spots a large pine tree across the courtyard. He turns toward me with a huge smile lighting up his face and reaches for my hand. Tilting his head in the direction of the tree, he gives my hand a light tug, "Come on, let's go check it out!"

I laugh, enjoying his enthusiasm, and speed up my pace to walk alongside him. We step up to the tree, and I can't help but be entranced by the boyish joy on his face as he stares at the tree in wonderment. He glances toward me, his cheeks coloring pink as he realizes I'm watching him. "I really like Christmas," he admits proudly with a shrug.

I grin, asking playfully, "Doesn't everyone?"

He chuckles as he looks into my eyes before clearing his throat and looking away. Nodding toward the tree, he asks, "So, what do you think?"

I think I could stare at you all day, but I'm not about to tell him that. Taking a deep breath, I turn toward the tree and quietly take in the sight in front of me. The evergreen tree appears to be at least eight feet tall, with small colored lights wrapped around the branches shining down on the courtyard. A beautiful white angel with golden wings lights the top of the tree. I step closer to take a look at the delicate ornaments hanging from the branches. Various decorations include colorful glass bulbs, sleighs, wagons, trucks, famous animated characters playing in the snow, big cities, a baby Jesus, Christmas cookies, elves, reindeer, and even Santa Clause ornaments. "I think it's absolutely beautiful," I murmur reverently.

"Should we take a guess on what we think the theme might be this year from looking at this tree?" he prods, giving me a crooked smile.

I tilt my head to the side, reassessing the tree and the variety of ornaments. Finally, I shrug, admitting, "I have absolutely no idea. This looks like a normal Christmas tree to me."

He chuckles and tilts his head to the side, questioning, "Normal?"

I shrug, making him laugh harder. "I know there's really no such thing as normal when it comes to decorating a Christmas tree. I mean, I could see this Christmas tree in just about anyone's house I know."

He nods in understanding and glances back toward the tree, continuing to stare. "Maybe it's Christmas present," he suggests. My eyebrows scrunch together in confusion, so he elaborates, "You said before you did one of Christmases past, so maybe it's Christmas present."

"Huh. Good idea. Why don't we find another one and see if it fits?" I propose, tilting my head to the side in a challenge.

"Sounds good to me," he agrees, nodding. We walk a little further into the festival hand in hand, warming my body from the inside out with the sweet gesture. It's been a long time since I held a man's hand, and I'm grateful it's this man by my side.

I catch a glimpse of a Christmas tree just to our left and startle, jumping at the sight, my free hand flying to my chest as I take a step back right into Jack, making him laugh. Turning, I glare playfully at him before I shoot my glare at the tree. "I don't like spiders! Why would you decorate a Christmas tree with spider webs and spiders over all the branches?" I whine, a disgusted chill going right through me as I step closer to Jack as if for protection.

Jack smirks and opens his mouth to answer, mumbling, "Well."

"Ah!" I interrupt excitedly, bouncing on my toes. "Maybe the theme is holidays!"

"Maybe," he concedes, shrugging. "Let's keep looking," he prods, giving my hand a small tug. I step toward him and meet his slow easy stride. Quietly, I take in my surroundings while just enjoying walking next to this man. Everything about him makes me feel at ease.

Food trucks are lined up around the outside of the festival grounds. A large group of men and women dressed up in black, white, and red begin singing "Carol of the Bells" on a small stage next to the tallest Christmas tree I can see. We wander toward the chorus, completely drawn to the light, joyous sound. As the last note echoes around us, we drop one another's hands, and both clap appreciatively before the beautiful harmony starts right back up, this time singing, "Wonderful Christmastime."

"They're so good," I murmur.

He nods in agreement. "They're fantastic."

"Look! There's another tree." I point just to the left of the stage.

We wander closer to the tree by the stage, trying to figure out what the shiny red decorations might be hanging from the branches. As we get closer, I giggle at the sight of bright red apples covering the tree. As I glance toward Jack, an easy smile graces his lips, making my stomach flip-flop. "I know the theme," he announces confidently.

My eyebrows rise in surprise. "Because of apples?"

His grin grows as he nods. "Yup," he declares, popping the p.

I tilt my head to the side, narrowing my eyes as I attempt to read him. "Then tell me what you think it is,"

"Are you sure you don't want to guess first?" he prods playfully.

I glance toward the tree and then look back at him, shrugging. "I don't have any clue," I confess, arching my eyebrows and waiting for his answer.

"It's Christmas around the world," he states simply as if the answer were obvious.

"Why would you think that?" I prompt, still puzzled.

"I know a lot about Christmas," he concedes, giving me a crooked smile.

"Really?"

Nodding, he elaborates, "Yeah. I guess you could say my father is kind of an expert on anything Christmas, and he passes his knowledge on to me."

"Okay..." I mumble, dragging out the word, hoping for more of an explanation.

He sighs as we turn around and begin walking past more of the tables, searching for more trees. He bites his bottom lip as if he's thinking about what to say. Finally, he takes a deep breath and explains, "I guess you could say my dad has a passion for Christmas. Since I was a little boy, he has always taught me a lot about Christmas, its history, traditions around the world, beliefs, and anything you can think of when it comes to Christmas. Even when it wasn't the holiday season, he would find something Christmas in the day-to-day to talk about or teach me."

"It kind of sounds like it was Christmas all year in your house," I murmur, piquing my curiosity. I wonder what it would be like to grow up in a house where you always had a feeling of Christmas. The idea warms my heart.

He nods and rubs his free hand uncomfortably on the back of his neck, watching me out of the corner of his eye. "Yeah, I guess you could say that."

"That's every child's dream." I grin.

He relaxes and smiles down at me, nodding his head. "Yeah."

"So, what's with the apples? Or the spiders, for that matter?" I prompt, crinkling my nose in displeasure as I stop to look at him.

He chuckles and lightly taps my nose, instantly heating my face to bright red and warming me from head to toe. "You're adorable," he murmurs softly. Then he clears his throat and continues walking. "The spiders and spider web decorations are from a Ukrainian folktale about a family who couldn't afford to decorate their tree. It was said that a Christmas spider decorated their tree with spider webs. The family awoke on Christmas morning to the webs being turned silver and gold, and they were never poor again."

My eyes widen in surprise. "Wow, I've never heard that before. That's a great story." He nods in agreement. "So, the first tree was a typical American Christmas?"

"I believe so, although there's not really a typical Christmas tree when it comes to the US."

"True. What about the apples?"

"Well, in France, they used to decorate all their Christmas trees with fruit. Then one Christmas, there was a shortage of fruit, and all the people started making glass ornaments of fruit to decorate their trees instead. Since Christmas is the celebration of Jesus's birth, a lot of people stuck with only using apples to decorate their trees because of the religious symbolism from Adam and Eve in the Garden of Eden."

"Wow," I mumble, enjoying the stories. I can't believe he knows so much about Christmas. I've never even heard these stories before. "How do you know all of this?"

He chuckles, shrugging like it's no big deal. "I told you, my father. I guess you can say that he's the one who gave me my love for Christmas."

"Hmm," I murmur, smiling up at him in amazement. This man is really taking me by surprise. "I'd love to hear more."

He grins, appearing pleased. "I'm happy to share more with you."

"Excuse me," a tall, lanky teenage boy about seventeen with brown hair, brown eyes, and light brown skin stands in front of me with a shy smile.

"Yes?" I prompt.

"Where did you get your flowers?" he questions, gesturing toward the Amaryllis in my hand.

I glance toward Jack and smile before looking back at the boy. "Well, one was a gift."

"Oh," he mumbles, his face dropping. "So not here."

"No, I'm sorry. Why?" I push.

"Well, there's a girl over there from school I want to ask out," he begins, nodding toward a small group of teenage girls. "And those flowers are beautiful, like her. I thought it was a good idea," he mumbles, sounding defeated.

"It is a good idea." I hold out the flowers to the boy and smile. "Here."

His eyes widen in surprise. "You're offering me your flowers?"

"Of course. I'm sure she will love them."

"Thank you!" He grins wide, taking the flowers from me. "Thank you so much," he reiterates as he spins around. Pushing his shoulders back, he stands taller as he strides toward the group of girls. Then he taps one on the shoulder and smiles as he holds the flowers out for her. I watch as she takes them, returning his smile and warming my heart.

"That was really nice of you," Jack murmurs, pulling my focus back to him, a small smile tugging at his lips.

I shrug, murmuring, "Young love."

CHAPTER 8
Jessica

We approach a set of tables covered with large sheets of white paper like a tablecloth. Upon closer inspection, we find Christmas drawings and writings of all kinds doodled on the paper, most likely by the kids and parents surrounding the tables. Christmas craft supplies, including stickers, scissors, glue, glitter, paints, paintbrushes, wooden pieces with directions to make a truck or sleigh, felt, colored construction paper, and so much more, are scattered on nearly every available surface.

Jack lets go of my hand and steps up to one of the tables near a few kids to get a better look at all the different creations. He glances at the young couple behind the kids, assuming they're the parents, and gestures toward the children in front of them, nonverbally asking permission to look at their projects. The couple smiles appreciatively and nods in agreement.

Jack kneels down between a little boy and a girl, both with brown hair and about eight years in age. He notices the intense concentration on the little girl's face, with her tongue barely peeking out between her lips and smiles. Turning to the boy first, not wanting to break the little girl's concentration, he asks, "What are you working on?"

Looking up, the boy grins, proudly holding up a small wooden truck he's painting red with a tiny Christmas tree lying in the back. "I'm making an ornament for our Christmas tree. It looks exactly like my dad's truck."

"That's incredible. You're doing such a great job. Your dad will love that!" Jack praises the little boy, who instantly preens at the compliment.

"I'm making a plate of Christmas cookies," the little girl with dark ringlets announces from across the table. Jack smiles over at her, assessing her circle picture covered in various shapes, all practically drowning in glitter.

"I bet the glitter is the sprinkles?" he asks curiously, arching his eyebrows.

The little girl's eyes widen, lighting up as she nods vigorously. "Yup! I love sprinkles! Just like Santa Claus!"

"Santa sure does love sprinkles. It looks delicious," he tells her, licking his lips for emphasis.

"You can't eat them, silly!" She giggles and rolls her eyes in exasperation. "They're paper!"

He chuckles and nods. "Oh, okay. Thanks for telling me. I'm sure that wouldn't taste too good."

"They would taste yucky," she agrees, scrunching up her face and sticking her tongue out for emphasis. Then she looks at Jack and adds, "I promise to make some real ones for Santa, and they will taste really good."

"You're not going to have any of the real ones?" he prompts, giving her a crooked smile.

She plants her hands on her hips and narrows her eyes at Jack, insisting, "Not of Santa's!" I lift my hand, covering my mouth to hide my amusement. These kids are melting my heart, right along with the man talking with them.

"You know who makes the best Christmas cookies?" Jack prompts. She shakes her head as Jack smiles up at me. He reaches for my hand and pulls me closer to them. "My friend, Jessica. I've only had her gingerbread cookies, but they were the best I've ever had!" He leans closer and holds up his hand like he's telling her a secret but speaks in a loud whisper, "And I've eaten a lot of gingerbread cookies!"

The little girl giggles and then nods solemnly. Leaning up from behind her, the little girl's mom asks, "Do you sell them? The cookies, I mean. We love gingerbread!"

I blush and nod, informing them, "Yes. Actually, I work at the bakery in town."

"Excellent!" she exclaims, grinning. "I can cook, but I'm not much of a baker. I think I may have to stop in to see you."

Jack stands to join me and praises me again, "It would definitely be worth it. She should have her own business." I feel myself turn a deeper shade of red with all his compliments.

"We'll definitely be stopping in."

"Thank you," I whisper. "I hope to see you soon." She smiles, and I offer them all a small wave.

Jack turns toward the families and waves. "Merry Christmas, and great job on all your projects! Thank you for sharing them with me."

"Thank you!" the kids yell in unison before turning back toward their artwork as we walk away.

When we're only a few steps from the tables, I glance at him in awe. With admiration clear in my voice, I tell him, "Jack, you were absolutely incredible with those kids. What can't you do?" I tease.

He laughs joyfully and proudly admits, "Bake."

I laugh, enjoying myself more and more as this date progresses. We come across another Christmas tree by the man-made ice rink. Alongside various ornaments, a garland of a nation's blue and yellow flag is strewn around the branches. "I know this one. It must be Sweden," I announce proudly.

"What gave it away?" he teases, smirking at me. He gestures toward the rink next to us and prompts, "Do you want to go ice skating?"

"Why don't we save that for another night?" I suggest, hopeful for a second date.

He grins wide. "Already planning another date? Does that mean you think this date is going well?" he prompts sweetly.

As I feel myself blushing again, I glance down at my feet. I take a deep breath, and instead of changing the subject or blowing off my comment like it was no big deal like I normally would, I gulp down the lump in my throat as I gather my courage and look him in the eyes as I quietly admit the truth. "It is for me." A shy, nervous smile plays on my lips as I await his reaction.

He chuckles, his smile growing and his eyes sparkling, making my heart beat faster. "Well, that's good, real good," he emphasizes. "I think this date is going pretty great too."

I feel my body relax at his admission. Suddenly feeling playful, I pinch my lips together, holding back my laughter, before I joke, "I didn't say it was going great."

His head falls back as he bursts out laughing, causing my heart to feel full.

As we make our way around to the other side of the ice rink, we notice a "Wish Tree," causing my heart to skip a beat with the sadness of my own memories. Jack squeezes my hand, and I look up at him, his eyes questioning and full of concern. "Are you okay?"

I nod and attempt to gulp down the lump in my throat. "Yeah," I croak. "This is the 'Wish Tree,'" I declare as an explanation for my reaction, nodding toward the tree. He remains quiet, waiting for me to continue. Heaving a sigh, I attempt to release the tension from my shoulders. I'm suddenly aware that, for the first time, I'm comfortable enough with a man to tell him this story, which causes my stomach to flip at the realization.

Giving myself a mental shake, I stare at the tree as I speak. "This tree holds wishes of kids whose family doesn't have the money to buy them things or of kids who don't have families to give them gifts. They write one wish on a star or angel and decorate it if they want. Then they put it on the tree. Anyone can pick a wish off the tree and grant it or buy that present and wrap it." I grin, thinking about the generosity of so many when we needed it most. "Then you bring the presents here before Christmas Eve so they can be delivered to the kids in time for Christmas. There's another one for kids in the local hospital, too," I inform him. "I'm sure it's around here somewhere."

"That's a pretty wonderful thing." He pauses, tilting his head as he assesses me. "You sure seem to know a lot about these trees."

Nodding in agreement, I mumble, "I do." I exhale slowly as I guide him toward the green wooden bench next to the tree and sit with his hand still linked with mine in support. I glance up at him, looking into his eyes, seeing nothing but warmth, kindness, and support. I feel like it's time to share.

"Are you alright?"

I nod, quietly admitting, "A few years ago, my sister had her name on that tree." He grips my hand tighter, and his free hand gently covers our clasped ones causing my chest to tighten. "Our parents died when I was twenty-one, and she was only ten. It happened right after Thanksgiving." I shake my head, almost in denial of the memory. "The first year, I found a few things my parents had already bought for her, but..." I trail off and take a deep breath, pulling myself together. "The next year, someone told me about the tree. I had my sister write down one of her Christmas Wishes and I gave it to the organization to put on the tree. It really meant a lot to us for a couple of years," I confess with a sad smile. "I would always make her something, too," I shrug without looking at him, feeling the tears welling in my eyes. "But I just wanted her to have as good of a Christmas as she could," I explain, pushing back the tears I pray don't fall.

After I pull myself together, I finally glance up at him from underneath my eyelashes to gauge his reaction. "You're an amazing woman, taking care of your sister like that," he softly proclaims.

"Thank you," I rasp, my whole body warming with the compliment. "It's the most important thing I've ever done, and that's what you do for family, for someone you love," I declare.

He nods. "I agree, but who took care of you?" he asks, his eyes full of empathy.

My heart jumps up to my throat as I inhale quickly in surprise, my whole body tingling instantly. Licking my lips, I fight to get any words out. "Seeing her happy made me happy," I insist, knowing it's true.

His eyes sparkle with admiration as he stares at me. My face heats, and I quickly avert my gaze. "How old is she now?" he probes.

Relaxing, a smile tugs at my lips. I glance over at this man beside me, wondering how he can pull a smile out of me when I'm talking about this. "So, you want to know how old I am?" I ask, quirking my brow. He laughs but doesn't agree or deny my accusation. "She's fifteen, which means I'm twenty-six, but my birthday is two days after Christmas," I reply with barely suppressed laughter.

"We will have to celebrate," he proclaims, his eyes lighting up.

I gasp as soon as I realize what he just said. He wants to celebrate my birthday with me weeks from now. Could this actually work between us? This is just our first date. I feel like I'm getting ahead of myself, but he's making it so easy. I clear my throat and attempt to push his comment out of my mind. "Anyway, Christmas is about her for me," I tell him. He stares at me momentarily, but I can't tell what he's thinking. Biting the inside of my cheek, I ask nervously, "So, is this conversation scaring you away now? I have a fifteen-year-old at home," I tease, feeling slightly uneasy as I await his response.

He shakes his head in denial and clears his throat. "No, that doesn't scare me. I'd love to meet her." My eyes widen, and my heart skips a beat at the thought. "You would?"

"Definitely. She sounds amazing."

"She really is."

He squeezes my hand, his eyes pinned to me as he tells me sincerely, "I'm so sorry for your loss."

"Thanks," I mumble and begin fidgeting with an imaginary string on my coat as I look away.

Sensing my unease, he changes directions on the subject, making me grateful. "Why don't we pick a few names off the Wish tree, and we can go Christmas shopping together for a few of these kids before Christmas?"

I smile, his suggestion causing my heart to stop before restarting. I love this idea more than he could begin to understand. But I don't have the money to contribute to more than one gift. "I would love to. Although I can't buy for a few kids, I could help with one. I believe it's important, and I try to give back to them whenever I can, especially after everything they did for Holly and I."

He gives me a comforting smile and suggests, "Well, you can help me with the ones I'd like to buy presents for too. That is if you don't mind?"

"I would love that!" I nod in agreement, the lump immediately returning to my throat.

We stand and walk over, picking three names off the tree, noticing a little boy with blonde hair curled up underneath the branches. Jack crouches down and gently nudges the boy on the shoulder. "Are you alright little man?" he asks gently.

The boy lifts his head. His eyes are red and swollen from crying. He shakes his head and whimpers, "I can't find my mommy and daddy. They told me to meet them by the big tree if I got lost, but they all look big to me," he explains, whimpering.

Jack gives him a comforting smile and offers, "We'll help you find them. Can you come out from under the tree?"

"I'm not supposed to talk to strangers, but I need help," he reasons, shaking his head. Lifting my hand, I cover my mouth to hide my amusement; at the same time, my heart hurts for this little boy knowing how scared he must be. I watch him cautiously take Jack's hand and climb out from under the Christmas tree.

He stands the little boy next to me and introduces us, "Owen, this is my friend Jessica."

Owen's eyes snap up to Jack and narrow on him curiously. "How do you know my name?" he accuses.

Jack smiles warmly and explains, "Your tag is sticking out of your coat, and it's written on there." Owen relaxes as he nods in acceptance. "Stand here for a minute with Jessica. I'm just going to stand up on this bench right here and see if I can find them," he informs him.

"How will you know what they look like?" Owen asks as he slips his hand into mine, making me smile.

"Don't worry about that," Jack advises as he steps up onto the bench and cups his hands around his mouth like a megaphone. Taking a deep breath, he yells, "We have a little boy here who is looking for his lost parents. Do we have any lost parents searching for a little boy?" he reiterates loudly.

"We are," a mother screeches as two hands fly into the air and come charging toward us. "Owen," she croons with tears in her eyes, overwhelmed with relief at the site of her son. She wraps him up in her arms tightly as he buries his head into her shoulder.

The father nods gratefully toward me. "Thank you," he mumbles, his voice catching.

I grin and gesture toward Jack. "It was all my friend, Jack."

"We," he emphasizes, "are happy we could help."

The woman looks at both of us and wipes a tear away, still tightly clutching her son with one hand. "Thank you."

"Bye," Owen calls as we both wave to him. He wipes the last of his tears and smiles broadly before he waves goodbye with his free hand.

"Merry Christmas," Jack calls.

"Merry Christmas," they reply in unison.

I glance up at Jack, butterflies swarming my insides. "You're not at all like I expected," I giggle.

"What did you expect?" he asks curiously, giving me a look without judgment.

"I don't know, but not...this," I smile shyly, my face turning a deep shade of red. "You're like a knight in shining armor," I tease him, thinking he's like the man of my dreams. It makes me wonder if he's too good to be true.

He laughs, shaking his head. "I'm no knight."

"Well, you're a good man," I insist, thinking about all the things I witnessed in just one night.

"Thank you," he acknowledges, his cheeks turning rosy, making my heart skip a beat. "I think you're pretty incredible, too," he proclaims and takes a step closer to me, holding my gaze.

My heartbeat speeds up, and I gasp for breath as he steps into my space. He glances down at my lips, making me want nothing more than for him to kiss me. But this feels like it's happening too fast. The loud ringing of bells startles me out of my haze, and I break our heated gaze.

Swiftly, I step back and look away as I try to catch my breath and calm down my racing heart. Digging into my pocket, I pull my phone out, noticing the time. "Wow, it's late! I'm so sorry, but I need to get home. I have another early day at work tomorrow, and my sister has school," I blurt out.

He grins, nodding his head in acknowledgment. "That's okay. I understand. Can I give you a ride home?"

I shake my head. "No, thank you. I actually walked. It's a beautiful night." He nods in agreement. "I better go; I'm sorry," I repeat awkwardly.

He shakes his head. "No apologies. May I walk you home, at least?"

Breathing a sigh of relief, I grin, nodding in agreement. "Sure, thanks."

We fall into step together as we walk toward my house. After a few beats of silence, he glances at me hesitantly before he comments, "This date has not only been longer than my last three dates combined, but it has also been a million times better." He pauses, staring at me. "I had a wonderful time, Jessica. I just want you to know that."

"I had a great time, too," I state simply. "I haven't been to any of the Christmas festivals in a really long time and..."

"Why not?" he interrupts. "Don't you live here?" he asks, perplexed. "I asked you before when you mentioned it's been a long time, but you just said you were busy. Has your answer changed?"

I nod. "I do live here, and yes, my answer has changed, but I think I'll have to tell you more another time." I've told him more tonight than I've ever told anyone, and this is just our first date. I think I need some time to process before I confess anything else to this man.

"Gives me a reason to see you again," he teases, his lips quirking up in a smile.

I blush, my gaze drifting away. Taking a deep breath, I look him in the eyes and whisper, "I'd really like that."

"Good. I think I may start coming up with reasons to see you blush. You really are beautiful, Jessica," he compliments, causing me to turn a deeper shade of red. "Besides, according to the festival brochure, it looks like there's a lot of other things we haven't been able to see or do yet," he comments, holding up the brochure as proof.

"That's true," I agree, nodding.

"How about after work tomorrow, we do some shopping for the kids we picked from the tree? I can pick you up, and we can go to the toy store and wherever else you think we should try," he suggests. "What do you think, Jessica?" He pauses, adding, "I'd really like to see you again."

I nod. "I'd like that too. Just let me just check with my sister first if that's okay?"

Releasing a sigh, his body relaxes as he grins. "Of course. She is welcome to come with us too if you'd like. Only if she wants to, of course," he adds as an afterthought.

I chuckle, appreciating the offer. "I'm not sure but thank you." We stop in front of my home, the front porch light on as well as a light illuminating the inside both in the front and the back of the house where the kitchen is located. "This is me," I inform him, gesturing behind me. "Thank you again for a great night, Jack."

He smiles. "You're welcome, and thank you, Jessica." He leans down toward me and tilts his head to the side, placing a sweet kiss on my cheek. I savor the light touch of his lips against my skin with a soft smile, sending small shock waves to my heart.

Turning around, I step toward the front door and glance over my shoulder to wave, finding Jack still standing in the same spot, watching me. His smile warms me from head to toe, and I force myself to turn back toward the house. I push the door open and quickly step inside, closing the door behind me. Then I fall against it with a happy sigh.

Before I left, I hoped my date would be with someone like him, not even knowing exactly whom I might be meeting. I can't believe I'm lucky enough to not only have my date be the man I had been thinking of but to find out he's impossibly better than I imagined in my dreams. I just hope he's not too good to be true.

CHAPTER 9
Jack

"Those first few dates you sent me on were terrible, and that's putting it nicely. I definitely can't give you any credit for those, Allie. Don't get me wrong, each of them is probably perfect for someone else, but not me," I emphasize as I walk another box of ornaments over to the corner of my ranch office. "Although, I have to admit you were right about Jessica," I mumble, trying to hide my smile.

"Say that again!" She grins as she hangs the blue ornament on the tree from her perch on the small ladder. I arch my eyebrows in question, and she elaborates. "You know, the part about me being right."

I smirk and tease, "I don't need your head to get any bigger." She places her hands on her hips and glares at me. I hold my hands up in surrender, laughing. "You know I'm kidding. The problem is, I still don't think it can work down the road."

"You don't know that."

"I really do like her, though," I concede, thinking about her bright smile. I hand Allie another red glass ornament to place on the small Christmas tree. "She's different," I add thoughtfully.

"I knew it!" she squeals happily. She spins and hangs the ornament in her hand on one of the higher branches.

I laugh as I hold my hand up to steady her before she knocks over the whole tree. "Whoa, be careful!"

"I'm fine!" She waves me off, steadying herself as she hangs another ornament. "You two are absolutely perfect together!" she declares triumphantly.

"Don't get ahead of yourself," I warn, chuckling. "We've only been on one date. Unless you count the date I had with the other woman at the bakery when I met Jessica, I did talk to her more than the woman I was supposed to be on a date with," I joke, making Allie giggle.

I sigh heavily, already feeling defeated. "It doesn't matter how much I like her, though. Even if we go on a few dates and everything goes perfectly, it's not like I can tell her who I really am, then bring her home and introduce her to my parents. You know it's not that easy for me," I remind her, feeling a pang in my heart.

"Why not?" she challenges, shrugging as she reaches for another ornament. "If she's the right one..." she trails off, arching her eyebrows.

I shake my head and drop my hands to my sides, my heart lurching in protest with my thoughts. "It's not about her being the right one, and you know it."

"I don't believe that Jack, and neither should you. Her being the right woman for you and you being the right man for her should be the only thing this is about," she declares in exasperation.

"I wish that were true."

She stops decorating the tree and puts her hands on her hips, staring me down furiously. "Nicholas Jack Claus, stop complaining! If she's the right woman, she'll love you as you are, parents and all," she maintains.

"It's not really about my parents either. It's more about the Christmas baggage that goes along with being a part of our family legacy," I attempt to explain, knowing she should understand this better than anyone since she's been with our family for so long. "I'm proud of who I am. I really am," I insist, "but my family legacy is not something that's easy for adults to believe in. If they can't believe in our family legacy, then you can't believe in me."

She drops her hands to her sides with a heavy sigh, all her fight gone. "Jessica is not like every other adult you meet."

"That's definitely true."

Heaving a sigh in exasperation, she maintains, "You just need to try, Jack, and give her a chance. Everything else will eventually fall into place," she encourages.

As I groan, I run my hand over my face in frustration. I have to let it go. I'm not going to win this conversation right now, or ever for that matter. "Anyway," I stride over to my desk and glance at my calendar, "I have a meeting late this afternoon on the shipping of the new tech toys. I need to make sure they're ready on time," I insist, attempting to focus on my job.

She nods in agreement. "Yes, you do," she mumbles, stepping off the ladder as she reaches for her tablet to take a few notes. I quickly recap the rest of my schedule for the rest of the week with her, which is thankfully relatively light.

"Got it," she declares. "Good luck." She turns for the door, pausing and turning back around with a mischievous smile. "Oh, by the way, we need you to handle everything for the Christmas train in Mistletoe Haven this year. I know it's last minute and all, but the company we scheduled to coordinate it this year accidentally overbooked, so your dad volunteered you for the job."

"Great."

She adds cheerfully, "He figured since you're in the area and the ranch isn't too far from there, it should work out perfectly."

I nod in agreement, knowing I'll do everything I can to help out my family, especially this time of year when they need it the most. "I can handle that," I confirm. I honestly wouldn't be surprised if Allie was the one who volunteered me for the event so I would be closer to Jessica during the holidays, but I'm not about to complain. I may not tell her, but I will admit it to myself, I'd love to spend more time in Mistletoe Haven. More time there means more time with Jessica, and although I have my doubts, the possibility of things working out with her has me wanting to try.

I want to get to know her better and maybe even meet her sister if she will let me. I'm just going to keep all that information away from Allie for now. I can only imagine what she and my mom would do if I didn't. Honestly, they would probably start planning my wedding. My heart lurches at the thought. I want that someday. I just don't know exactly how I'm supposed to get it. As I take a deep breath, I mentally shake my head, forcing myself to return my focus to the work in front of me.

"Jack?" Allie nearly shouts, making me realize she's been trying to get my attention.

"Sorry, I'm going over some things in my head," I mumble smoothly. Hopefully, she'll assume I mean regarding the Christmas train and not about the girl. However, her eyes narrow, and before she has a chance to say anything, I ask her a question, attempting to keep the conversation on business. "Do we have a passenger train ready to handle all the children and families for the event?"

She purses her lips and stares at me for a moment before she answers. "Yes, it's on the way into town today. I told the transportation coordinator you would be there later this week to inspect everything. For now, we just need to work on servers for the hot chocolate, which we'll make using your mom's recipe, of course. We need treats, a baker to make the treats, music, a few games, tickets, decorations, marketing, and I'll also make sure Katie brings you a suit down from the North Pole so you can be Santa on the train," she declares happily. "She'll be coming down to help since we added this event for you last minute."

My eyes widen in surprise. "Can my mom and dad afford to be without Katie at the workshop right now?" It's hard to believe she would be helping anywhere but at the North Pole, with Christmas only a couple of weeks away.

She nods. "They've got it covered up there. Besides, she's been working a lot more of the Christmas events in the last few years anyway. We want her here."

I nod at the reminder. "That's right. It seems I could definitely use her help then." I tap a pen on my desk and begin mentally running through everything I need to do for the Christmas train event in my head. "Allie, can you put that list together for me now so I can have everything in front of me?" I request. "I want to get right to work on the event."

"I already have that for you right here," Allie declares, standing a little straighter. She walks over to the small table near the tree and pulls a folder out from underneath her tablet. She steps up to my desk and hands me a green folder with a satisfied smile.

"Thank you," I mumble appreciatively as I take the folder from her. "And thank you for coming up here and helping me decorate this office, too," I add quickly.

"You're welcome. I also figured we might be here a while, and if that's the case, it needs to feel more like Christmas in here. I have some of the elves brightening up the rest of the house this afternoon." She grins.

"Thanks," I mumble, amazed at how fast and efficiently she works.

She nods, then turns and walks back to the table, picks up her tablet, and begins typing. She stops and looks up at me, grinning. "There! I just emailed you the file as well, so you can't tell me I never gave it to you," she teases.

"Of course you did," I grin. "You and Katie are so efficient with everything," I state confidently. "Between the three of us, Christmas should be easy this year," I joke, making her giggle. In all honesty, I don't know what I'd do without her.

"Our part of it anyway," she jokes.

I chuckle. "Anyway, I'll also need some elves to help with the trip and gifts for all the kids onboard," I remind her, and she nods in agreement. "Will we be able to get ahold of a passenger manifest at least a few days before the event?" My job is much easier when I know who will be onboard the train."

She nods. "Yes, we should have it the day before the event if it doesn't sell out, but around here, the train has historically sold out at least a few days before the event, if not sooner. If that's the case this year, we should have the list in our hands early. When we get it, we'll make sure to compare our list with your dad's list, so we don't have any crossovers. Either way, I'll make sure you have whatever you need for the kids on the train," Allie confirms.

"Wonderful, thank you," I murmur. She nods and turns to leave again.

When she's walking out the door, an idea crosses my mind, and I stand up to stop her. "Allie, wait!"

She freezes and spins on her heel, looking back at me again, arching her eyebrows in question. "Yes, Jack?"

I feel my body warm nervously with the thought of what I'm about to ask. "Could you do me a favor?"

"Of course. It's my job."

I force a smile and ask, "Would you send Jessica a bouquet of Amaryllis flowers, maybe mixed with some pine and winter berries?" I request.

She grins wide and with a clap of her hands, exclaims, "Absolutely!"

Attempting to ignore her exuberance, I instruct, "And on the card, have them write, 'I had a wonderful time with you last night. I can't wait to find more reasons to hear your laugh, see your smile, and to beautifully color your cheeks like these flowers.'"

She jumps up and kicks her leg out as she spins toward the door as if she's dancing across a ballroom floor. She calls over her shoulder, "I'm on it!" I laugh and shake my head in amusement as she rushes out of the room, probably afraid I might change my mind.

As I sit down, I lean back in my chair, smiling to myself as I hum, "Wonderful Christmastime." I open the folder Allie just handed me and begin looking over the list. My eyes widen as they focus on one item, in particular, forming an idea in my head. Quickly standing, I grab my coat, pulling it on as I stride for my office door.

I step out of my office, striding to Allie's desk. "Allie," I say to get her attention as she hangs up the phone.

"The flowers for Jessica are all taken care of," she declares as she looks up at me with satisfaction.

I nod in appreciation. Feeling my cheeks heat, I simply say, "Thank you." She smiles her acknowledgment, and I continue, "I just wanted to let you know I'm headed out for a few hours. I'll be back for the meeting later this afternoon. There's something on this list I hope I can take care of right now," I inform her, my stomach turning in anticipation.

She nods. "Sounds good. Don't forget your phone, so you can call me if you need anything while you're out," she reminds me. I chuckle at how well she knows me since I'm the one who often leaves it on my desk or somewhere at home.

"I will," I concede with an appreciative smile. "I have my phone," I inform her waving it gently in front of me so she can see it. "I will make sure I'm back for my meeting this afternoon, too, so don't worry."

She chuckles and shakes her head. "Okay, good. You can go then," she states, shooing me away with a small wave of her hands.

I cross my arms over my chest as my eyes narrow on her. "Are you trying to get rid of me?"

"Yes," she declares with a smirk, making me laugh. "Get out of here," she demands playfully, "so I can call your mom and give her an update on how all of your dates went, especially the one with Jessica." She grins with a sparkle in her eyes.

"I'm leaving!" I chuckle and shake my head as I turn and walk away. I'm sure that's exactly what she's going to do as soon as I'm out of earshot. I pick up my pace, wanting to get away from here as quickly as possible.

CHAPTER 10
Jessica

Careful to get it exactly right, I touch up the white frosting on the last tray of Santa hat cookies before setting down my frosting bag. Then, I slip on my brown and white Gingerbread cookie oven mitts and take the two steps toward the oven just as the timer goes off, indicating the candy cane cookies are done. I open the oven and pull out two full sheets, inhaling the sweet scent of the warm sugar cookies with a satisfied smile. As I set the cookie sheet down, I let my eyes skim over the twisted red, white, and green dough in admiration. I nod to myself, happy with how the cookies came out. Quickly, I yank the right oven mitt off my hand and place it next to the tray. Then, I reach for my spatula and begin carefully removing the cookies from the tray and placing them onto the cooling rack sitting next to it.

"Jessica," my boss Betty calls from the front of the bakery.

"Yes, Betty?" I call back.

"One of the customers is asking about your cookies. Can you come here for a few minutes, please?" she requests.

"I'll be right there," I respond sweetly as I remove the last of the candy cane cookies off the baking sheet and onto the cooling rack. Then, I set the spatula down along with the other oven mitt before grabbing the tray of finished Santa hat cookies to bring out to the front to put in the display case.

I approach my gray-haired boss standing next to the large display and gently set the tray down on the counter. "Hi, Betty. I just finished the Santa Hat cookies."

She turns to me with a broad smile and exclaims, "Wonderful!" She eyes them, her coffee brown eyes lighting up, appearing pleased. Then she turns her focus back on me. "I'll put them in the case while you go ahead and help this gentleman. He asked about some of your cookies and would like to try some," she informs me, gesturing over her shoulder.

I turn and gasp as my eyes immediately lock with Jack's intense blue gaze. He grins, his eyes sparkling as he greets me, "Hi, Jessica."

"Jack, hi," I whisper, feeling my heart pound erratically inside my chest at merely the sight of him. "What are you doing here?" I blurt out.

He chuckles. "I actually came to see you." I feel the heat rush to my face and glance down at the case filled with cookies and other treats as I pull myself together. "I was hoping I could taste test anything you may have made today," he proclaims, grinning.

"What?" I ask, confused. "Why?"

His smile broadens. "Well, do you mean besides the obvious reason that I really like your baking?" I blush an even deeper shade of red as my eyes wander toward his flat stomach. I can't help but think there's nothing obvious about him liking dessert as much as he claims. He chuckles again, informing me, "Actually, I'm here on business, but I knew you were the one I needed to speak with. Do you have any Christmas cookies for me to try specifically beside the gingerbread ones I tried the other day?"

"Of course I do. I just finished these," I reveal, gesturing to the tray of Santa cookies Betty is currently unloading into the display cases, "I have a few others I made today as well. But what kind of business do you have where you get to taste test my cookies?" I smirk.

"A fun one," he claims, grinning. I reach for a plate as he continues. "I just found out I am now in charge of organizing everything for the Christmas train that leaves from here in Mistletoe Haven for this year anyway. The company that was supposed to do it accidentally overbooked, and now I need to finish all the planning as quickly as possible to make it happen. One of the first things I have on my list is finding some delicious Christmas treats."

My eyes widen in surprise. "Oh, wow. That's gotta' be a lot of treats. And you want the bakery to help with the event?"

He shakes his head, prompting my eyebrows to draw together in confusion. "No, I want *you* to help me with the event," he emphasizes.

"What?" I ask, my mouth falling open before I quickly snap it shut.

"I wasn't kidding when I said your gingerbread cookies were the best I've ever had, and believe me, I know a thing or two about Christmas cookies," he claims, his blue eyes sparkling mischievously.

I shake my head, my stomach turning as disappointment overwhelms me. "Betty won't let me do something like that. She won't have enough help if I'm not here."

"I already talked to Betty, and she thinks it would be a great idea," he informs me. My eyes widen again as hope consumes me. "How about this," he proposes, "make me a plate with a few of your Christmas cookies, all the ones you have ready today, and I'll pay for them. Then come and talk to me about what you made while I try them. Then we can figure out where to go from there."

I open my mouth to argue, "But, Jack..."

He immediately interrupts, pleading, "Please, humor me. It doesn't have to mean you'll work with me on this, but wouldn't it be wonderful if it worked out?"

I take a deep breath to calm my anxiety and quietly agree, "Okay." He thanks me with a heart-melting smile causing butterflies to take flight in my stomach.

Taking a deep breath, I attempt to focus on what I'm doing instead of Jack watching me. I reach for a white plate, setting three different Christmas cookies on it. Then I carry them to the register and ring up the cookies. "That comes to seven dollars and eighty-nine cents."

He hands me the money as I hand him the plate. I glance back at Betty for approval. She smiles, and she waves me away with her hands. "Go ahead," she encourages me to go with him.

I nod and turn around, following him as he strides over to a small round table for two directly in front of the large front picture window, looking out onto Main Street. I wipe my hands on my apron as I sit down, and he slides into the seat directly across from me.

"So, what do I have here?" he asks, pointing to the treats in front of him.

"Well, unfortunately, I don't have too much," I ramble, scrunching up my nose. "I didn't know you'd be coming, so I'm not really prepared."

He grins and looks me in the eyes, attempting to calm my nerves. "It's okay, Jess. I don't expect you to read my mind. This is more than enough," he insists, gesturing to the plate in front of him.

My heart skips a beat at the nickname. I take a deep breath and exhale slowly, willing my nerves to calm down. Honestly, I don't know why I'm so nervous. I love making cookies and other treats for people, especially Christmas cookies. Maybe I'm anxious because he's the one trying something I made, and I really want him to like it. I care what he thinks. Pointing to a chocolate cookie with peppermint cream and sprinkled with crushed candy canes, I enlighten him, "That's one of my new ones this year. I don't have a name for it yet."

I watch as he picks up the cookie and consumes nearly half of it in just one bite. He closes his eyes as he chews, his whole body relaxing as he takes in the flavor. "Mm, this is delicious!" he mumbles as he finishes chewing. "Is everything here one of your recipes?" he questions as he opens his eyes and focuses on me, his eyes full of curiosity.

I shake my head. "No, a lot are Betty's old recipes, but I've been adding things on my own over the years. She trusts me and tells me to make what I'd like as long as I make the ones her customers have come to expect when they walk in the door. All of the Christmas cookies are mine, though," I admit.

"You should have your own bakery. You're really talented."

I feel my face heat at his compliment. "Thanks. I appreciate that, but I can't do that right now. It's a lot of money to invest in a place," I tell him honestly, shrugging.

He nods. "Yeah, but with these cookies," he gestures with his head toward the plate in front of him, "You could have investors lining up to be a part of your business. I know I would be the first in line. These are seriously fantastic!" he emphasizes.

"Thank you," I repeat. "My own bakery, though?" I question, pressing my lips together as doubt creeps into my mind. I shake my head, quickly brushing off the idea. "Betty needs me. Besides, I couldn't do something like that by myself, and where would I go? I would never want to compete against Betty. She's always taken very good care of me. Besides, one bakery is more than enough for this town, but I couldn't go somewhere else with Holly and school." Pausing, I shake my head. "Plus, I'm so busy already, and I have Holly to think about."

"Exactly," he mumbles inaudibly, sighing. As he bites his lip, he stares intently at me like he's trying to read every single thought in my head, only making me wonder what he's thinking. He tilts his head to the side and finally asks, "Do you do all the baking?"

I nod. "Most of it. It's too much for Betty now that she's older. Holly sometimes helps on weekends and after school. Plus, Betty has a niece and nephew who sometimes work here too, but they both have full-time jobs. They just cover when I'm not here."

He picks up a thin sugar cookie, pressed simply with green sugar. His eyes widen as he swallows. "I think this just melted in my mouth," he murmurs. He picks up the last cookie, the Santa Hat I just finished decorating. After he takes a bite and swallows it, he sets the rest of the cookie down and declares, "You're making the cookies for the Christmas train. You have to," he pleads with a confident smile. "It needs to be you."

I sigh in defeat, my lips tugging up at the corners, knowing I don't want to say no to him. I have the strongest urge to do whatever I can to help him. "Okay, I'll do it," I agree, nodding as my stomach twists into knots the moment the words leave my mouth. "But I need a lot more information if you want me to do a good job."

He laughs, his whole body relaxing into his seat. "That's the easy part now that I have you." Heat rushes to my cheeks as a storm takes over my insides with his comment, feeling like his meaning has more behind it than just baking. "I'll make sure you have help too. I realize I'm asking a lot. I don't expect you to do it all by yourself."

Shaking my head in disbelief, I smirk. "You're a bit eager."

He sits up straight and grins broadly. "Must be all the cookies I ate." I laugh, and he chuckles along with me, warming me from head to toe.

I reach my hand up to brush my hair back behind my ears and drop my hands back into my lap. He freezes, giving me another look that takes my breath away. Then, he licks his lips and opens his mouth as if to say something, but no words come. Instead, he leans over the table and gently brushes his thumb over my cheek, eliciting a soft gasp from my lips. He pauses with his hand, gently cupping my jawline. I stare at him, afraid to move and breathe, not wanting the moment to end.

Breaking our gaze, he finally clears his throat and drops his hand as he leans back in his chair. He mumbles an explanation, "You, ah, had some flour or something on your cheek."

I smile and look down at the table, murmuring, "Thank you. That seems to happen to me a lot." I shrug. "It's a hazard of the job."

He grins and takes a deep breath, popping another bite of cookie into his mouth. His phone beeps with a text message. I watch as he checks his phone, a bright smile lighting up his face. "Looks like I just got the rest of the day off," he announces as he looks at me.

"What?"

"I was supposed to head back to my office after this for a meeting this afternoon, but they just rescheduled for tomorrow morning." I nod in understanding. "So, what time are you done with work today?"

I shrug. "I just have to drizzle some icing on a batch of candy cane cookies I just finished. I think that's all I have left for today. Why?"

"More cookies? Can I try one of those too?"

I laugh, shaking my head in amusement. "How can you eat any more cookies right now?"

He chuckles, claiming, "There's always room for dessert. Are they peppermint?"

I shake my head. "No. It's colored sugar cookie dough twisted together, and I drizzle a white glaze icing over them after they cool. Pretty simple." I shrug like it's no big deal. "They should be cool enough to finish about now."

"Sooo," he drags out before continuing, "do you think I can try one while I wait for you?" he reiterates with a hopeful smile.

I arch my eyebrow in question. "Wait for me?"

He nods. "Yeah, after you're done, we can go shopping for the Christmas Wish gifts we picked off the tree last night."

"I need to go home and get cleaned up before I go anywhere." I glance down at my clothes covered in flour, sugar, frosting, and food coloring and laugh at myself. "And I definitely need to change out of these clothes. I'm a mess."

"I'll wait for you and bring you home then. If that's okay with you," he adds sheepishly. "Did you walk here?"

I shake my head. "It was too early to walk. I usually come in to start baking when it's still dark, so I drive to work."

"I'll drive you home. And then you can pick up your car when we come back into town to go shopping."

I smile over at him and happily relent, "Okay. Let me go finish up these cookies, and then we can go." He nods in agreement appearing pleased with my response. "I'll see you in a few minutes, Jack."

"Don't forget to bring me one of those cookies!"

I laugh as I push through the swinging kitchen door.

CHAPTER 11
Jack

I follow Jessica through the front door of her house and right into a living room full of stacks of boxes along with large red and green colored storage bins. "You can sit down on the couch while I go clean up," she tells me, gesturing toward the filled room.

I chuckle, looking around me with wide eyes. "Where is it?"

She stops and glances over at the living room, immediately dropping her hand down at her side. She blushes a deep shade of red, causing my heart to pound. "Oh," she grumbles, scrunching up her nose in distaste. "I forgot about those," she murmurs adorably.

I laugh harder and prod, "Really? That looks like a lot of things to just forget about."

She shrugs. "My sister got them out from the basement last night while we were out. She wants to decorate for Christmas. She figured it would get done a lot faster if there was an obvious reminder in our living room," she explains, the corners of her lips tugging up in amusement.

I grin, nodding in understanding. "That would do it. Let me help you."

Her mouth drops slightly open in surprise. With her disbelief clear in her voice, she looks up at me and asks, "You want to help me decorate my house for Christmas?"

I nod, enjoying the way she's looking at me. "Yes, I would love to help you. I'm good at it, too," I brag, a smile tugging at my lips.

She laughs. "You are, huh?" I nod, no longer trying to wipe the huge grin from my face. Her eyebrows scrunch together with doubt, and she hesitantly prompts, "Are you sure?"

I step toward her and look into her eyes, confirming, "I'm positive. It will be fun!" Looking around, I ask, "Where should I start?" I turn toward the box closest to me and reach for the one on top.

"Not those," she says, stopping me by gently laying her hand on my forearm, heating my skin. She quickly pulls her hand back as if she were burned and continues to explain. "Those are ornaments, and since we don't have a tree yet," she mumbles, trailing off.

"We definitely need to get you one."

She ignores my comment and informs me, "I'm going to go change. I feel like I have cookie dough all over me."

"I like cookies," I tease, smirking.

She blushes and backs toward the hallway. "I'll be right back."

I nod and turn back toward the boxes as she disappears. Walking to the other side of the room, I pull the lid off a bin, finding several strings of white and colored Christmas lights. I lift it off and open the one underneath it, finding more of the same. Then, I take the top off the bin to my right and pull out a mini artificial tree. Underneath that, I find two more mini trees and bags of mini ornaments, including some handmade ones, bringing a smile to my face. I startle at the sound of the front door opening and look toward it.

"Jess, are you here?" a teenage girl with light brown hair, a white winter coat, jeans, and tall black boots calls as she steps into the house. "I'm home!"

"I'm in here, Holly. I'll be there in a minute!" Jessica's muffled voice comes through her bedroom door.

"I didn't see your car."

"I left it in town."

"Hi," I greet her.

She startles and spins toward me with her hand on her chest. "You scared me. Where did you come from?"

I smirk at the small tree in my hand and answer, "The North Pole?" She rolls her eyes and takes a cautious step toward me. "You must be Holly."

"Yes," she answers hesitantly, "and you are?"

"I'm sorry, I'm a friend of Jessica's. I'm Jack," I introduce myself, holding out my free hand for her to shake.

Her whole body instantly relaxes as she smiles like I just gave her the best gift. "Jack!" she exclaims, slipping her hand into mine and shaking it firmly. "I should've recognized you from your profile picture!"

"Ah! So, you're the one I need to thank for helping set us up?"

She nods vehemently. "Absolutely! It's so nice to meet you! I heard you and my sister had a lot of fun last night at the Christmas festival," she tells me, her smile growing, "and now you're here...in our living room."

I chuckle, nodding. "Yeah, we were going to do some Christmas shopping, but it looks like we have some decorating to do instead and maybe even a Christmas tree to buy."

She drops my hand and puts her hands on her hips with a bright smile on her face, declaring, "We definitely need to buy a Christmas tree!"

"What about a tree?" Jessica asks as she steps back into the room wearing black leggings and a long dark green cable-knit sweater, taking my breath away.

Holly leaps toward her sister in excitement. She stops abruptly right in front of her, bouncing on her toes. "We're going to get a Christmas tree!"

Jessica laughs. "Okay, okay. You're like a little kid again."

I grin. "Isn't that part of the fun of Christmas?"

She blushes and smiles shyly up at me, shrugging her shoulders. "I guess it is."

"Let's go right now before you decide we have something else we have to do first," Holly encourages. She grabs her sister's hand and tugs her toward the door, making me laugh.

"Let me grab my coat and my purse first, Holly," she mumbles, barely containing her laughter. Holly drops her hand, and Jessica turns toward me. I reach for her coat and hold it out for her, helping her slip it on. "Thank you." She nods in appreciation. Spinning around, she grabs her purse, only to find Holly holding it out for her making her laugh again. "I get it; you want to go," she teases.

We walk out front, and Jessica freezes on her front walkway, nearly causing me to bump into her. I reach for her arm to steady myself and immediately apologize, "Sorry."

"It's fine, but I don't have a car," she reminds me.

"That's okay; I'll drive."

We walk up to my red truck and pull the back door open, holding it for Holly. She quickly climbs in, and then I do the same for Jessica. She smiles and whispers, "Thank you." I nod in acknowledgment and jog around the front of my truck, swiftly sliding in behind the wheel.

"The best tree place is just on the other side of town," Holly instructs as I back out of the driveway.

"The one just past the church?" I question, glancing at Jessica out of the corner of my eye.

"Yes," both of them reply in unison.

"You seem to really like Christmas, Holly," I state, grinning.

"Of course! Don't you?" she questions with wide eyes.

"I do." I laugh and joke, "I'd probably be kicked out of my family if I didn't."

Holly giggles and shares, "That's why our parents named us Jessica and Holly. They always loved Christmas. It was their favorite time of year, and they wanted us to have names that reminded them of something that had to do with Christmas."

"Really?" I ask, arching my eyebrow in surprise.

I see her nod in the rearview mirror before she continues, "Yeah, my dad wasn't sure at first, so Jess was named after Mrs. Claus." She smirks.

My stomach twists as I laugh and mumble, "Well, one of them, anyway."

"He had forgotten it was one of her names. Our mom didn't bother reminding him until after her name was on the birth certificate, Jessica Layla Moore." She giggles as if her parents were retelling the story bringing a smile to my face.

I glance over at Jessica as I pull into the parking lot in front of rows of Christmas trees. Her face appears pink, even in the dim light, as she casts her head down, a small smile on her lips, giving me goosebumps. "You've always loved that story," Jessica murmurs.

"Of course. It's a great story! My name is a little more obvious, although I know another Holly who doesn't remind me much of Christmas at all," Holly grumbles, scrunching up her nose in displeasure, the same way I've seen her sister do several times already.

I barely have my truck in park when Holly jumps out, narrowly escaping the snap of the seatbelt as it flicks back into place. Chuckling, I step out of the truck and walk around to meet Jessica, just closing her door. "Your sister is full of energy." I grin, letting her know it's a good thing.

She laughs. "That's an understatement. The closer we get to Christmas, the less she sleeps," she jokes. She sighs and takes a step toward the Christmas trees scattered all around the lot in staggered rows, the smell of pine thick in the air.

We walk together slowly, Jessica seeming lost in thought, unable to mask her sadness. My eyebrows draw together in concern, wishing I could take away her pain. "Are you okay?"

She nods sadly and pastes a smile on her face, but it doesn't reach her eyes. My heart squeezes in protest. "Yeah, I'm fine. Let's go find a tree."

"Jess," I prod as I reach for her arm, stopping her. She pauses as I give her a look of doubt and plead with her to talk to me without saying the words. I want more than anything to help her feel better and see her genuine smile.

She grimaces and sighs heavily. "I'm sorry. I guess it's like Holly said, our parents loved Christmas so much that both of us even have names that reminded them of Christmas. I guess you could say there's so much about Christmas that reminds me of them, and sometimes it hurts. I want to feel like that again," she blurts out quickly, nodding in the direction Holly disappeared. "But it's just hard for me sometimes to pretend to be happy when I miss them so much."

I nod, my heart full of empathy for her, desperate to ease her pain. "I can't say I understand where you're coming from completely since I still have both of my parents, but I can imagine how hard it will be when I don't have them anymore." I slip my fingers through hers and squeeze her hand in reassurance. "I guess I would think of it this way, celebrating Christmas is also celebrating your mom and dad. They're always in your heart, but I also believe they're still with you, especially at Christmastime. I'm sure all they really want is for you and Holly to be happy."

She smiles up at me, her eyes watery as she nods her head. She opens her mouth and closes it again before she takes a deep breath and reaches up, brushing away her tears. "You're right." Then she turns toward a long row of pine trees, giving my hand a light tug, urging, "Let's go find Holly and pick out a Christmas tree."

I nod in agreement, taking her hint. "Do you have a tree stand?" I ask as we begin looking through the various Christmas trees. There seem to be hundreds of different shapes and sizes, short needles, and long ones here, making me wonder what kind of tree they like best.

Jessica nods. "Yeah, we have one of the big stands." She stops and opens her mouth like she's going to say more when suddenly we're interrupted by a loud, gleeful shout from Holly.

"Jessica! Over here! I found our tree!" We follow the sound of her voice to the next aisle finding Holly holding a full, nearly eight-foot Douglas Fir. "Isn't it perfect?" she asks reverently as she grins up at the tree.

"It's beautiful," Jessica whispers, a small smile tugging at the corners of her lips.

I nod and reach for the tree. "Then it's yours."

"Do you want help?" Jessica asks.

"I got it," I insist, grabbing the trunk with both hands.

"Thank you. I'll go pay for the tree. Would you mind putting it in the truck for us?"

"No, this is my treat," I insist, easily walking the tree toward the cashier. I've done this so many times I've lost count.

"You don't have to do that, Jack. We just enjoy having you with us," Jessica protests.

I grin, my stomach twisting. "I'm happy I'm doing this with you too, but I want to buy the tree for you and Holly." I turn, setting the tree next to me as I dig cash out of my pocket and hand it to the man with a nod of my head, mumbling, "Thanks. Merry Christmas!"

"Merry Christmas!" he replies.

Then I lift the tree again and walk it to the back of my truck, laying it carefully in the bed and securing it gently with some twine before I climb behind the wheel. "Have you guys ever cut down your own tree?"

Holly laughs as Jessica shakes her head, replying, "No."

"Maybe next time we could try that," I suggest, my heart squeezing, hoping they're around next Christmas to do that with me. "It's a great experience."

"As long as you're the one with the ax, I'm okay with that," Holly jokes, making all of us laugh.

On the short drive to Jessica's house, I listen to Holly happily chatter about school and her friends, a warm feeling washing over me I can't quite explain. As I glance over at Jessica out of the corner of my eye, I notice all her focus is on Holly, making me wonder when the last time was that she did something for herself.

I pull up to her house and park in the driveway. We all pile out of my truck, and I grab the tree while Jessica opens the front door for me. "Thank you," I mumble as I step inside.

"I should be thanking you," she insists. "You drove, you paid, you carried the tree..." she trails off, shaking her head in disbelief.

"It's no problem. I don't mind at all. Where do you want it?"

"In front of the large window in the living room," she instructs. "Oh wait, the tree stand!" she recalls, spinning around.

"It's right here," Holly announces, walking in from the back door with the tree stand in her hand. "It was in the garage," she informs us, shrugging her shoulders.

"Thanks." I grin. She sets it down by the window, and I carefully set the tree in the stand. "Do you two want to hold the tree up, and I'll tighten it to make sure it stays in place?"

"Sure," they both answer and reach their arms in between the branches, grabbing onto the trunk on opposite sides.

I lie down on the floor, easily tightening the tree. As I finish, I brush my hands together and pop up, reminding them, "Now we just need to add water and your Christmas tree is all set."

"Can we decorate now?" Holly asks, biting her lower lip in anticipation.

Ignoring Holly's question, Jessica looks at me, insisting, "You really don't have to help us with all of this. You've already done so much."

I take a step toward her and smile softly in reassurance. "I promise you, I want to help you. I wouldn't be here if I didn't. I guess you could say I'm definitely a Christmas guy." I smirk. "When it comes to Christmas, I'm all in. Just don't ask me to bake, especially cookies, because even Santa won't eat them," I joke, knowing it's the truth.

She laughs and shakes her head in amusement. "What about decorating cookies?"

I nod thoughtfully. "I could do that as long as someone else makes the frosting, but they won't be as pretty as yours."

"Isn't that half the fun?" she prompts, teasing, using my own words against me. My heart clenches. I love it.

Holly bounces back into the room with a pitcher of water. I didn't even realize she'd left. She wiggles under the tree, pours the water into the tree stand, and quickly pops back up. "So, are we decorating or what?" Holly pushes, smirking at both of us.

Jessica nods, confirming, "We are, but let's start with the stuff around the house and do the Christmas tree last." She reaches past the boxes to grab something behind it.

"Yes!" Holly cheers and tears off the top of one of the bins. She pulls out a Santa figure. I hold back my laughter as I look closer, realizing it's a pretty good replica of my grandfather, except his nose appears way too small. It's always interesting to see what people come up with each time.

Grown-up Christmas list begins playing, bringing my attention to Jessica as she sets a speaker down on the table. "Is this okay?" she prompts, arching her eyebrows. "We like to listen to Christmas music while we decorate."

"It's perfect," I admit. It makes this feel like home. The thought overwhelms me. Taking a deep breath, I try to push it out of my head and enjoy my time with them.

We spend the rest of the evening talking, decorating, laughing, listening to Christmas music, and singing along. It's not long before Holly requests, "Can we order pizza? I'm hungry."

"What kind do you like?" I inquire.

"Pepperoni," she hums.

"Okay, I got it," I declare.

"You've done enough," Jessica insists, wide-eyed. I offer her an innocent smile with my phone to my ear, already connecting to the local pizza shop. I quickly order and disconnect the call before she has a chance to stop me. She shakes her head, grinning. "Thank you again, Jack," she emphasizes.

"It's my pleasure," I tell her because I mean it. Usually, when I'm doing something like this, it's either with my parents, the elves, for an organization, the business, or something. I can't believe I'm spending the day decorating for Christmas with this beautiful woman and her sister. I don't think I could've asked for a more perfect day.

"Well, if that's the case, I think we can start on the tree if you want," Jessica murmurs.

Deciding on the adjustable lights, we string them onto the tree and barely begin hanging the ornaments when the doorbell rings. Setting the elf ornament in my hand down, I stride to the front door and pull it open. Smiling, I reach for the pizza, handing the delivery girl wearing a Santa hat a sizable tip. "Merry Christmas."

"Thank you!" she exclaims, grinning from ear to ear as she runs back to her car.

As I close the door, I ask, "Where do you want the pizza?"

"Let's just eat right here," Holly suggests as she lowers herself to the floor and sticks her legs underneath the pine coffee table with the armchair as her backrest.

"Okay," Jessica agrees as she sits on the couch.

I set the pizza on the coffee table and slowly lower myself to join her on the couch. We all grab paper plates and dive into the pizza. "This is good pizza," I mumble as I swallow my first bite.

"Mm," they both moan in agreement, making me chuckle.

"Your house looks good," I tell her, looking around the room.

"Thanks to your help," she emphasizes again between bites.

"When can we do the outside?" Holly asks, making me laugh.

"One thing at a time," Jessica requests, causing Holly to make a face at her before she bursts out laughing.

"You look tired," I observe as I look at Jessica, staring at her in admiration.

"I am," she admits with a soft sigh. "It's those early mornings at the bakery. I really do love it, but it's a lot sometimes with everything here too."

"She never does anything for herself," Holly adds, confirming my suspicion.

"I went out this weekend," Jessica reminds her, blushing as she says it.

"Yeah, because I pushed you to do it," Holly reminds her.

"You didn't want to go out with me?" I tease, arching my eyebrows.

Jessica turns an even deeper shade of red and shakes her head, "No, that's not it. I didn't know it was you; I mean, it's just," she grimaces, and Holly laughs, covering her mouth with both hands.

I place my hand gently over hers and concede, "It's okay. I get it. I didn't really want to go on a date either."

"You didn't," she questions, her eyebrows drawn down in confusion.

I shake my head. "No. Honestly, I was frustrated with dating, and this time of year, I'm way too busy, but my assistant, Allie, made a deal with me. I agreed to go on a few dates. She insisted and even signed me up on the dating site. My date with you was the last one I promised to go on, but it was the *only* one I can say I'm glad I didn't miss."

She looks down at her lap in embarrassment, a small smile playing on her lips, her soft skin warm under my touch, igniting my insides. "I'm glad I didn't miss it either."

I smile, my chest tightening as I look at this incredible woman. She sets her plate down on the coffee table with a tired sigh. "Why don't you rest here and let Holly and I finish the tree," I suggest.

"I look that tired, huh?" she prods, grinning sheepishly.

"You should be tired. We can handle it. Right, Holly."

She nods. "Absolutely. Take it easy for a few minutes, Jess."

Jessica sighs and relents, "Okay."

She sits back with a sigh, making me grateful she agreed. I wipe my mouth and set my plate down on the table as I stand. Tugging the folded red and green knit blanket off the back of the couch, I cover her up, brushing my lips over the top of her head. Then I stand, going back to decorating the tree with Holly. Barely moments later, Jessica falls into a peaceful sleep.

"She really did have fun with you this weekend," Holly reveals, bringing a smile to my face.

"Good. I had a lot of fun with her, too, and you," I add, nodding at Holly.

She smiles, her cheeks turning pink before she quickly schools her features. Then attempting to look firm and intimidating, she demands, "Be good to her."

I nod. "I will," I murmur and wait for her to continue.

"She does everything for everyone, especially me. I think since we lost our parents, she thinks whatever she needs doesn't matter anymore." I wince, hating that Jessica feels that way, but after only knowing her for a few days, I believe Holly's right in her assessment. "I want her to find someone who will love her and take good care of her like she does for me. She deserves it."

"It seems to me that you take very good care of her," I tell her honestly.

"Thanks, I try," she admits, shrugging. "But with school and everything else…" she trails off, shaking her head. "She just deserves the best," she maintains.

I nod in agreement, already knowing it's true. Holly and I continue decorating the tree, with the unwrapping of ornaments and the soft Christmas music the only sounds. While we work, I plan the outside lights and decorations in my head as we finish the tree, knowing I can easily decorate outside for both of them before they even have a chance to think about it again.

CHAPTER 12
Jessica

I stand in my front yard and look around me, my eyes wide with awe. White lights line the roof, windows, and sides of the house, making it look like a large gingerbread house. Garland, weaved with lights, sweeps along the banister of the front porch and wraps around the front post light. The same garland borders the garage and front door. The trees and bushes are wrapped with lights. A small wooden sleigh led by three wooden reindeer sits off to the side of the porch filled with colorfully wrapped boxes. I walk toward the wreath on the front door, made with evergreen roping, pine cones, berries, and a red and white ribbon and bow. Slowly, I reach toward the door handle as if I'm afraid to disrupt the picture-perfect setting when it suddenly flies open, shaking the wreath and making me take a step back in surprise.

Holly pops out and holds her arms out, spinning around with a huge smile on her face. "Isn't this incredible?"

"Did you do all of this?" I ask without answering her question.

She huffs a laugh and grins, shaking her head. "Nope, definitely not."

"Then how?" I ask, my eyebrows drawn down in confusion.

"I bet it's the same way your car ended up in the driveway this morning." She wiggles her eyebrows, still smiling.

"Jack?" I question, already knowing it's true. "How?"

She shrugs and teases, "I don't know, but you better be going out with that man again."

I huff a laugh and nod slowly, feeling overwhelmed. "We were going to go shopping for some Christmas Wish gifts." At the reminder, I glance at my phone, checking the time. "In fact, I need to get ready before he gets here. I'm a mess," I mumble, scrunching my nose up in displeasure.

"You're always a mess," she jokes, smirking.

"Thanks," I mumble, monotone.

"Are those for me?" she prompts, eagerly reaching for the bakery box in my hands.

I swiftly pull the box back. "No!"

Her eyes widen, and she quickly blurts, "Sorry."

I shake my head, "No, I'm sorry. I didn't mean to snap. I just made some cookies for Jack to thank him for helping us with the Christmas tree and decorating everything," I explain. I stop and spin in a circle again, taking in the beautiful decorations, "But if he did all of this, I think I need to do a lot more baking."

Holly laughs, nodding in agreement. "Definitely. But for now, go get ready, and I'll guard these treats with my life. I promise," she adds, her eyes gleaming mischievously.

"Not even one, Holly," I insist, narrowing my eyes at her in warning as I step past her into the house.

She smirks and declares sarcastically, "Yes, Ma'am!" Adding a mock salute before I move.

Sighing, I stride for the hallway in a hurry to get ready. I jump in the shower and quickly wash my hair, my mind on Jack. I can't believe he would do all that for Holly and me. It feels like he's too good to be true. I can't help but think my parents would absolutely adore him. But who wouldn't? I sigh again and finish rinsing my hair before quickly running conditioner through it and cleaning the rest of me, trying to focus on the task at hand instead of the man I'm getting ready to see.

I swiftly step out of the shower, dressing in dark blue jeans and an ice-blue turtleneck cashmere sweater. Grabbing my hair dryer, I quickly dry my hair and apply a minimal amount of makeup. I finish adding lipstick and give myself one more glance in the mirror before I step out into the hallway.

I walk toward the sound of voices at the front of the house, finding Holly and Jack laughing. Both the sound and the vision cause my heart to skip a beat. "Hi," I barely squeak out.

Jack spins toward me, his smile lighting up his whole face and taking my breath away. "Jessica, you look beautiful," he tells me, his eyes full of sincerity.

I gulp down the lump in my throat and whisper, "Thank you." He stares at me, and I blurt out, "Did you do all of this?"

He chuckles softly, arching his eyebrows in question. "What?"

I shake my head in disbelief and ramble, "My car, the house, our yard, the lights, the decorations. Did you do all of it?" I stare at him in wide-eyed amazement, already knowing it's true and overwhelmed by his kindness.

He chuckles and jokes, "Someone decorated your car? I have to see that."

I huff and shake my head, no longer able to hide my smile. "You know what I mean. You brought my car home for me before I had to get to the bakery this morning. You would've had to walk back to town to get yours."

"It wasn't far," he replies, brushing it off.

"Then you decorated our whole house on the outside after you spent the whole night decorating our house with us on the inside," I continue.

He shrugs like it is no big deal, but it's a huge deal to me. I don't remember the last time someone other than Holly helped me with anything, and I've always tried to make it, so she doesn't see the amount of work everything entails because I don't want her to feel bad. He did so much.

"Do you like it?" he asks, biting his lower lip anxiously.

"We love it!" Holly chimes. "It looks incredible, Jack!"

I turn to look at her, and her eyes widen as she backs away slowly. "You know, I have some homework I have to do. I'll see you when you get back. Have fun!" She spins on her heel and quickly strides for her room, closing the door behind her.

I turn my gaze back to Jack and insist, "You really didn't have to do all of this. You did so much!"

He nods. "You're right. I didn't have to do anything, and I hope I didn't overstep, but I need you to know that I only did what I wanted to." He slowly approaches me and takes my hand in his, holding my gaze. "It really wasn't that much for me," he claims, biting the inside of his cheek. "Do you like it?" he repeats, still wanting an answer.

I nod, trying to push back the tears welling in my eyes. "It's absolutely beautiful, and it's one of the nicest things anyone has ever done for me," I inform him choking down the lump in my throat.

"Maybe I did it for selfish reasons," he prods, watching me closely.

My eyebrows arch with doubt, not believing that for a second. "Oh?"

The corners of his mouth twitch upwards as he nods. "Yup, three reasons, all of them completely selfish." I giggle and snap my mouth shut, waiting for him to continue, my breath speeding up with every word he utters. "The first reason is because I thought if you had more time, you might agree to help me out with the Christmas train. I still need the best baker there is to make cookies for the event." I nod, a smile tugging at my lips as I realize I never gave him an answer. "My second reason is that I want to spend more time with you, so if I can give you more free time, I'm going to do it," he insists, making me blush. "And my third reason is I love having a reason to see you smile," he admits, butterflies instantly taking flight in my stomach. "And I love even more when I'm the one to do it."

I take in a deep, shaky breath, wanting desperately to kiss this man, but I don't know if it's the right thing to do. Holly is my priority, and she's just in the other room. This thing with him can't last, can it? He steps closer, invading my space, and tilts his head down slowly. My heartbeat becomes erratic, thrashing against my ribcage feeling as if it might burst right out of my chest.

His phone rings, and I exhale, taking a quick step back to pull myself together. "You can answer that," I mumble flippantly, needing a minute.

He stares at me for a moment before he steps back as well, sighing softly. Then he pulls his phone out and glances at the screen before pressing a button and lifting it to his ear. "Hi, Dad. What's up?" I force myself to breathe in through my nose and out through my mouth while I stare at him talking with his dad.

I've never wanted something to work so badly, but I can imagine having it all with him. I really like him, not just because he does incredibly sweet things for me, but because he makes my heart race. He's incredibly handsome, generous, and kind. He's amazing with Holly; then again, he's been wonderful with everyone we've come across when we've been together. I don't know many people like that. What I don't understand is how Holly seems to be actually pushing me toward him, too, so what's holding me back? I want to be with him, but at the same time, something is making me anxious, and I'm not sure what it is. I need to figure it out before I do something stupid like fall in love with this man. My heart stutters at the thought, causing me to take another deep breath. In all honesty, I'm afraid I started to fall the day I met him.

Jack ends his call and looks down at me. "I'm sorry about that," he apologizes. "My dad and I do a lot of business together, and he needed something from me. Christmastime is our busiest time of year."

I wave my hand, dismissing his apology. "That's okay. I understand. So, what does your dad do? Is he in the toys and technology business too?"

He smirks, his eyes drifting away from mine and his cheeks turning a soft pink as he replies, "Yeah, I guess you could say that."

"It must be nice to be able to work together," I tell him honestly. I can't imagine being able to work with my mom or dad when I would give almost anything just to have them around again in any part of my life and Holly's.

He pinches his lips tightly together and nods, answering softly, "Yeah. Eventually, I'm supposed to take over the family business."

"Oh, really? I thought you planned on staying at your job in New York. Where is his business based out of?" I ask, suddenly realizing he's not here permanently, my heart dropping like a lump of coal into the pit of my stomach.

"We're pretty far north," he says generally, "but my New York Company will still be a part of the corporation even after I take over there. I'll always still do some work around here."

I bite my lip, afraid to respond. He's too good to be true because he's not going to be sticking around. I can't be with someone who's only around part-time. My stomach continues to churn, my anxiety increasing with every second that passes. I should've known better. No one is permanent in my life. They come and go so easily but always leave me in the end. "Oh," I finally mumble and pull my hand away, suddenly feeling all alone, even with him by my side.

He tilts his head to the side, his eyes narrowing as he assesses me. "Jessica?"

I need a subject change, fast. As I turn toward the coffee table, I spot the box of cookies I made for Jack right where Holly left them and pick them up. The ribbon falls loosely, having already been untied, making me grumble, "Holly."

"What?" Jack asks, quirking his eyebrow in question.

Spinning toward him, I smile sadly, holding up the box for him. "I made these for you, but it looks like Holly may have gotten into them already."

He chuckles. Gesturing toward his chest, he clarifies, "For me?"

I nod and hold out the box to him, pasting a smile on my face. "Yeah. I know it's not much, but I wanted to do something for you, and you said you like my cookies, so..." I shrug.

My fingers brush his, giving me goosebumps, as he carefully takes the box from my hands and opens it. He closes his eyes and takes a deep breath, inhaling the scent of the sugary goodness. He exhales slowly as he opens his eyes to find mine. "These smell delicious. Thank you so much." He smiles appreciatively.

I grin stiffly back at him. "You're welcome."

He pulls one out of the box and holds it up. The cookie is made up of two cake-like chocolate cookies sandwiched together with a marshmallow whipped cream in between. "What is this?" he prompts, curious.

"It's a hot chocolate cookie."

His eyes widen, and he takes a bite, closing his eyes. "Mm," he moans in satisfaction.

"They're even better when they're warm," I divulge, enjoying his reaction.

"Oh, that sounds so good. I have to try that!" he exclaims. As he finishes the cookie, he reaches in for another one. He pulls out a chocolate ball about an inch in diameter. "I smell peanut butter." He grins. I nod, and he pops the whole thing into his mouth. "Mm, this is fantastic!"

I smile, feeling slightly calmer. "Thanks. I've been calling them chocolate peanut butter snowballs, but since there's no coconut, I'm not sure if that's the right name," I admit, grimacing.

He licks his lips and nods in understanding. "I get it, but I like the name. They are a little round ball of chocolate...and peanut butter."

I laugh, feeling my body relax again. "I guess you're right."

"Well, maybe I should quit while I'm ahead." He smirks, making me laugh. He closes the box and looks into my eyes. "Thank you, Jessica."

"You're welcome," I repeat. "And thank you," I add.

He ignores my additional praise and prompts, "So does that mean you'll bake for the Christmas train?"

My lips pinch together nervously. I don't know if I can handle it. A lot of families go on the Christmas train. That's a lot of baking and a lot of prep work. Even with help, I'm not sure I'm the one to do an event like this, no matter how much I want to be me. "I don't know," I murmur.

"Please, Jessica. I don't want anyone else. I only want you," he declares, causing my heart to skip a beat. I know he's not talking about me, but that doesn't seem to matter to my stupid heart. He takes a step closer to me and pleads, "Please. I'll beg if you want me to." I shake my head, and he pleads once more, "Please."

I take a deep breath and give in with a huge exhale. "I think I just need to think about it a little more. Maybe we could go over more of the details."

"We can do that, but I promise, if you do this with me, you won't regret it!" He grins broadly. "I'll make sure you have all the help you need. I just need to know when and where you need them as well as anything else you might need from me," he informs me.

I smile awkwardly at him as I remind him, "I thought we were going shopping for some Christmas Wishes today."

He nods happily. "We are. Are you ready to go?"

"Yes." I nod, needing to do something to keep my mind occupied, but I don't know if doing anything with Jack is the smartest idea. He's the reason I need a distraction in the first place. But I don't want to give up my time with him either.

"Let's go," he encourages. He grabs my coat, helping me slip it on. Then, I grab my purse and call to my sister, "I'll be back soon, Holly. Call if you need me!"

"I'll be fine! Have fun," she yells back.

Jack puts his hand on the small of my back, sending shivers down my spine. He reaches around me, pulls my front door open, and escorts me back outside, his nearness and demeanor already pulling me back to the present and how much I'm enjoying every minute I spend with him.

CHAPTER 13
Jessica

Jack reaches into the back of his truck and pulls out one of the large red velvet bags filled with some of the gifts we just purchased and tied at the top with a thick, gold, braided cord. "Is this one too heavy for you to carry?" he asks, holding out the lightest one.

I take it from him and toss it over my shoulder with a grin, testing it. "I can handle it." He reaches for the other two red velvet bags and throws them over his own shoulder, bringing a smile to my face. "You look like Santa Claus," I tease.

He chuckles and mumbles something under his breath that sounds like, "You have no idea," piquing my interest.

"What was that?" I prompt, arching my eyebrow.

He shakes his head. "Nothing. Let's go."

I nod and lead the way. "I can't believe you bought all of this," I tell him with awe in my voice.

"I will do anything I can to make someone's Christmas brighter," he informs me honestly.

My heart clenches with his response. "I can tell," I reply, grinning. I love that about him.

We approach the Christmas Wish table and stop in front of two women volunteers, one with wavy, graying hair and the other with similar dark brown hair, appearing to be the younger version of the woman standing beside her. "Hi," I greet them.

Both of them lift their gazes, taking in the large bags over our shoulders, and stare at us with wide eyes. "Can we help you?" the older woman prompts.

Jack smiles almost shyly, surprising me. Then he clears his throat, informing them, "These bags have presents for the Christmas Wish tree." Both of the women gasp, their mouths dropping open in shock. "We wrapped and tagged everything from the names we picked over the weekend, but we bought some extra presents to save for names that don't get pulled too. We left those unwrapped, so you can decide what to do with them if that's okay?" he questions.

Both women nod vigorously. The younger of the two women walks around the table and wraps her arms around me in a huge embrace, pinning my arms awkwardly to my sides. "Thank you," she whispers, her voice catching.

I laugh, feeling myself blush. "You're welcome, but these were all him," I proclaim, gesturing with my head toward Jack standing beside me.

She instantly releases me and throws her arms around Jack, causing him to stagger back a step at the unexpected contact. "Thank you so much! You're doing such a good thing! You have no idea how much this means to us, the kids, and the families!" she rambles.

"You're welcome," he rasps, pinned in her embrace. My hand covers my mouth as I burst out laughing, unable to hide my amusement. He chuckles and adds, "We're happy to help. But do you think I could set these down somewhere? Some of these presents are pretty heavy," he adds.

Instantly, she drops her arms from around him, blushing. "Oh, I'm so sorry! Yes, yes, of course! Can you just bring them over here?" she requests, scrambling back around the table.

"Sure," he agrees. He nods for me to go first. I walk around and set my bag down behind the table. While Jack steps up behind me, placing the other two bags right next to the first. "Are you ladies going to need help with moving all of these things later?" he questions. I didn't even think of that.

The older woman shakes her head. "No, thank you. We have some people coming to help us gather everything at the end of the night. Thank you so much for your donation," she repeats, narrowing her eyes as she looks quizzically at Jack as if she knows him and she's trying to figure out who he is.

"No problem." He nods.

"Wait, I know who you are," she mumbles in excitement, her eyes going wide. "You're the gentlemen that donated all those toys and electronics to our group effort."

I turn and stare at Jack, his cheeks flushing a rosy pink. "It's no big deal," he claims, attempting to brush the comment aside.

The younger woman gasps in shock. "You're him?" He shrugs in response, not able to deny it. "That was so much more than just a few toys and electronics; we almost filled a truck with nearly everything on our list. This is going to be a memorable Christmas for so many people! Thank you so much! You are like Santa Claus!" she exclaims, her eyes bright.

Jack smiles and turns to leave. I spin on my heel, following behind, desperately wanting to know what they're talking about, when the woman stops us both. "Wait!"

We stop, turning to face them. "Yes?" Jack prompts, glancing at them.

"These are really nice bags. We can empty them really quick and give them back to you," the older woman offers.

Jack smiles and shakes his head, waving them off. "Keep them. They make great Santa bags, and I have plenty more of them at home."

Both women grin, and each shout their appreciation, "Thank you so much! That's so kind of you!"

We turn to leave for the second time and I can't help but look up at Jack in amazement. "What?" he asks sheepishly, his cheeks a rosy pink.

"That really was incredible," I insist, shaking my head in awe.

His cheeks darken again, and he shrugs, claiming, "Just doing what I can to help."

I huff a laugh and shake my head. "You do a lot more than most people."

He shakes his head. "Nah, I just do what I can, the same as everyone else. I'm just able to do more than most."

"Jack," I mumble, my stomach flip-flopping. "What about the Santa bags, though? They were right; those were gorgeous! There's no way you have a bunch of those just lying around," I add incredulously.

He chuckles, shrugging. "You'd be surprised." I want to ask him more, but he stops me when he lifts his head and points to a drink cart only a few steps away. "I'm thirsty for some hot chocolate. Would you like one?"

I nod my head. "Sure." I stare at him, full of curiosity, as he orders and pays for our two hot chocolates. It's obvious to me he doesn't do any of it for attention or recognition. He turns shy whenever you try to praise him for it. There aren't many people like that in this world, no matter what he claims. I'm grateful to have met him. My heart skips a beat as he turns and walks back toward me, grasping a cup in each hand. I just hope he doesn't crush my heart because it seems it already jumped in with both feet, no matter what my brain thinks.

"Here," he offers me a cup of hot chocolate.

I reach for one, wrapping my fingers around the cup, his fingers lightly brushing mine. "Thank you." I smile up at him, my heart feeling full.

He grins. "You're welcome." Then he takes a sip of his own drink. "Want to walk over and listen?" he asks as he points over my shoulder.

I twist and turn my head to see what he's pointing at, finally spotting a small group of young teens bundled up in winter coats who appear to be singing. As I look back at Jack, I nod happily. "I'd love to."

"Let's go." He holds his arm out for me making my stomach flip and my insides warm. I step beside him and slide my free hand around his arm as we stroll toward the music.

As we approach, I begin hearing the soft sounds of "Where are you, Christmas?" My heart stutters at the hauntingly beautiful and innocent sound.

"How old do you think those kids are? They sound incredible," I declare, blown away by their young talent.

He nods, agreeing. "They really do. I would guess thirteen, fourteen, fifteen," he pauses, "maybe a couple of sixteen-year-olds, but they're definitely all under eighteen, probably in high school."

"Wow," I murmur under my breath, realizing they're Holly's age.

We begin walking slowly as we listen to the music. I'm fully aware of my hand still wrapped around Jack's arm, my skin feeling as if it's on fire everywhere we connect, even through the thick material of our coats.

We reach a wide aisle of tables on both sides, displaying Christmas crafts, and gifts and stroll slowly through. The first table we stop at is filled with various colors of sweaters and hats made of soft yarn. "Holly would love one of these sweaters. She loves anything soft," I inform Jack. "I think I'll buy her the blue one for Christmas."

"I think that's a great idea. I'm sure she'll love it," he agrees.

I pay for it and slip the bag over my shoulder with the sweater inside. "Thank you," I murmur to the woman who made them. We turn, walking to the next booth, covered with hand-painted Christmas ornaments. "I love these. My parents used to get us each a new ornament every year."

"You don't do that anymore?" he questions, arching his eyebrows.

I shake my head sadly but don't elaborate. Instead, I turn and walk to the next booth, finding jewelry with silver or gold as well as some with colorful beads. I walk around the table, admiring the different pieces, when my eyes land on a thin, rose gold chain with angel wings making me gasp. I pick up the necklace to take a closer look. "It's beautiful, isn't it?" the vendor asks.

Lifting my gaze, I look back at kind brown eyes and nod my head, unable to speak over the lump in my throat.

"Very pretty," Jack murmurs from just over my shoulder. The heat of his breath sends chills down my spine.

I again nod in agreement and set the necklace down. "Thank you," I rasp.

Spinning on my heel, I quickly stride past the rest of the booths toward the ice rink, struggling to breathe, knowing Jack will follow.

"Are you okay?" Jack asks as he catches up with me.

I nod and take a deep breath before I'm able to answer him. "Yeah, I'm fine. Thanks." I clear my throat and add, for his benefit, "I honestly don't remember the last time I enjoyed this part of Christmas this much."

He reaches toward me, but I turn my head, and my eyes skim over the ice rink before continuing to roam the rest of the area. My breath hitches at the site of a family getting off a sleigh. "They have sleighs?" I murmur, flooded with a memory from my past, my chest tightening.

"Would you like to go on a sleigh ride?" he asks, following my gaze.

Gulping down the lump in my throat again, I shake my head. "No, that's okay. I just didn't think they had that here anymore. I haven't been on one in a really long time," I emphasize, trying not to let my emotions get the best of me.

"I hear that from you a lot. I think we need to remedy that right now." He grins as he steps toward the sleighs. Momentarily holding my breath, I'm not sure what else to do besides follow behind him. We approach a tall man with a short white beard and a friendly smile. "Two for a sleigh ride, please," Jack requests.

"Of course," he murmurs, accepting the money from Jack. He glances curiously at me, his head tilting to the side as he assesses me. "Aren't you Frank and Judy's girl?"

My breath hitches, and my eyes narrow; not quite sure who he is, but I nod in confirmation. "Yes."

"I thought so!" He grins. "I was a friend of theirs. I'm Gus," he introduces himself holding his hand out for me to shake.

I place my hand in his, shaking it as I smile nervously up at him. "It's nice to meet you, Gus."

As I turn toward Jack, I see him already holding his hand out for Gus with a genuine smile. "Hi, I'm Jack."

They shake firmly, both men immediately turning their attention back to me. "I don't think I've seen you here since before..." Gus trails off and looks away. No one ever knows how to finish that sentence. I don't blame him. I don't either, but it's never easy to hear, even unfinished, making my stomach twist into knots.

He clears his throat and smiles at me. "It's just been a long time. I miss your mom and dad. They loved helping with all of this every year," he proclaims, gesturing around the festival. I nod in agreement, remembering how much time we used to spend here. He smiles again. "They always seemed to be both the first and the last ones on a sleigh ride." He chuckles at his memory, smiling to himself. "I think this and the Christmas train were probably their favorite events."

"Really?" I ask, arching my eyebrows in surprise.

He nods. "Absolutely."

"I didn't know that. I know they always helped with all of this, but I guess I got so busy the last few years with school." I wince, wishing I had taken the time to do this with them more back then and hating that I'll never have that chance.

"Here you are," he announces, gesturing toward a red and silver sleigh drawn by a beautiful black and white Clydesdale horse that saunters up next to him.

I attempt to gulp down the lump in my throat as I look at the picturesque sight. "Thank you," I rasp. He offers me his hand to help me into the sleigh as Jack's hand slips behind me and lands on the small of my back, ensuring my safety. I sit down and slide across the bench seat to make room for Jack, comforted the moment he sits down next to me. He tilts his head to the side, assessing me. "What?" I ask, rubbing my hands on my legs to keep warm and calm my nerves.

"When was the last time you were on one of these?" he gently prods as the driver nudges the horse into motion with a click of his tongue. I pinch my lips tightly together and glance down at my lap as my heart rises to my throat. "You don't have to answer me if you don't want to," he murmurs softly.

As I close my eyes, I heave a sigh and shake my head, opening them back up and meeting his concerned gaze. "It's not that I don't want to; it's just that it has been so long since I talked about any of this, but you seem to bring it out of me. Plus, it seems I keep getting flooded with memories of them lately, especially tonight."

He covers my hand with his in silent support, giving me the courage to speak. "It was the last Christmas before I left for college, about three Christmases before they died. It was just the four of us, and we spent the whole weekend doing things to get ready for Christmas." I smile softly at the memory. "It was so much fun," I admit reverently.

"I'm sure it was," he responds with conviction.

I look up into his blue eyes, appearing to glow in the dim light. Shaking my head in disbelief, I blurt out, "How are you still single?" He chuckles, and I ramble on, my face growing warmer with each word I utter. "I mean, you're smart, caring, kind, generous, humble, funny, and incredibly handsome."

"You think I'm handsome?" he questions with a wide smile. My cheeks go from a blush to flaming red instantly. He chuckles and gives my hand a light squeeze. "You are all of those things too. Besides being strong, beautiful, creative, talented, and so much more," he insists, staring into my eyes.

My heartbeat becomes erratic inside my chest, and I struggle to breathe, wondering if he's going to kiss me. He leans forward slowly, glancing at my lips, letting me know his intentions, and I tip my head toward him, my lips tingling in anticipation.

My cell phone rings in my coat pocket, interrupting the moment again, and prompting me to pull back. "Sorry," I mumble. I pinch my lips tightly together and reach for my phone. Holly's name flashes across the screen, making my eyes widen and my heart drop in fear. I quickly connect the call and put my phone to my ear, "Holly? Is everything okay? Are you alright?"

"Yeah, everything is fine, but is it okay if I order some Chinese food? I'm hungry."

I breathe a sigh of relief, at the same time feeling like the worst sister in the world. "Oh my gosh, Holly, yes! I completely lost track of time. I'm so sorry. I'll be home soon. Order extra," I instruct.

"Okay, thanks, Jess!" she mumbles and hangs up without saying goodbye.

I slip my phone back into my pocket and turn toward Jack, my eyebrows drawn down in apology. "I'm so sorry, but I have to get home. I completely lost track of time."

He shakes his head. "No need to apologize. This was fun," he insists. Small, soft, white snowflakes slowly begin to fall, bringing my attention to our surroundings. The snow-covered path in front of us is lined on both sides with pine trees, the branches heavy with snow. The moon is full and bright, the light from it glinting off the snow and making it sparkle like diamonds. A light wind whistles in the trees as the sounds of Christmas music I can't decipher can be heard in the distance. "It's so peaceful, isn't it," he murmurs with admiration and wonder.

"It's truly stunning," I proclaim quietly.

He glances back at me with a soft smile and agrees, "Yes, it is." My heart lurches, feeling as if his meaning is more than his simple words. Tilting his head, he looks at me, smirking as he asks, "So, your parents used to help with the Christmas train, huh?"

"Apparently." I grin. I raise my eyebrows and wait to see if he'll say more. He remains quiet, the sparkle in his eyes growing stronger with every passing second. Finally, I sigh and give in, knowing I'm not going to give him any other answer. "I'd be happy to help you with the Christmas train."

His smile lights up his whole face making my heart skip a beat. "Really? You're going to do the Christmas treats for the train?"

I grin, nodding. "Yes, I'll do it."

He laughs happily and wraps me up in his arms. "Thank you! Thank you! Thank you!" I fall into his warm embrace and close my eyes, soaking in the moment with my heart feeling full. "You've just made me a very happy man, Jessica," he claims.

He loosens his hold on me, and I slide back to look at him. My breath hitches at the look in his eyes as we suddenly jerk lightly to a stop. "Whoa," the driver urges the horses to a halt.

I push back from him and clear my throat. "I really have to get home."

He nods in acceptance. "I know." He releases me and easily jumps out of the sleigh. Turning toward me, he reaches his hand up to assist me.

I take his hand, gasping as his fingers briefly brush my side while he helps me out of the sleigh. "Thank you," I rasp, forcing the words out.

He keeps hold of my hand and whispers, "Let's get you home."

CHAPTER 14
Jessica

I stick my lower lip out in an attempt to blow my hair out of my eyes and wipe my hands on my white apron decorated with Christmas holly as I glance around the kitchen. Colorful Christmas cakes and cookies are spread out on every available surface. I smile to myself in satisfaction as I take it all in. Reaching for the back of my neck, I lift my apron over my head and walk over to the laundry chute just off the back of the kitchen. I pull the handle and stuff my apron in, letting it drop to the basement as I release the handle.

"Whoa!" Holly exclaims as she walks into the room with wide, hungry eyes. She turns slowly in a circle, taking it all in. "This is a lot of desserts! No wonder it smells so good in here." Holly reaches for a cookie. I swiftly step toward her and lightly bat her hand away. "Hey!" she exclaims, glaring at me. "You can let me have at least one. You have so many," she whines.

Planting my hands on my hips, I glare right back, narrowing my eyes. "Not until Jack gets here, please. I asked if he could stop by to try some of these, so I know what he wants me to make for the Christmas train."

"How long do I have to wait?" She grimaces.

I glance at the clock on the oven and my eyes widen in surprise. "Oh, no. He should be here any minute," I mumble, suddenly in a panic.

She looks me up and down and smirks. "Jack's coming over right now? You went all out getting ready for him, huh?" she giggles.

I narrow my eyes further and state flatly, "Not funny." Gasping, I plead, "Just please help me! Find me something to wear while I clean up."

"Fine, I'll help because I like him, and I like you two together. He shouldn't see your normal mess until you're married," she teases. I groan, making her laugh as she follows me down the hallway.

I run into the bathroom and strip out of my black leggings and gray Hallmark Christmas sweatshirt. Reaching for a washcloth, I wash my face and the rest of my body before brushing my teeth. Yanking the rubber band from my ponytail out of my hair that's barely hanging on anyway, I mutter, "Ow," forcing myself to slow down. I run a brush through my hair and spritz on some perfume just as Holly charges into the bathroom without knocking. "Hey!"

Ignoring me, she demands, "Here! Put this on!"

"Thank you." I grab the clothes from her and pull on the black skinny jeans and ivory cowl neck sweater just as the doorbell rings.

My eyes widen in panic as Holly grins and spins on her heel, striding toward the door. "I'll get it," she calls over her shoulder toward me.

As I glance in the mirror to assess how I look, I smooth the sweater over my hips. Taking a deep breath, I mumble, "Not that bad." I reach for my vanilla cupcake Chapstick and run it over my lips before slipping it into my jeans pocket. Then, straightening my shoulders, I take another deep breath to calm myself down and step out of the bathroom, turning toward the front of the house.

I hear Jack's laughter as I approach the kitchen, causing my stomach to do somersaults. "She said she was the tinsel queen, and of course, I was the princess!" Holly grins as she shows him a picture of us decorating a Christmas tree when Holly was five and I was sixteen, both covered in tinsel.

"Thanks so much for sharing, Holly," I murmur as I walk into the room, red with embarrassment.

Both their heads swing over to me, Holly laughing and Jack grinning making my chest tight. "Should I bow to the tinsel queen?" he jokes. He chuckles and takes a step toward me. "You look beautiful."

"Thanks," I murmur, blushing.

Holly grins proudly behind him mouthing, "You're welcome."

I fight my own laughter as he stops in front of me, still grinning. He whispers, "You were cute then too."

My body heats even more at his compliment. I clear my throat and gesture to all the surfaces behind him. "I have a few treats for you to try."

"I see that." He nods appreciatively. "They all look so good. I'm going to need some help trying all of these though. I love Christmas cookies, but this is quite a bit, even for me. I think we could all be on a sugar high in just a few minutes without even trying," he jokes, arching his eyebrows in mock challenge. "Who's with me?"

Holly reaches for a cookie and takes a bite without answering, making both of us laugh. She holds up the chocolate cookie and mumbles through her bite, "Mm, these are my favorites."

"Holly," I scold.

She covers her mouth with her free hand and murmurs, "Oops, sorry."

I laugh and shake my head. "I had no idea how many things I should make for you to try," I tell him honestly, shrugging my shoulders. "How many different kinds of treats do you usually offer for something like this?"

He shrugs. "It depends, but I will have chocolates and candy canes as well as drinks like homemade hot chocolate." He looks around the room again with wide eyes and asks, "Wait. Did you go out and buy all these ingredients?"

"Of course," I reply, my eyebrows drawing down in confusion. "How else would I make all of this?"

"I need to refund you for all of this."

I shake my head. "No, that's okay."

He holds up his hand to stop my refusal. "I'm the one who is asking you to do this for me. Whether you're testing desserts or making them for the event, you're doing it for me. I'm paying for all the ingredients as well as all of the time you spent baking," he insists, leaving no room for argument.

Knowing he's not going to give in, I whisper a partial agreement, hoping he lets it slide. "Okay, fine. You can pay for the ingredients."

He grins, pushing, "And I'm paying for your time!" He grabs a triple chocolate cookie and looks at me, winking. "Didn't think I'd catch that did you?" He smirks and takes a bite of the cookie, moaning in appreciation. "These are delicious."

"Thank you." I smile appreciatively.

"These cakes are like artwork. They're beautiful," he tells me sincerely as he walks along the counter,   looking at everything I made.

"You really think so?" I reply, biting the inside of my cheek, my nerves going haywire.

He nods vehemently. "If you want to make some cakes, you can, but you don't have to. I don't want you to over-work yourself," he insists. "But if you decide to make some, I think we could have some at a snack station on the train. Depending on how many you're able to get done, we'll keep most of them in a display case at the train depot for people to buy to bring home with them for their own holiday celebrations."

"Oh, I like that idea. Depending on how much help I have, I should have time to make a good amount of cakes and extra treats for that and for the snack stations," I tell him, not quite sure about exact numbers yet until I have more information. "So, what kind of treats do you want on the train? Is it just for snack stations, or are you bringing cookies around to the passengers?"

"Both. The plan is to have staff bring the first batch of cookies around to everyone. Then we can have extras at snack stations throughout the train. After the staff goes through the first time, they can refill their platters and go through for seconds. I was thinking about four or maybe five kinds of cookies? Maybe only one with nuts since there are so many kids with nut allergies," he suggests. "What do you think?"

I nod. "I think five different cookies is doable, and it gives everyone a good variety. I like your idea about only one cookie with some kind of nut too. I don't want kids to feel left out if they have allergies, so only having one cookie they can't eat should definitely help and it's definitely something I can handle. Plus, the nut cookies will need to be kept separate for their safety."

"You're right. We'll make sure of that."

"What if I make the nut option something with peanut butter? That always tends to be a favorite."

"Good idea. I love peanut butter. Now, in my opinion, the hard part for me is going to be deciding on just five. Everything you make is incredible." He grins.

Heat rushes to my face, and I quickly point to a chocolate gingerbread cookie, hoping to change the subject. "You should try this one if you like chocolate. I know you liked the gingerbread, so…" I trail off as he picks up the cookie and takes a bite.

He holds up the cookie with a nod. I watch as he finishes chewing and swallows before stating, "Definitely this one."

Holly and Jack try a couple more cookies, and between the three of us, we come up with a short list of five Christmas cookies. I smile in satisfaction and glance at Holly. "Thanks for helping."

She grins and strides out of the room. "Thanks for the cookies," she calls over her shoulder.

I laugh, shaking my head at my sister. I look up at Jack and remind him, "Now I just need more help getting them done."

He nods in agreement. "I told you I would provide help for you. I meant it. You're going to make everything here?"

"Mostly. Betty said I can use the bakery in the evenings if I need to for the extra ovens."

"That's great. So, when do you need people here to help?"

I bite my lower lip as I think. "Hmm," I mumble as I release my lip and explain my thoughts. "Well, I guess two days before the event and of course the day before as well. I want the cookies to be as fresh as possible. I'll get all the ingredients beforehand and have everything set up so it will be an easy process for whoever is helping. Holly can help me with all of that," I add.

He interrupts, "I need to know where you're getting all your ingredients so I can set up payment beforehand. I don't want you to have to think about any of that."

I nod in agreement. "Okay, that's no problem. I get almost everything from the same place."

"Are two or three people enough? I want to make sure you have all the help you need, but I also don't want to crowd your kitchen. I know that can be counterproductive, so tell me what you think will work best for you."

I nod mumbling, "You're right. I think three should be perfect as long as they know what they're doing in a kitchen and don't mind taking direction from me."

"I promise, they're experienced," he emphasizes.

"You already have people in mind?" I ask, arching my eyebrows in surprise. He grins, eliciting a smile from me.

"I have some people in mind."

"That would be wonderful! I'll have Holly to help, too," I remind him.

He nods, and we quickly finalize the numbers while I move on to a grocery list. His cell phone rings, interrupting our conversation. He glances at the screen and grimaces as he picks up his phone, apologizing, "I'm sorry, I have to take this."

I smile and wave him off. "It's okay. I don't think you can help with the list of ingredients anyway."

"True," he mumbles, chuckling as he answers his phone, lifting it to his ear. "Hey, Dad."

I watch him for a moment as he walks to the front of the house, enjoying just having him here in my space. Sighing happily, I look away and focus on my shopping list. "I hope I can do a good job with this," I murmur to myself.

Moments later, Jack strides back into the room and claps his hands together, startling me. I turn my head to him, and he announces, "It's time to take a break. I need to work off some of these cookies." He smirks, patting his flat stomach.

I laugh. "What did you have in mind?"

"How about ice skating?" he proposes. "We said we would go back another time."

I open my mouth to answer just as Holly bounces into the room. "Did I hear someone say we're going ice skating?" she asks sweetly. "Hannah and I were just talking about going to the rink. Can we have a ride?"

Jack and I laugh, and I nod my head in agreement. "Sure. Text her and let her know we'll be at her house to pick her up in about ten minutes," I inform her.

"Thank you!" she yells as she spins around, heading straight for her room.

I smile at Jack. "I guess we're going ice skating." He grins down at me, making my stomach flip-flop. This man does so much for me; it's overwhelming. "Thank you," I tell him sincerely, knowing I'm thanking him for so much more than I can begin to express.

"You have nothing to thank me for," he claims.

I sigh happily and let it go for now. I'll just have to find a way to thank him besides through his stomach. I stand and walk toward the living room. "We rent our skates there, so I just have to get my coat and gloves and then we can go," I tell him.

He follows behind me and grabs my coat from me, helping me slip it on. "I knew we would get back there," he teases grinning. He pulls his own coat on and pauses in front of the door to look at me, causing my heart to pound so hard it feels as if it will jump out into his arms. "I might have to head back to the office for a few days after tonight," he reveals.

My head drops down as my heart sinks. I focus on the zipper of my coat before I force a reply, "Okay." I take a deep breath, slowly zip up my coat, then pull my gloves out of my pockets and tug them on. Hopefully, I can get my emotions under control before I look at him. I don't want him to see the overwhelming disappointment in my eyes. I'm more attached to this man than I probably should be.

He steps into my space, and my whole body instantly heats from his nearness. His fingers lightly grasp my chin, making me gasp and freeze, holding my breath in anticipation. He gently nudges my head up until I meet his gaze. As he stares intently into my eyes, he insists, "But I'd really like to see you again, Jess, and not about work. I know the Christmas train is next weekend, and we're both going to be busy, but do you think you might be able to make some time for me? Go out with me again?"

I meet his tender gaze and exhale slowly, trying to get my nerves under control. Feeling my cheeks flush, I nod shyly and admit, "I'd like to see you too, Jack."

His smile lights up his whole face, taking my breath away. He slowly leans toward me, and my heart speeds up, heating my already overheated body. I feel his warm breath on my face, our lips only inches apart. My eyes begin to close in anticipation of his long-awaited kiss.

"I'm ready!" Holly announces as she bounds into the room, startling both of us apart.

Jack chuckles lightly and shakes his head as I slowly inhale and exhale a few times before finally responding, my voice overly cheerful, "Okay, let's go ice skating."

CHAPTER 15
Jack

I open the door and gasp in surprise at the sight of my mom. She's still beautiful with mostly gray hair, along with a few blonde streaks, pulled loosely back, her round cheeks rosy from the cold. Her blue eyes, so similar to both my dad and me, quickly assess me from head to toe as if to make sure I'm okay. "Mom, what are you doing here?" I blurt out.

She giggles and smiles warmly up at me, her eyes crinkling at the corners. She scrunches her button nose in displeasure and asks, "Is that any way to greet your mother, Nicholas Jack?"

I shake my head and apologize, "I'm sorry, Mom. It's so great to see you! You just caught me by surprise is all," I tell her as I step into her warm embrace.

"I'm happy to see you too, my boy," she proclaims sweetly as she squeezes me tight.

As she releases me, I step back and open the door further, gesturing for her to come inside. "May I help you with your coat?" I offer, reaching for her thick, white, winter wool coat accessorized with a red scarf. She slips it off and hands it to me with a nod. Spinning around, I hang it in the closet by the door before turning back toward her. Underneath her coat, she's wearing black pants, a white turtleneck covered with a red cardigan sweater, and a long necklace of tiny jingle bells. I smile at the simple familiarity, warming my heart and making me feel closer to home.

She holds her hands up toward me, offering, "I wanted to come down here and help you. You know how busy your dad is this time of year, but he has a whole community helping him. It sounds like you need my help much more than him this time."

"Thanks, Mom, but I've got it covered," I insist with a wave of my hand.

She pats me gently on the chest, placating me. "I'm sure you do, dear, but it sounds like there are some other things I needed to check on as well." She grins and takes a step back as she drops her hand to her side and begins looking around as if she's looking for something.

My eyes narrow, and I tilt my head to the side, assessing her expression while she appears to be avoiding my gaze. Stepping toward her, I probe, "What are you really doing here, Mom? You never come to help me this time of year. Dad's the one who needs all the help he can get for obvious reasons."

She purses her lips and waves her head, insisting, "Your Dad is just fine. He has more than enough help with all the elves and the reindeer. I'm here to see my son and help him out with his event. I've always enjoyed the Christmas train and it has been a long time since I've been able to help with it."

I huff a laugh and shake my head in amusement. "The Christmas train in Mistletoe Haven is a much smaller event than Christmas itself," I emphasize, continuing to watch her closely. She's obviously up to something.

Her head falls back as she laughs, both of us knowing that's an understatement. She purses her lips and sighs, finally admitting, "Well, I also heard you might need some extra hands in the kitchen to help that baker of yours, and I couldn't say no to baking some Christmas cookies. You know me."

"Baker of mine?" I question, ignoring the rest of her statement as I cross my arms over my chest. "I think your words just gave you away, Mom," I smirk, arching my eyebrows in challenge.

She huffs a laugh and waves her hand, dismissing her comment, "Oh, you know what I mean." She spins around and clasps her hands together as her grin takes over her whole face, her eyes sparkling. "You know exactly what I mean, Nicholas," she insists. My mom is the only one that calls me by my first name, but not all the time. She usually has a reason for doing so. Well, my dad does, too, when he's mad, but that's the same for so many.

I laugh, "Yeah, I do, Mom." I relax and smile widely at her. "I know you and Allie have been doing a lot of conspiring lately when it comes to me."

"Is that what you call it?" She sighs and shakes her head, casting her eyes at my feet before looking at me again. "She had to be the one who told me about this woman you're dating. How come you didn't?" she asks, her eyebrows arched in challenge.

My eyes widen at the hurt on her face causing my heart to clench. "You and Allie were the ones who put me on a dating website after I told her no," I stress.

Her smile fills with satisfaction as she straightens her shoulders, looking me in the eye. "Well, someone needed to do it for you. You should be thanking me."

I huff a laugh. "Don't get your hopes up quite yet. I'll thank you if she survives meeting both you and Dad," I emphasize, "and the reality that is my life." Saying the words out loud brings reality crashing into me like a Mack truck. She's going to think we've all lost our minds.

She grimaces and tilts her head to the side, studying me. "So, you do like her," she proclaims, her tone gentle.

"Mom," I warn, feeling defeated.

"You just said you're ready for her to meet your father and me." She grins full of hope.

Heaving a sigh, I run my hand down my face in frustration. Apparently, I speak from my heart before my brain processes what I want to say. "Can we just start slow?" I request, my stomach churning. "I don't know how to handle an introduction with Dad yet," I admit, the idea daunting.

She nods in agreement, "Okay, Jack. We can go as slow as our family circumstances allow."

"Thank you," I mumble, sighing in relief. At the same time her comment reminds me that our family circumstances won't allow me much time at all, especially with Christmas so soon. My brain searches for ways to ease her into the idea of my family, wondering how she'll react.

Mom claps her hands to get my attention, startling me from my thoughts. She smiles. "Anyway, I'm ready to meet her. Can we go now?" she asks politely. "I came all this way," she adds dramatically.

I chuckle softly and sigh in resignation. "Okay, Mom." I nod in agreement. "Let me text her to see if she's available." I grab my phone off my desk and send a quick text to Jessica. "Are you home? I have someone I want you to meet," I tell her simply, not wanting her to worry about meeting my mom.

The bubble pops up, indicating her typing a response. I stare at my phone, waiting for it to come through. "I'm home, but who am I meeting? Can you give me a few minutes to cleanup? I just got back from the bakery."

"Okay, we'll see you in about a half hour," I reply, hoping that gives her enough time to do what she wants to do before we arrive.

"Sounds good! Who's coming with you?"

I look up at my mom and take a deep breath. This is a big step. I'm nervous this will push Jessica away and that's the last thing I want. Then again, my mom's right. With Christmas so close, I guess it's time to figure it out one way or another. I just hope we come out on the other side of this together. "Okay," I murmur as I exhale. "We can go in a few minutes. She just got home from work."

She nods emphatically as she smiles broadly. "Perfect!" She claps making me chuckle.

"Do you want to check on the train before we go over?" I propose. "Maybe see what I've been working on? You know, your excuse to meet Jessica?"

She giggles, non-apologetic, and declares, "Sure, Let's go." Spinning around, she opens the closet and grabs her coat off the hanger. Then she quickly pulls it back on as she walks out the door without even checking to see if I'm trailing her.

I chuckle and follow behind her. As I reach for my coat and slip it on, I realize I never told Jessica whom I was bringing for her to meet. Bringing my mom without letting her know probably wouldn't be the best idea. I reach for my phone to tell her when my mom calls over her shoulder, sounding slightly impatient, "Nicholas Jack, let's go!"

Sighing, I slip my phone into my pocket and jog after my mom. It's never a good idea to make her wait. "I'm coming, I'm coming!"

About forty-five minutes later, we pull up in front of Jessica's house, my mom still chattering about the Christmas train. "The snack stations will be just perfect…"

"We're here," I interrupt as I turn off my truck.

She stops and looks up at Jessica's house, decorated in white lights, garlands, and bows. "She did a wonderful job decorating," she comments, smiling proudly.

I grimace, knowing how much something like decorating for Christmas means to my parents, but I can't lie to my mom. "Actually, I did the outside for her as a surprise one night. But we all decorated the inside together," I inform her.

She looks approvingly at me, gently patting me on the cheek. "Of course you did. You're such a gentleman." I feel myself blush and look away. Taking a deep breath, I reach for the handle and get out of the truck before she has a chance to say anything else. Then, I jog around to the passenger side and hold my arm out to help my mom out of my truck.

My heart skips a beat as we take a step toward Jessica's front door. My stomach twists into knots. I never told her who was coming. I take a deep breath, attempting to gulp down my nerves, hoping she'll take this in stride. Then again, if she doesn't, she's not the right woman for me. My heartbeat speeds up at my thoughts. I'm not ready for this to be over. I shake my head, attempting to mentally pull myself together as I force myself to ring the doorbell.

"Coming!" I hear her muffled yell through the door. The door swings open and she smiles up at me, taking my breath away. She has her wet hair pulled back into a neat ponytail. Her legs appear longer than I know. They are covered in black leggings. My gaze glides up over her fuzzy gray sweater until I meet her curious eyes. "Hi," she says almost shyly as her gaze flits from me to my mom.

I can't stop my smile, even if I tried. "Hi, Jessica," I greet her, my voice sounding raspy. She glances anxiously over to my mom and back to me. I shift on my feet nervously and clear my throat. "Um, I had a surprise visitor today and she wanted to meet you. Jessica, this is my mom," I inform her, forcing her name from my lips, "Carol Claus."

Her face pales slightly, making my stomach turn as her eyes widen in surprise. "Oh! Um, Hi! It's so nice to meet you," she stammers awkwardly. She sticks out her hand for my mom to shake.

My mom smiles warmly and gently pats Jessica's hand down before she holds her arms out. "I'm more of a hugger if that's okay with you?" Jessica barely begins to nod when my mom embraces her, squeezing her tight. I watch as Jessica slowly returns the gesture before she slips out of her hold, her eyes glistening. "Did Jack tell you his grandmother's name is Jessica?" she asks, arching her eyebrows.

"No, he didn't." Jessica shakes her head.

"It's such a beautiful name for an incredibly beautiful woman," my mother compliments.

Jessica's cheeks turn a beautiful shade of pink, making my heart skip a beat. "Thank you," she whispers. Her eyes widen, and she steps back suddenly. "I'm so sorry. Where are my manners? Would you like to come in?"

My mom giggles as she steps into the house and right past Jessica while I follow. I lean down next to her ear while I pass. "I'm so sorry to drop in like this. I hope this is okay. It's something my family seems to think is acceptable," I whisper, desperate to know what she's thinking.

She smiles and nods reassuringly. "It's fine," she quietly insists.

I slowly release the breath I didn't know I was holding, feeling the tension ease out of my shoulders with the sincerity of her affirmation. I look around the room, noticing the quiet house, and return my attention to Jessica. "Where's Holly?"

"She went over to her friend's house to study for a big test," she informs me.

My mom spins back around, facing Jessica and asks, "So I heard you're a baker?"

Jessica nods nervously. "I am."

"You must be really good at what you do because Jack has been raving about your cookies and he's very particular about his dessert," she emphasizes. Jessica blushes as she glances over at me.

I smile at her in encouragement, agreeing with my mother. "It's all true."

"He also said you agreed to bake the cookies for the Christmas train event and hopefully some cakes for the train depot and maybe the snack stands. I know that's a lot to take on. I would be happy to help you. I definitely know my way around a kitchen. Plus, I've worked the Christmas train before. It may be a lot of work, but it's also a lot of fun, and it's definitely worth the effort to see all those smiles on all the children's faces."

"That would be wonderful! Thank you. I must admit, I'm looking forward to watching everyone take it all in, especially the kids," Jessica concedes.

"Allie and Katie have both offered to help with the event, too, and unlike Jack, they're wonderful in the kitchen," she informs her.

Jessica giggles before her eyebrows scrunch together in confusion. "Who are Allie and Katie?"

"Allie is my assistant..." I begin.

Jessica nods. "Oh, that's right. You've told me about her. But I haven't met her yet."

I nod, adding, "And Katie is my mom's assistant."

Jessica's eyes widen as she shakes her head. "You don't have to do that. I could probably find someone local to help."

My mother steps toward her and grips her hands between hers. "I insist. This is Jack's event, and we will do everything we can to help. We always take on big projects for Christmas," she proclaims with a wink in my direction. I internally roll my eyes at my mom's dramatics.

Jessica giggles and nods, accepting our offer. "Okay, thank you then. I really appreciate it! I have some cookies for you to try if you'd like," she offers, turning toward the kitchen. "You said you know your way around a kitchen, but do you like to bake?"

"I dabble here and there," my mom answers evasively.

I huff a laugh. "Don't let her fool you. She's an excellent cook and baker," I enlighten her.

Jessica stumbles over her feet as she enters the kitchen and begins fidgeting. "Oh, well, um, I hope you like them," she stammers nervously.

My mother eyes me sternly, making my stomach flip as I realize my mistake. "But Jess, I was serious when I told you I've never tasted anything like your cookies. They really are the best I've ever had."

Jessica eyes me skeptically. "Thanks," she mutters halfheartedly.

Smiling, I declare, "It's not something I would ever admit in front of my mother if it wasn't true. I like my mom's baking, but yours is more than spectacular."

Jessica turns a deeper shade of red, seeing my sincerity, and turns to busy herself at the counter. I watch her as she fills a plate with different cookies. Then, she turns and sets the plate in the middle of the counter, keeping her eyes on the display. "Can I get you something to drink?" she offers.

"I would love some milk," my mother requests making Jessica smile.

"Me too, please?" I request, grinning up at her as I sit at the counter.

She finally meets my gaze, settling my own nerves. "Okay," she replies, nodding. I watch as she fills three glasses of milk and sets them on the counter. "Have a seat," she insists, briefly glancing at my mother and quickly returning her attention to rearranging the small plates and glasses.

My mom steps up to the counter, and I reach out, putting my hand on her elbow to assist her into the high bar chair. "Thank you, Jack." She returns her attention to Jessica and, without preamble, proclaims, "My Jack is a good man."

My face heats as Jessica smiles in amusement, glancing up at me with her green eyes sparkling. Then she turns to my mom, giving her attention to her. "Yes, he is. He's really good at taste testing cookies, too," she teases, giving me a crooked smile making my chest tight.

We all laugh, and I watch as the tension leaves Jessica's body, helping me to relax. "Yes, I am."

"He's just like his father," my mother informs her. My mom picks up a cookie, taking a bite of one of the candy cane cookies, her eyes widening in delight. She swallows and licks her lips, declaring, "Jack is right. This cookie is wonderful!"

"Thank you," she whispers shyly.

My mom turns to me and gives me a quick pointed look before turning back to Jessica. I know what that look means. It means my mom likes her and she wants me to do something about it, but I don't know how to deal with telling someone about my family life. Would she even accept it? Would she run? Would she think it's my excuse to escape? Would she be able to handle everything that comes along with being a Claus if she did accept it? A lot of family responsibility would fall on her shoulders if she chooses to be with me after she knows the truth. I know it's a lot to take in, no matter what she believes or what she decides. In the end, I know with all of my heart I want her to choose me.

I give myself a mental shake and try not to think about it for now. Instead, I smile, warmth filling my body as I watch and listen to the two of them chatter about Jessica's cookies and the Christmas train.

CHAPTER 16
Jessica

Crouching down, I pick up the last bag of flour and set it on the counter. I look around my kitchen and my table. Almost every available counter space is covered with ingredients, measuring cups, measuring spoons, bowls, mixers, scrapers, cookie sheets, cooling racks, and anything else I might need for each recipe. I take a deep breath and smile to myself, satisfied with the various stations.

The doorbell rings, startling me. "I'll get it," Holly yells and bounds for the door before I have a chance to move. As she opens the door, the instant sound of chattering alerts me to our company. I tentatively take a few steps toward the living room to greet the women when I'm suddenly embraced in a warm hug. "Jessica, it's so good to see you again," Jack's mom croons sweetly in my ear as I savor the feeling of his mother's arms around me.

I take a deep breath and step back, out of her embrace. Smiling, I proclaim, "It's good to see you again too!" knowing it's true. I see where Jack gets his heart. I know I haven't met his dad yet, but his mom is an incredible woman.

"Hi Jessica," Jack greets me with a warm smile, causing my entire body to heat.

I glance up at him from under my lashes and whisper, "Hi, Jack. Thank you for bringing everyone over to help."

"Anytime," he nods, offering me a small smile. He steps toward me and places his left hand on the small of my back. Holding out his right hand, he gestures to the two women behind him. I tear my gaze from him as he introduces me to a petite blonde with blue eyes and a bright smile first. "Jessica, this is Allie. She's my assistant."

"It's so great to finally meet you, Jessica!" Allie exclaims as she steps toward me, wrapping me in her arms. I awkwardly pat her back and lean toward Jack for support so I don't fall over making him chuckle against my ear and giving me goosebumps.

"Okay, Allie, you don't need to scare her with your enthusiasm," he teases.

She steps back, narrowing her eyes on Jack, making him laugh. As I take her in, my mouth drops slightly open, realizing how young she looks. She looks more like a college student and way too young to be a long time assistant to the owner of a big company. I guess I expected someone older, more like his mom. "You're so young," I blurt out without thinking.

Allie laughs, the sound light, almost musical. "Thank you! I do hide my age very well. I'm much older than you think," she claims, leaning in and whispering loudly like it's a secret. "Katie and I are both lucky like that. It runs in our family," she emphasizes and gestures toward the woman with light brown wavy hair behind her who appears even younger than her, almost childlike.

"Um, I...wow," I stammer. "I'm sorry, it's just that I wouldn't think either of you were old enough for a driver's license. You both look so young," I say honestly, feeling my face heat with embarrassment.

Everyone laughs, and Katie grins, nodding. "We get that reaction a lot. That's one of the reasons I work so far up north. It's hard to explain myself to so many people, but if you live and work where everyone knows you, it's not a problem." She shrugs like it's no big deal. Then, she steps forward, smiling brightly at me. "It's very nice to meet you, Jessica. I've heard so many wonderful things about you."

I feel myself turn a deeper shade of red and give myself a physical shake, apologizing again, "I'm sorry. It's really nice to meet you both," I mumble, briefly wondering what they've heard about me. "Thank you so much for coming to help. I'm sure you have so many other things to do this time of year other than helping me bake cookies."

"It's Christmas! There are always things to do, but we want to be here," Allie insists.

I nod in acknowledgment. "Okay, good. Jack said you both have experience baking?"

They glance at each other out of the corner of their eyes, their lips tugging up with a grin as they both nod, confirming, "We do."

I clap my hands together in excitement. "Then, we should get started. There's so much to do." I turn and take a step toward the kitchen, but Jack's hand reaches out, lightly grabbing my arm to stop me.

"Before you get into it..." I turn and look up at him, standing right behind me. My breath catches in my throat as our eyes meet. "Can I have a minute?"

As I nod in agreement, I swiftly clear my throat and repeat my appreciation, "Thank you, Jack."

"I'm happy to help. I wish I could do more, but you don't want me anywhere near your cookies unless I'm eating them." He smirks. I giggle in response and he continues, "I have to meet with a few people at the train station to finalize some of the details for the weekend. I'll come back later to check in with you if that's okay with you?" he prods, arching his eyebrows in question.

"That sounds good. I'll see you later!" He leans down slowly, causing me to freeze. I'm not sure what he's doing in front of everyone, but I admit I'm excited to find out. He pauses when our faces are only inches apart, and I feel his breath on my cheek. He tilts his head slightly and closes the distance between us, brushing his soft lips against my cheek. My body heats before he pulls away. He pauses to look into my eyes, assessing my reaction and giving me his sweet smile, making me melt at his feet.

"Thank you, Jess," he whispers. "I'll see you later," he promises.

He steps back, and I release my breath, quickly refilling my lungs again and again. Then, taking one more deep breath, I pull myself together as I watch him walk out my front door. I finally turn around with a smile for everyone. "Ok, everyone ready?" I question.

"Wow, he's really crazy about you!" Katie exclaims.

Instantly, I blush a deep shade of red. "Don't embarrass the poor girl, ladies," his mom gently warns. She steps over to me and wraps her arm around me, giving me a squeeze. Then just as I begin to relax, she leans in and whispers in my ear, "They're right, you know."

"What?" I ask, shocked, my heartbeat skyrocketing again.

"He is crazy about you!" she tells me, nodding her head. "A mother knows these things," she insists giving me a secretive smile.

My brain suddenly goes into overdrive. I want to ask how she knows these things. I want to ask what it means because isn't he supposed to be taking over the family business really far from here? I want to know what happens after besides the fact that his job is in the city now. He's just in Mistletoe Haven because he's working on the Christmas train. Then again, why would he agree to go on so many dates here in town if he didn't think it could ever work? I shake my head and take a deep breath, refusing to give in to my insecurities, and ask his mother. That's a surefire way of making me appear desperate, and I'm anything but. Jack just has a way of getting to me and making me crave more.

"Anyway," I murmur, attempting to change the subject. "We have a lot of cookies to bake. I set up stations. You can let me know if there's something you'd prefer to do or something you think you'll do well with since I don't know everyone's talents."

"Just put us where you want us," his mom murmurs cheerfully.

I glance up, finding all three women smiling broadly at me, causing my stomach to flip-flop. Then, I quickly shake it off as Holly comes striding back into the room. "Where did you go?" I question, then shake my head as if it doesn't matter. "Did you meet everyone?"

She smirks and arches her eyebrows like I've lost my mind. "Yeah, I met them all when I answered the door and let them in."

"Oh yeah," I reply and shake my head feeling flustered. I walk over to the counter and begin walking through each station, attempting to bring my focus back to the cookies and away from Jack, which seems to be much easier said than done. "Anyway, at each station, I have the recipe along with everything you need to put it together. Just let me know if you have any questions."

"Okay," all three mumble in acknowledgment.

I take a deep breath and rush on nervously with my explanation. "Here, I have a station for the chocolate and peanut butter snowballs since they don't need the oven. Then after they sit in the refrigerator for a little while, we can make room at the stove for dipping. I have another station for the candy cane cookies. I already made the cookie dough and broke it up into three bowls, coloring it as needed, so it just needs to be rolled out, twisted together into the shape of a candy cane, and then drizzled with the glazed icing after they cool. There's extra dough in the refrigerator. Whoever does this can use the top oven. Then over here," I begin, walking to the other side of the oven, "I have a station to make the chocolate peppermint cookies. Whoever does this can work with the bottom oven. Holly and I will make the icing, filling, and glaze, plus we will make the chocolate gingerbread dough."

"Will we have anything left to do tomorrow? This will be a lot of cookies!" Katie exclaims.

We all laugh, and I begin feeling more relaxed and focused on the task at hand. "Yes, tomorrow will be for all the cut-out cookies, decorating and assembling anything we need to, like the chocolate peppermint cookies, as well as any cakes and pies I'm able to squeeze into our schedule either today or tomorrow," I inform them, my excitement growing.

"You are very organized. I'm impressed. I knew you would be absolutely perfect for Jack!" Allie exclaims smugly.

"I helped," Jack's mom adds proudly.

"Me too," Holly murmurs.

My head falls back as I laugh and immediately attempt to ignore their comments the best I can as I feel my face redden again. I watch as they all decide where they want to begin working. Then, I gather the ingredients for the buttercream frosting and for the whipped cream frosting and place everything between Holly and me on the counter. After doing this together so many times, we don't even have to discuss who is doing what and we both seamlessly get to work.

As I stir a large batch of buttercream frosting, I remain quiet, waiting until everyone gets into a rhythm. Then, gathering my courage, I take a deep breath and finally respond to Allie's comment. "According to Jack, you aren't a very good matchmaker. He said he didn't have very good luck with the first few dates you sent him on. I even witnessed one of them," I admit, sighing at the memory.

Holly freezes, her mouth dropping open in shock. "You did?"

"Yeah," I admit shaking my head with disbelief as I think back on it. "The woman was so busy with her blog, constantly taking pictures and thinking about her next post that she couldn't see what was right in front of her."

"So, you noticed him then?" Allie asks smiling mischievously.

I shrug noncommittally. "He's hard to miss."

"Mm-hmm," his mom murmurs, grinning to herself.

My face floods with heat, and I quickly continue, "Well, anyone with eyes could tell his date wasn't going well. He was talking to me more at the counter than he was talking to his date. The woman barely looked at him, and then she turned her nose up at all the treats. I don't even think she noticed him leave."

Katie laughs as Allie turns to Carol and mumbles under her breath, "I told you it would work." Carol smiles happily in response.

I freeze at the comment and drop my spatula into the large mixing bowl. I lean on the table with both hands and look at Allie with confusion. "What?" I ask, my curiosity overwhelming me.

Her eyes widen in surprise, and she rambles, "Nothing, I was just showing Katie how I mix the dough like Carol taught me; it works so much better."

I arch my eyebrows in question, not quite believing them as all three of them nod in confirmation, but I don't know what to say either. Heaving a sigh, I give myself a mental shake. I stare at Allie and redirect the conversation the best I can instead. "Anyway, he said all the dates you set him up on before me were a complete disaster."

Allie grins. "If that's what he wants to call it. I do know he wasn't happy with me," she admits, scrunching her nose up in displeasure. "He called me within fifteen minutes of the start of every date to tell me it didn't work out." She laughs at the memory. "But the way I see it, everything worked out just how it was supposed to," she proclaims, grinning proudly.

"I agree with that," Katie chimes in. She pauses before glancing at me and asking, "By the way, do you happen to have any of these cookies for us to sample?"

I laugh, grateful for the reprieve, and reach for a plate of cookies hidden on top of the refrigerator. "Of course!" I answer happily.

"Thank you," she responds as I peel back the saran wrap and hold the plate out while everyone reaches for a cookie. I replace the saran wrap and set the plate down in the center of the table.

We quickly get back into a rhythm. Images of Jack as a little boy run through my head, prompting me to look at Jack's mom and ask, "Mrs..." I begin.

She puts her hand up with a stern look in her eyes, interrupting me, "No, Mrs. Please, call me Carol."

I nod in agreement, smiling in appreciation. "So, Carol," I pause, "What was Jack like when he was growing up? He always seems so attentive to other people," I contemplate, momentarily lost in thought. "I was just trying to imagine him when he was younger," I finish quietly, shrugging.

She smiles, her eyes going soft as memories go through her mind. "He was always like that. He always wanted to see what he could do to help, but many times that got him into a lot of trouble too."

"Really?" I ask, her comment piquing my interest.

"Yes," she grins, nodding as she continues adding ingredients to the mixing bowl in front of her. "I remember one year one of our reindeer," she halts instantly, glancing at me. "Did Jack tell you we have a ranch? We have animals, like horses, reindeer, dogs..." she trails off in thought.

I shake my head. "He told me you had a ranch, but I didn't know you had reindeer."

She continues without acknowledging my answer. "Anyway, one of the reindeer hurt his leg, and Jack didn't want him to be alone while he was in pain. He snuck out of the house at night, and we found him the next day in the barn sharing his blanket with the reindeer. This happened three nights in a row, even after we tried locking him in his bedroom. He still found a way out," she proclaims, grinning fondly. She sighs and shakes her head in disbelief. "He ended up with pneumonia because of it and was sick for weeks. The entire time, he was still more worried about the reindeer than himself. In fact, he tried arguing with the doctor when he told him he had to sleep inside if he ever wanted to get better."

I burst out laughing, along with everyone else. I couldn't help but picture Jack as a little boy asleep in the barn, attempting to take care of a hurt animal. The vision is one of the sweetest things I can imagine.

"Was the reindeer okay?" Holly asks hopefully, squeezing my heart. She's always had a soft spot for animals of any kind. I look up, curious about Carol's answer.

Carol grins and chuckles. "He was up and running before Jack was allowed out of bed!" She shakes her head, a proud smile covering her face.

I know, listening to her, he's the same man I've been seeing since the day we met, which fills me with both happiness and anxiety. The story causes my heart to fill with even more love for everything he is. Unfortunately, I still don't understand how we could ever work in the long run, and that's what leaves me on edge. He doesn't live around here full-time, and I have Holly to think about. She's always my priority. If it's not too late, the rest of my life can begin after she goes to college.

I grimace at the thought, my heart hurting, making it difficult to breathe. I can't imagine dating anyone besides Jack. Sighing heavily, I can't help but wonder why I ever let Holly put me on a dating site in the first place. If she didn't, I wouldn't have to worry about how I'm falling in love with a man I just met who won't be sticking around long enough for a full-time relationship. I sigh, reach for a spatula and begin vigorously stirring the frosting in front of me. I need the distraction of baking without thinking about what might or might not happen between us.

CHAPTER 17
Jessica

"My hands and arms hurt," Holly whines. "In fact, my entire body hurts." She stands, slouched over, staring at the trays of cookies, cakes, and pies stacked neatly in the bakery van Betty let us borrow to deliver all the desserts to the Christmas train.

I give her a pointed look, raising my eyebrows in disbelief, knowing we have to unload everything before she can rest for a few minutes. "We can't stop yet, but very soon, I promise."

She huffs a sarcastic laugh arching her eyebrows in challenge. "So, you're telling me your body doesn't hurt?"

I shrug my shoulders, knowing it doesn't matter. I still have to get this done, no matter what I feel. "Come on, after this, you can sit down and rest until the guests begin boarding the train. Work and then rest," I reiterate, trying to remind myself at the same time.

She narrows her eyes at me and groans. "Sometimes I wonder if you agree to do these things to torture me as some kind of punishment. What did I ever do to you? I thought you loved me."

My head falls back in laughter, making me feel lighter and able to keep going. "You know I do!" I grab a tray and tease, "Besides, I think sampling too many cookies might be a better explanation as to why you're feeling a little tortured."

She groans dramatically. "I don't think I'll ever eat another cookie again."

"Don't make promises you can't keep," I taunt. She shrugs and pushes herself up as she reaches for a tray. I take a deep breath and spin on my heel, balancing the trays in my hand as I head for the train.

Just as I reach the platform, Jack steps out of one of the cars with a wide grin. "You look like you have your hands full. Would you like some help?" he offers.

I breathe a sigh of relief. "That would be wonderful! Thank you!"

He takes the tray from my hands, and then he steps back into the train. "Why don't you and Holly bring the trays to Charlie and me, then we'll deliver them to the kitchen? That way, you're not stepping in and out of the train trying to balance the trays," he suggests. "Less chance of losing any cookies."

"It sounds like you're joking, but with how tired we all are you're probably right," I concede.

"See, I knew you were tired," Holly exclaims as she steps up next to me, making me laugh.

"I never said I wasn't." She rolls her eyes in response. "That sounds great, Jack. Thanks. But who's Charlie?" I ask as Jack reaches down toward me and takes the trays out of my hands.

He looks behind him and calls, "Charlie? Can you come help us with the cookie trays?"

A young teen boy wearing a red and green hat with his dark brown hair sticking out of it in all directions steps up behind Jack. He's wearing green pants and a red, white, and green top, making him look like an elf, bringing a smile to my face. He looks up at Jack in admiration with friendly brown eyes and a crooked grin. "Did you say cookies?" he asks happily.

Jack laughs and nods in confirmation. "I did. The cookies are here. Can you help me bring them back to the kitchen?"

"Of course," he readily agrees. He steps past Jack as he strides away with the first tray of cookies and turns toward me, smiling broadly. Stopping in front of me, he holds his hand out and introduces himself, "Hi, I'm Charlie."

"Hi Charlie, I'm Jessica, and that's my sister Holly," I respond, gesturing toward my sister as I shake his hand.

"Hi," he grins. As he let go of my hand, he turns to Holly, again holding out his hand.

She glances down at it smirking. Then, she gestures to his hand with her eyes, mumbling, "I'm sorry. I'd shake your hand if I could, but my hands are kind of full at the moment."

He visibly startles. "Oh, yes, of course! I'm sorry." He reaches for the tray and takes it out of Holly's hands, appearing flustered.

She laughs lightly and murmurs, "Thank you."

He nods and steps back into the train. "I like your costume," I call to him.

He halts in the doorway, momentarily appearing confused as he glances down at his clothes. Then his eyes widen in realization, and he quickly replies, "Oh, thank you."

I chuckle, nodding, "You're welcome."

As he walks away, Katie and Allie slip past him, both in costumes similar to Charlie's. "Hi, Jessica! Hi, Holly! We saw cookies," Katie declares with a grin.

"So, we thought you might need some help," Allie offers before giving a small wave in greeting. "Hi, guys."

"Hi!" Holly and I both greet them. "And thanks," I tell them appreciatively as we all turn back toward the van. Holly jumps inside and grabs a tray. Katie reached up and took the tray right out of Holly's hands, immediately turning for the train. Holly hands another tray down to me as Allie jumps into the van and grabs her own. Between the six of us, the cookies, as well as the extra cakes and pies, are swiftly unloaded onto the train and into the train depot in very little time.

With a sigh, Jack steps off the train and inquires, "Is that it?"

I raise my eyebrows and smirk. "You don't think it's enough?" As I ask the question, joking, my heart drops suddenly, my face going pale as I wonder if I miscalculated. What if I didn't make enough? I want this to go well for Jack and all the families planning to come aboard. Did I not make enough?

Seeing my face, he steps toward me, swiftly reassuring me. "It's perfect, Jess. It's just what we need." His words and his calming tone ease my mind. Then, his lips quirk up as he chuckles, joking, "But are there ever really enough cookies?"

I giggle. "Apparently not with you around," I mumble playfully, making him laugh harder. My stomach flips at the beautiful sound while the light in his eyes causes my breath to catch.

His laughter quiets, and he again emphasizes with his lips twitching, "There's more than enough for everyone that will be on the train today. Don't worry." I nod, grateful for this man. "I can't believe you made pies too! You amaze me, Jessica." I blush and shrug like it is no big deal. "Would you like me to show you around?" he offers, tipping his head toward the train.

"Sure, I'd love that!" I readily agree.

He steps into the train, then turns around and holds his hand out for me. I gulp down the growing lump in my throat and take his hand. He pulls at the same time I do, making me fly toward him and crash into his hard chest; a gasp escapes from my lips. I use the hand that landed on his chest to push back, but collide with a wall almost immediately, keeping us close together. I meet his eyes, feeling my entire body heat with embarrassment and chemistry from his physical proximity. The corners of his mouth twitch up as I get lost in his gaze.

Suddenly, a dull thump drags my attention away from him, and I turn to look outside. I search for the source of the sound and notice Holly's feet barely sticking over the tailgate of the bakery van. "Holly?" I question loudly. "Are you okay?"

Her voice echoes off the walls inside the van as she replies, "Don't worry about me. I'm not moving a muscle until you absolutely make me!"

Jack and I both chuckle at her dramatics. Turning around, I step in front of Jack and the rest of the way into the train. Pausing, my eyes begin taking everything in as I look around the compartment we're standing in. A large red mailbox with a white and red sign labeling it, Santa's Mail catches my eye, bringing a smile to my face.

Stepping past the mailbox, I find rows of seats in gray vinyl, mostly three on each side, lining the compartment, with a snowflake labeling each row on the side of the first seat. A small wreath with a red ribbon bow hangs over each window by a twisted red and white ribbon. Red and white streamers are twisted and draped from one end of the compartment to the other on both sides. I begin walking down the middle of the aisle and notice a small card placed on each seat. I pick one up to admire a picture of a red and white lamppost amidst a deep snowdrift in the moonlight. I glance at the cards next to it, realizing each one has a different winter picture printed on the front.

"I believe there are twelve different pictures, mostly images from the North Pole, but there are a couple of different ones with Santa," he explains. I offer him a soft smile and flip the card over. The back of the card contains the activities for the train ride and even a list of the various cookies we made, acknowledging me as the creator. "What do you think?" he asks softly.

My eyes flash back to him at the sound of his voice. "I think it's wonderful," I tell him honestly.

I watch as he exhales, causing his shoulders to relax. Then, he nods in satisfaction. "Good."

"And thank you," I add, nodding toward the card. "You didn't have to do that."

He grins, shrugging like it's no big deal, but it is to me. "I believe I did. You worked so hard on this, Jess. I really appreciate it, and so will everyone riding the train. You deserve the credit," he insists.

I blush and look away, feeling overwhelmed by his compliments. "Thank you."

He nods and thankfully moves on. Gesturing in front of us, he suggests, "Let's keep going to check out the dining cars."

I continue through two cars similar to the first until we reach one of the dining cars. The tables have bench seats facing each other with a table in between, all covered with white tablecloths. As I step closer, I realize the tablecloth is a white paper. Red and green paper napkins alternate back and forth for each setting, with a coffee mug and a water glass at every spot. A small bouquet of red and white flowers with pine and other greens sits low in the middle of the table. A red or green cup filled with crayons sits on each side of the flowers.

On the other end of the dining car sits a small bar. "I have some people helping to serve the hot chocolate and coffee or tea if the adults prefer. Then, I have others going around with trays of your cookies. Each dining car has a bar like that, even if it's a small one that they can work out of for both the treats and the drinks."

"That's perfect."

He continues, his voice animated with excitement. "I also have someone doing activities and entertainment in each car. The dining cars cost more, but the cars with just the seats will have the same amenities, just with less room. For example, they will have small travel hot chocolate cups and small paper plates so they can eat on their laps. We'll have to send people around to collect garbage in there a lot more often."

"That makes sense." I nod in understanding.

"The next car is reserved for the kids from the orphanage as well as a few special VIP families who wouldn't be able to do something like this otherwise," he informs me, a reverent smile on his face. Of course, the company took care of those tickets."

My heart lurches, loving how he always thinks of everyone else. "Sounds like this train will have everything a child desires at Christmas.

"Yes! I almost forgot. Santa Claus will go from compartment to compartment to talk to every child and give them a candy cane and a small gift to take with them, making sure each one of them feels special."

"Santa?" I prod, arching my eyebrow as I look up at him.

He glances at me curiously and nods his head, confirming, "Yeah, with the help of a few elves of course. He can't carry everything."

"Hmm," I respond thoughtfully as Jack continues to stare at me, almost as if he's waiting for some kind of reaction from me, but I'm not sure what he's looking for.

He exhales slowly and eventually tears his gaze away from me, continuing, "Anyway, we have Christmas music piping into each compartment, but we will turn that off during any sing-alongs."

I grin. "This really is wonderful, Jack."

"Thank you," he replies, his cheeks turning pink, making my heart race.

"When is Santa getting here?" I prod sweetly.

"Well, technically, it's Santa's apprentice," he answers, blushing a deeper shade of red, causing butterflies to erupt in my stomach.

I nod in understanding as his gaze studies me as if looking for an answer to a question I don't know. "Is there something you want to ask me or tell me?" I finally inquire after an uncomfortable moment of silence.

He opens his mouth and quickly snaps it shut. I tilt my head to the side and wait patiently for him to say something. Instead, he eventually heaves a sigh and shakes his head. "No, it's nothing."

"Okay," I mumble, my heart sinking into the pit of my stomach, suddenly feeling apprehensive.

"Jessica," he begins, taking a step toward me an anxious expression on his face.

Allie pushes through the door of the compartment interrupting. "Jack, I'm so sorry to interrupt, but your mom has your dad on a video call, and he needs to talk to you right away," she prattles immediately. "It's urgent."

He nods, sighing. "Okay, thanks, Allie. I'm coming." Allie spins around and walks back through the door she just came from as Jack turns back to me. He hesitates before asking, "Do you want to come with me? She's in the kitchen where we put all your desserts."

I shake my head, feeling his hesitation and not wanting him to be uncomfortable. "No, that's okay. I should go check on Holly, and whatever your dad needs sounds like it might be important," I explain, not wanting to get in the way. It doesn't feel like he wants me to meet his dad, even via video. It makes me wonder if he regrets introducing me to his mom too.

He gives me a fake smile that hits me square in the chest. Then he nods in acknowledgment, appearing relieved, making my stomach churn. "I'll see you in a little while," he mumbles and spins to leave, suddenly in a hurry to get away from me.

Exhaling harshly, I walk back through the cars and exit the train at the same place we boarded. I find Holly still in the same position, appearing as if she didn't move, just as she promised. I sit down next to her on the tailgate with a defeated sigh. "Are you okay?" I ask, nudging her knee, knowing it's easier for me to check on her than even think about the storm brewing inside me.

She leans up on her elbows and narrows her eyes, assessing me. "That sounds like the question I should be asking you right now," she accuses.

I grimace and fall back, lying down next to her. "I'm fine. I'm just tired, like you said. Everything looks great. It looks like it will be a great event," I reply robotically.

She huffs a laugh of disbelief. "Are you sure about that?"

I fold my fingers over my stomach and begin fidgeting with them. "Yeah. It will be great," I admit, this time with a little more confidence. It's not the event I'm worried about; it's the gorgeous man running it and why he looked like he was happy to get away from me.

After a brief pause, she encourages me to keep going. "But..."

I scrunch my face up before relaxing and answering honestly. "I'm just confused about everything with Jack. I really like him, Holly," I confess, my voice barely audible. Goosebumps instantly cover my flesh at my admission.

She grins, obviously happy with my admission. "What's wrong with that? Isn't that the point of dating someone? And Jack is a good man."

I groan in exasperation. "Yes, but what happens when he leaves? And what if he doesn't feel the same way about me? I don't know how I let you talk me into all of this."

She sits up completely and looks down at me. "First of all, I think it's pretty obvious how into you he is. He's always looking for reasons to see you and going out of his way to do things with you and for you, like helping us with our tree, helping us decorate, even doing the outside by himself, and getting your car from town for you. There aren't many men that do things like that. And second," she gulps and lowers her voice to a whisper, "the way Jack looks at you is the exact same way that dad would always look at mom."

I gasp and meet her eyes. "Holly," I murmur, overwhelmed with emotion, my insides feeling like a hurricane is attempting to make its way through.

She nods emphatically, gulping hard as she wipes her tears away. Leaning forward, she reaches for me, grabbing my hand and gripping it tightly for support as she offers me an encouraging smile. "It's true, Jess. That's one look I will never forget."

My tears overflow onto my cheeks, and I swiftly slip my hand away from hers and push myself up. I quickly wrap my arms around Holly and pull her close as she does the same, while silent tears stream down both our cheeks. "I love you, Holly," I whimper. "You know that, right?"

She nods and leans back, looking into my eyes. "I love you too, Jess." Reaching up, she wipes her face again and emphasizes, "Which is why I want you to have this. You deserve to be happy."

I sigh, loving how heartfelt her gesture is, but at the same time, still hesitant. How do I not worry about what happens when he has to leave? Instead of voicing my feelings again, I whisper, "If it's meant to work out, it will work out, for all of us."

She smiles affectionately and confidently declares, "It will work out, Jess. I just know it!"

I sigh again and wipe my own tears away as I push out of the van. Reaching out for her hand, I urge, "Come on. Let's go see the kitchen. We can help everyone set up with the cookies and other desserts."

"Okay," she agrees and pushes up. She sniffles as she hooks her arm through mine, and we walk toward the train side by side. Talking with her reminds me how lucky I am to have her as my sister. She makes me feel like the luckiest person in the world.

CHAPTER 18
Jessica

I hand a box of pecan pie to the redheaded mother of two rambunctious seven-year-old twin boys with a smile. "Thank you. I hope you enjoy it," I murmur.

She laughs. "No worries there; I know we will enjoy every single bite if this is anything like those cookies you baked." I smile shyly, feeling my face heat from the compliment. "And pecan pie is both mine and my husband's favorite." She grins and leans slightly toward me over the counter. "If he wants to share this with me, he's going to have to help me with Christmas dinner and the dishes, or maybe I'll just have to keep it for myself," she whispers conspiratorially.

I burst out laughing, not able to hold it back, and quickly cover my mouth. I repeat appreciatively, "Thank you. I've always enjoyed baking, but the stories that go along with them make it even better."

"I agree with you on that. I'm going to need more of your desserts. I'll be back to visit that bakery of yours very soon!" she exclaims and spins away.

"Oh, it's not mine," I call after her, but she's already gone. I grimace and step out of the way as one of the hot chocolate servers steps up behind me to refill her teapots.

As Holly is helping the last customer in line, I glance up just in time to see Santa enter the compartment in a beautiful red velvet suit lined with white fur around the edges, shiny black boots, and his signature red and white hat. "Ho, Ho, Ho, Merry Christmas," he bellows joyously to everyone in the compartment.

He's met with loud, excited cheers and children waving and calling his name, "Santa!" He turns his head toward me, looking at me from across the train until he catches my eyes with his own sparkling blue ones. He grins beneath his white mustache and beard, causing my whole body to heat instantly and my chest and stomach to clench tightly with excitement, seeing the man behind the mask. He offers me a small wave, and I shyly wave back with a content sigh.

Santa turns to the table next to him to greet the family. Completely enamored, I watch as the two little girls' faces light up with pure joy at merely the sight of him. I chuckle to myself, thinking I know how they feel. I watch him interact with them, drawing something quickly on the table and making them both laugh. The girls jump up and stand on each side of him, one hugging him while the other one stands proudly, posing for the camera. Both their mom and dad scramble to grab their phones and begin snapping pictures.

After the picture, both girls clamor for his attention. Their parents quickly calm them down and have them sit to wait their turn. Santa turns toward one of his elves and then turns back with two small, wrapped gifts in his hands. He hands one to each girl and watches as they open them, a resounding squeal from one while the other jumps out of her seat and throws her arms around him, embracing him with a shy smile. He chuckles as the girls sit back in their seats before Santa says a few more words to both the girls and their parents and waves goodbye Then he turns toward the family at the next table and begins repeating the process with just as much enthusiasm and individual attention as he did with the first two children.

Holly slides up next to me and leans on her forearms on the bar. "So, we're watching Santa?" she questions happily.

I turn toward her with a shrug, not bothering to hide it. "It's incredible to watch him with all these kids. Even though I have no idea what he's actually saying, I just know he's making a huge difference with every single child onboard with the way their faces light up, and even the smiles on the parents' faces give it away. He's so good with them, Holly!" I emphasize, butterflies taking flight in my stomach.

She stares at me for a moment before she agrees with a nod. "You're right. He is very good with them. It seems to come naturally with him."

"Did you realize he has small gifts for every single child on this train? And not just a candy cane like most Santa Clauses give out?" I ask, astounded. "It's almost like the gifts are personalized, but I don't understand how he would even do something like that!"

She grins. "Well, as you have pointed out to me several times," she emphasizes playfully, "he isn't like most men."

I shake my head reverently and admit, "No, he's not."

"By the way, the man I just helped bought the last of your pies and cakes," Holly grins proudly. "We're all sold out," she adds, clapping her hands lightly to make a point.

I gasp, turning to hear with wide eyes. "Really? We sold out of everything?"

She nods in confirmation. "Yup! He's having a big Christmas party tomorrow night, and even though he already has all the dessert for the party ordered, he wanted yours."

"What?" I rasp.

She giggles and nods, absolutely gleeful to share this news with me. "Yup, he even asked if we had any more." My mouth drops open in shock, which only makes Holly smile brighter. "When I told him there's more at the depot, but we're all sold out here, he said he was going to grab everything he could when we get back. Then, he told me he would make sure to book you early for his parties from now on so he doesn't miss out on the best desserts."

I shake my head, not quite understanding. "What do you mean, book me? I've never been booked for parties or events before, at least not before today," I emphasize. "The bakery isn't mine," I reiterate, something we both know.

"Well, maybe you should have your own baking business," she suggests arching her eyebrows in challenge. "People should be able to book you so you can make whatever dessert they need for their parties and events. It's obvious they already want to, and after this, there will be so many who want you to bake something for a party or a wedding. Everyone is asking about you, Jess!"

"I don't have the money to do something like that, Holly! It takes a lot to get a business started," I blurt out, attempting to get her to see reason as my stomach turns.

She grimaces. "Maybe we could find some people who would want to invest in your business, in you. Everyone loves everything you make. You should have your own business instead of baking for someone else. You're doing the job without the money or the credit you deserve."

"I've always liked working for Betty," I insist, thinking about everything she's done for me. "I wouldn't want to compete with her. Besides, who would I find that would want to invest in my business?" I challenge.

"A lot of people," she claims, arching her eyebrows in challenge. When I remain silent, she shrugs and points to the man in red, spitting out, "What about Jack?"

I shake my head in refusal. "I can't ask him to do something like that, Holly."

"Why not?" she asks, perplexed. "He loves your baking, and he's the first person to brag about it."

"I just can't! I barely know him," I claim, not believing it myself.

She crosses her arms over her chest and arches her eyebrows in challenge. "Really? That's what you're going with?" She shakes her head, huffing a humorless laugh.

I purse my lips and continue, "Besides, I kind of like him. I can't use him to invest in my business and   try to start a relationship with him. It's just not right," I emphasize, shaking my head. "They say you shouldn't mix business and pleasure."

"Who's they?" she huffs in exasperation. "Besides, you wouldn't be using him, and you know it," she declares, her voice elevating slightly. "And he would know it too!"

I grind my teeth and hold my hand up, attempting to get her to quiet down. "Shhh! This isn't the place to talk about this. We can talk about this later."

She drops her hands to her sides and sighs deeply. "Fine," she grumbles, "but I'm not about to drop this. You deserve more in every part of your life. It's about time I see you go after it." She steps out from behind the counter and then glances back at me, announcing, "I'm going to wait for my turn with Santa Claus."

My hair stands on end as I warily agree, "Fine. I'll start cleaning up."

146

It's not long before we are back at the station and all the guests have exited the train. Jack walks up to me in his Santa suit and smiles. "It looks like you did well," he comments.

I nod in agreement. "Yeah, we sold out of all the extra pies and cakes during the train ride, and I just found out all the ones at the depot are all sold too."

"The cookies are all gone, too," he adds sadly, making me giggle.

"I can make more," I remind him. He grins at me, causing my heart to feel full. I look up at him with admiration as I think about watching him with the kids. "You were absolutely wonderful tonight, with everyone and everything," I emphasize, holding my arms out and gesturing around me.

His cheeks turn rosy as he whispers, "Thank you."

I shake my head, feeling like I can't put into words the extreme impact today had on me, especially watching him earlier, and insist, "No, I mean really wonderful." He chuckles. "Everything was fantastic, and everyone had such a wonderful time," I continue praising him. "I'm having trouble finding the right words," I mumble as my face heats in embarrassment. "Sorry, I'm better at baking than words," I state, shrugging.

"You're good at a lot of things and thank you. I think your words are perfect," he insists. He licks his lips and opens his mouth to say more when his mom enters the compartment and strides right for him.

"Hi, Mom," he greets her with a smile. "How did everything go for you in the kitchen?" he probes. He looks her over as if she might be hurt, his eyes going wide. "Mom, are you okay?"

Carol ignores his questions. She takes a deep breath, beaming proudly as she steps up to Jack and quickly embraces him, squeezing him tight. Then, she steps back with tears in her eyes as she looks him up and down. "Look at you," she murmurs happily.

He smiles shyly, his face turning pink as he reaches for her hands, giving them a light squeeze. "Mom, please don't cry," Jack pleads.

She grins and shakes her head. "These are happy tears. It's just this is really the first time it's just been you," she attempts to explain her emotions, and he nods in understanding. "You look just like your father, Nicholas. I'm so proud of you!"

My eyebrows draw together in confusion. I bite my tongue, not wanting to interrupt their mother-and-son moment, but why did she call him Nicholas?

"You were so good with everyone, especially the kids! I'm not surprised, but they absolutely loved you!" she exclaims. Jack glances my way, his cheeks turning a darker shade of red the more she compliments him. "Your father and I are both so proud of you," she reiterates for emphasis. "I wish he could have seen you tonight."

"Thanks, Mom," he repeats, rubbing the back of his neck with his free hand, seeming to get more uncomfortable by the minute. "Maybe we can talk more about this later?" he suggests, giving a quick glance in my direction.

"Oh, of course!" she agrees, with a smile in my direction. She drops his hand and lightly pats his cheek admiringly. "He was wonderful though, wasn't he?" she questions, glancing at me.

"He was spectacular."

She beams as if I just praised her, and Jack mumbles again, "Thanks, Mom."

"Okay, we'll talk later. I need to get back up north with Katie, Charlie, and the others to help your dad anyway. There are only a couple more days until Christmas, and there's still so much to do!"

Jack nods in agreement. "Yeah." He jokes, "I'm honestly surprised you got away for this long."

She rolls her eyes upwards, shaking her head. Then she leans in, gives him another hug and whispers to him, "I love you, Nicholas."

"I love you too, Mom," he replies and smiles down at her small form.

She releases him and steps back, immediately walking over to me. "Thank you so much for letting me help you with all those delicious desserts. They were all an absolute hit!" she praises.

I feel my face heat as I insist, "I couldn't have done it without you and the other girls. Thank you so much for helping me."

"I'm happy to be here to help you and Jack. He's a good boy," she tells me, glancing over at Jack, who suddenly looks extremely uncomfortable. I just nod in agreement, knowing it's true. "He has a lot of hidden talents he's been waiting to share with someone really special, someone he knows will stick by him no matter what they might question at first."

"What?" I question, my eyes narrowing, feeling as if her words have a hidden meaning I'm not privy to.

She purses her lips quietly for a moment, then reaches for my hand and holds it between us. "Just remember this, Jessica, no matter how old you are and no matter what you think you know, sometimes you need a little magic to make the unbelievable possible," she pauses briefly, giving me a knowing smile. "And when true love works together, there's magic all around you, as long as you keep believing in each other," she emphasizes.

I gulp down the sudden lump in my throat, trying to interpret the words that I feel deep in my soul are profound, but I'm stuck...true love, believing and magic? Does she think I'm Jack's true love? Or that Jack is mine? Or both? What does magic have to do with that? I give her a confused smile, feeling as if I'm trying to put a puzzle together. She grins sweetly before gently patting my hand in encouragement. "You'll understand soon, dear, one way or another. I'm truly happy I had the opportunity to spend this time with you."

"Me too. Thank you again for all your help. I'm really happy I had the chance to meet you too."

She nods in acknowledgment. Then, she takes a deep breath and informs us, "I'm going to gather Katie and Charlie and the others and head home."

"Have a safe trip home, Mom," Jack murmurs.

She leans toward Jack, and he tips his head down as she pushes up on her tiptoes and kisses him on the cheek. "Goodbye, sweetie." Then she turns and waves.

As I wave, I smile and call out, "Goodbye!"

We watch her walk away before I slowly turn toward Jack, desperate for answers but nervous about asking the questions, and I'm not sure why. Taking a deep breath, before I can change my mind, I blurt out, "Why did she call you Nicholas?"

He spins toward me with wide eyes. "What?" Instead of repeating myself, I just wait for an answer. He winces, admitting, "Um, well, Nicholas is my first name."

My eyes widen in shock. "What?"

Heaving a sigh, he explains, "My dad's name is also Nicholas. My middle name is Jack, so everyone started calling me Jack because it was easier." I nod in understanding, but I also feel like he might be hiding something else from me, and I'm not sure what it is. Unfortunately, I'm not really sure how to ask him about it either.

He stares at me for a moment as if waiting for the shoe to drop before he finally breaks the silence. "Tonight was a huge success," he declares, and I only nod in agreement. "You really were incredible, just like I knew you would be," he adds appreciatively.

"Thanks," I mutter, blushing again as I glance toward the ground.

"How about we go out tomorrow night and celebrate?"

My eyes snap up to his, suddenly feeling anxious. I think I almost expected him to clean up and leave town now that we're done with the Christmas train. Maybe that's what has me so on edge and skeptical of everything about him. "You want to go out tomorrow night?"

He nods, giving me his crooked smile. "Yeah. Let me take you to dinner, and then we can go to the festival of lights in town." I gulp down my anxiety as he continues, "Holly can come too if you want."

I exhale slowly and nod. "Okay. I'd like that. I'm not sure if Holly has plans tomorrow night or not, though. Is it okay if I text you to let you know after I talk to her later?"

He breathes a sigh of relief and grins. "Of course." Then, he leans toward me and lightly brushes his lips against my cheek, making me giggle and squeezing my heart. He stays so close I can feel his warm breath on my cheek when he asks, "My kiss makes you laugh?"

I attempt to suppress my laughter and respond with a shrug, but the shocked look on his face causes me to burst out laughing. "It's your beard," I admit, grinning up at him, "it tickles."

He chuckles. "Okay, that I can handle." He tugs his beard down under his chin and stares intently at me, glancing at my lips, then back into my eyes to let me know his intentions. Then, he slowly leans in, closing the distance between us. My heartbeat triples with every inch he diminishes. I can barely breathe as I clench my hands into fists at my sides. He's barely a heartbeat away. He's finally going to kiss me. I hold my breath in anticipation.

"Hey, Jess!" the sound of Holly calling my name causes me to freeze, wondering if I just imagined it. "Jessica," Holly calls again.

Heaving a sigh, I fall back onto the heels of my feet, realizing I'd been inching closer to him as well. "I'm coming, Holly," I yell toward the door.

I look back at Jack, my shoulders sagging as I point toward the exit. "I'm sorry, but I have to go."

He nods as he sighs with disappointment. "I know. It's okay, go. I'll see you tomorrow," he states sadly. I pinch my lips tightly together and nod in acknowledgment. He kisses my cheek, this time without the beard, making me sigh reverently. "Thank you again, Jessica, for everything."

Giving him a small nod, I whisper, "Bye, Jack." Then I force myself to turn around and walk toward the exit to find my sister.

CHAPTER 19
Jack

I pull up to Jessica's house and stare, feeling a slight tightening in my chest. The Christmas train was a success and no surprise to me; Jessica's treats were the talk of the event. I really need to finalize everything for Christmas back at the office, but I don't want to leave Mistletoe Haven. The truth is I don't want to leave Jessica. I want to see what happens with us.

The way Jessica looked at me last night, I can't help but feel hopeful that she could actually fit right in with my family. I'm incredibly grateful she agreed to go out with me tonight to celebrate. I want to spend every minute I can with her. Unfortunately, with Christmas so close, my life tends to become a little unpredictable, and I don't know how much time I have left here before I need to go to the North Pole.

I know it's probably time I tell her the truth. All I can do is hope she doesn't think I've lost my mind when I do. I need her to give me a chance. Pausing, I take a deep breath to steel my nerves as I step out of the truck.

Squaring my shoulders, I stride confidently up to her front door and ring the doorbell. Jessica pulls the door open with a shy smile, making my stomach flip. "Hi," she murmurs.

I gulp down the lump in my throat and quickly look her up and down. She's wearing a beautiful winter white sweater dress that falls just above her knees with black tights and tall black boots. She styled her blonde hair down so it fell in soft waves around her shoulders. My eyes pause at her ruby red lips before meeting her big green eyes. I open my mouth to greet her, but her beauty takes my breath away, and I snap it shut without uttering a single word. As I clear my throat, I try again. "Hi, Jessica. You look beautiful," I whisper in awe.

She blushes and offers me a soft smile. "Thank you." I grin patiently as she looks me over in my black pants, red button-down shirt, and black blazer. "You look pretty handsome yourself." She grins as her cheeks turn a bright shade of pink.

I love that she blushes when she compliments me. "Thank you." I grin appreciatively. "Are you ready to go?" I ask, gesturing behind me.

She nods. "Yes, just let me grab my things." Then, she turns and reaches for her coat. I step closer and grab it from her, helping her slip it on. "Thank you." I step back as she grabs her purse and follows me outside, pulling the door closed behind her.

"Holly's not here?" I question, knowing she wouldn't leave without letting her know.

She shakes her head and informs me, "She went to a friend's house to work on a history project for school."

I nod as I escort her to my truck and open the door for her. She lets me assist her as she climbs inside. I close the door and jog around the front, quickly sliding behind the wheel. "Do you like seafood?" I ask as I pull away from her house.

She nods, smiling. "I do. I'm relatively easy when it comes to food. I can always find something I like on a menu."

"Good. The Jingle House has delicious seafood. I thought we could go there for dinner."

Her breath hitches, drawing my attention. I glance at her out of the corner of my eye, trying to keep my focus on the road, noticing her wide grin and making my breath hitch. "I have to admit I'm astonished to hear you say you like seafood."

"Why?" I prod, my eyebrows drawing down in confusion.

She shrugs and smirks as she stares out the window. "I guess you always seem more interested in dessert, especially cookies, than actual dinner." She laughs at her own joke, and I cannot help but join in.

"Of course, I love cookies, especially yours, but I do need some nutrition," I answer playfully.

"Only a little," she teases, holding her thumb and pointer finger a millimeter apart. I chuckle as she drops her hands to her lap with a grin. "The Jingle House sounds wonderful."

I nod my head in acknowledgment as I glide to a stop at the corner. Tilting my head toward her, I glance in her direction, wondering what she will do when she finds out about who I really am. I grind my jaw and focus back on the road. "So, the Festival of Lights is something the town does every year?" I ask, delaying my confession.

"Yes, Mistletoe Haven has been doing it as long as I can remember. If you're willing to be cold, it's really a beautiful sight. They fill the park with a trail of Christmas decorations and thousands of lights. Then as you walk through, there are larger areas with elaborate Christmas scenes. Every year they try to make it a little different to keep people coming back," she explains, smiling fondly. "Then, if it's too cold for the walking trail, they also have a road path for the cars to follow, but it's not the same."

"No? Like they don't even see the same lights?"

She shakes her head, "No, not all of them anyway. There are some spots the cars can't get to. The road path includes people's homes, but it does start at the park. You can even tune the radio into the local radio station to hear the Christmas music that coordinates with the lights. It's pretty, but since the homeowners usually decorate their own houses, they don't have to follow any kind of flow. Each house seems to kind of do their own thing." She shrugs. "That's just not the same. Plus, the roof of the car blocks out so much, especially from the arches or overhead lights. When you're on the walking trails, being completely surrounded by the lights is almost like you're wrapped up in a warm hug of twinkle lights and happiness."

I grin, nodding in understanding. "I think I know what you mean. I'm looking forward to seeing it." She offers me a small smile as we pull into the parking lot of the restaurant. "We're here," I announce as I pull into a parking spot near the front. She reaches for the door handle, and I gently reach for her hand to stop her. "Wait."

She startles and turns around to look at me, slightly puzzled. I get out of the truck and jog around the front, swiftly pulling her door open. I offer her my hand. She giggles as she smiles up at me, taking my hand as I help her out of the car. "Thank you," she whispers softly.

I nod and clear my throat, turning toward the restaurant with her hand clasped tightly in mine. The outside entrance is decorated with garland and white lights overhead, as well as around the large oak front door with a large wreath hanging above the door. A host dressed in a black suit with a red tie pushes the door open and holds it for us, waiting for us to enter. "Welcome to The Jingle House."

"Thank you," we both acknowledge politely.

As soon as we walk through the entryway, we spot a large Christmas tree on our left decorated with red, gold, and silver ornaments and white lights. Every doorway has the same garland wrapped with white lights as outside. I step up to the podium, also draped with garland and white lights, and quietly give my name to the young woman with straight dark hair, brown eyes, and tan skin wearing a simple black dress with a red poinsettia necklace. She nods and smiles as she looks at her computer.

"What's your last name?" Jessica asks curiously. "I can't believe I don't know it. I think I heard you say it when you introduced your mom, but I don't remember what you said," she murmurs. "You surprised me that day, and I was so nervous about meeting her that's all I could think about."

"Right this way," the hostess interrupts as she reaches for two menus, causing me to breathe a sigh of relief. I want to at least sit down before we have this conversation. I'm fortunate and a little surprised I've been able to avoid it for this long. But my name alone tends to bring on questions.

We follow the hostess to a small table for two off to the right. The tables have black tablecloths and red napkins, accented with a small poinsettia plant in the center of the table. I pull Jessica's seat out for her, and she sits with an appreciative smile. After helping her slide in, I take the seat across from her.

"This is a really nice place. I can't believe I've never been here before. I've driven by so many times, but..." she trails off as her eyes return to me.

"I've been here a few times when I'm in the area," I respond vaguely.

"How often are you in the area?" she prods, suddenly sounding anxious. "I mean, your office is in the city, and your family's office is even further north. Are you really around here very often?" She quickly averts her eyes again, looking around the restaurant as she waits for my response.

I heave a sigh and reach across the table, pulling her hand into mine. She startles, her head snapping to me with wide eyes. "I know I have a lot of business that isn't here, but that doesn't mean we can't work." She winces as if I just read her mind, her gaze dropping down to her lap. I give her hand another squeeze and continue, urging her to listen to my truth, "Jess, I have a home just outside of town. I wouldn't have started anything with you if I didn't believe we could make this work."

She shakes her head, appearing defeated. "Jack, this isn't just about me. I have Holly to think about too."

"I realize that, but I think Holly is one of the reasons I like you so much. You're so good with her. She's lucky to have you as a sister. It's obvious what's important to you, and that means a lot to me. Family is the most important thing to me, too," I emphasize.

I see the sudden hesitancy in her eyes and on her face. My heart clenches tightly in my chest, and I can't help but hold my breath, steeling myself, waiting for a blow I feel is about to come. She opens her mouth but then snaps it shut, moving her attention toward our waiter as he steps up to the table. "Can I get you something to drink while you look over the menu?"

She exhales slowly, a look of relief covering her features, causing my heart to clench. "Sure, could I have a glass of cabernet, please?"

My shoulders relax with the subject change, determined for her to enjoy herself tonight and hoping she'll see how good we can be for each other. I don't know where her hesitation came from, but it's definitely there, and it scares me. I want to go through every day with her. I want to show her more of what we can be together because I believe we're magical when we're side by side. For the first time, I feel myself believing every word. I may have been interested in her since the first day I met her at the bakery, but she's inching her way into my heart and staking her claim. She's different. I'm confident she is exactly what I'm looking for, and hopefully, I can be the same for her if she lets me.

We order our food, and for the rest of dinner, I'm able to keep the conversation light and fun. With every laugh and smile she sends my way, I feel my heart fill, now feeling as if it's nearly bursting just for her. Her expressions as she animatedly tells a story, wearing her whole heart on her sleeve, causes my whole body to tingle, making me feel like I'm complete with her by my side. I don't want our time to end, not just tonight, but ever. It may be scary for both of us, but I know it's true. Now, I just have to convince her we belong together and tell her the truth about me and my family. My stomach twists as my anxiety increases.

When we're finished, I pay our bill and stand, holding my hand out for her. "Are you ready?"

She nods and smiles as she takes my hand. I pull her up, and we stroll out to my truck, hand in hand. "Thank you for dinner," she murmurs appreciatively as I help her into the passenger seat.

"It was my pleasure," I reply honestly. I walk around, sliding in behind the wheel. "I'm looking forward to seeing all these lights," I mumble as I start the truck and pull out onto the street.

Jessica's face lights up like a child's on Christmas morning. "I can't wait to see it this year, either! Can we walk through the trail in the park?" she prompts, her excitement evident.

I chuckle, nodding. "I don't think we have a choice. Why settle for good when you can have the best? What you described sounds incredible," I tell her sincerely.

She grins, nodding. "It really is. We may have to park a little bit further back, but that just means a little more walking."

I nod in agreement. "Well, I like walking with you, so that works for me." She blushes, looking out her window. Cars and trucks begin lining the streets in front of the homes a couple blocks from the park. Fortunately, I find an open spot on the corner where I can easily park my truck.

I climb out of my truck and walk around just as Jessica's feet hit the pavement, making me smile. "I'm excited," she murmurs, appearing almost giddy.

Warmth spreads throughout my body as I look at her, my heart lurching. "Good."

I reach for her hand, entwining our fingers, and squeeze gently, feeling like this is exactly where she's meant to be. She smiles up at me as we step onto the sidewalk. Then she glances toward the park and squeals in excitement, proudly announcing, "I can already see the lights."

I tear my eyes away from her and look ahead to the park. Christmas lights of white, red, green, blue, and some multicolored lights brighten the night in front of us. The lights blur against the blackened night sky, scattered with stars. I can hear the murmur of the crowd as we get closer to the park. The lights appear brighter and clearer with every step. As we enter the park, we approach an old-fashioned handmade wooden ticket booth wrapped with both red and white lights around the poles and then again around the ticket sign in front of the booth. As we reach the front of the short line, I hold out the money for the gray-haired woman behind the counter and request, "Two tickets, please."

The woman hands me our tickets with a kind smile. "Enjoy and Merry Christmas!"

"Thank you, and Merry Christmas to you too!" With a light tug of Jessica's hand, I step toward the white and red welcome sign, assuming it's the entrance to the walking trail.

She laughs, the faint twinkling sound giving me goosebumps as she stutter-steps up to my side. "You seem awfully excited too, Jack."

"Of course I am," I admit vehemently. "You have made this sound magical, and now I get to experience it with you." She blushes as we step into a tunnel of white lights, and I immediately slow my pace taking it all in. "Wow," I mumble, feeling as if the lights are enveloping us in our own little cocoon.

"If you think this is beautiful, you're going to be overwhelmed by the rest," she teases.

I chuckle and shrug my shoulders. "Bring it on."

We continue our stroll, taking in the beauty of the Christmas lights and decorations. As we make our way down the pathway, we come to an opening filled with nothing but live Christmas trees, each decorated with lights and ornaments in a single color. One row of trees is covered in blue, the next is red, the next is all white, the next is green, and the last one is an explosion of different colors adorned with multicolored lights.

As we keep walking along the lighted pathway, we approach another opening. I spot the red suited nutcracker first and then look over to watch Jessica's reaction to the lights. Her face almost glows under both the moonlight and Christmas lights glittering off the snow. Her eyes sparkle, and her smile is contagious as she points to something in front of her. She glances over at me, her breath hitching the moment she realizes I'm staring, but I can't help it. My smile grows as I stare at her making her cheeks turn a darker shade of red.

"Um, did, ah," she points to our right and starts over, trying again, "Did you see the ballerina?" I force my gaze away from her and look at an animated ballerina. She lifts her leg behind her, lowers it, turns, stops, and then repeats the process. "She's just magnificent, isn't she?"

I nod my head and look back at her. "Absolutely," I murmur as my heart clenches.

She appears flustered and finally turns back toward the pathway, pulling her hand away from mine. I instantly feel the loss as she prods, "Let's go see more."

I sigh and catch up to her in two long strides. A small blue and white cart with a sign for hot chocolate sits on the side of the pathway catching my attention. A boy and girl, both appearing about sixteen-years-old stand near the cart, both wearing a red sweater and a Santa hat. As we approach the cart, I take a deep breath, inhaling the sweet scent of chocolate and gingerbread. "Do you have gingerbread cookies too?" I ask, my eyes sparkling.

The girl looks at me at giggles, shaking her head. "No. Just the hot chocolate. Would you like some?"

I glance at Jessica and grin sheepishly at the knowing smile on her lips. I narrow my eyes at her, trying to read her expression. "I'd love some," she proclaims.

I nod and look back at the girl, holding up two fingers. "Two hot chocolates, please." She nods and turns, quickly making them. I glance back at Jessica curiously, but she's looking anywhere but at me, leaving me feeling uneasy. I turn back to the cart to pay before accepting the hot chocolates. "Thank you."

I turn back to Jessica and hand her a hot chocolate. She wraps her hands around the paper cup, smiling down into the cup. She whispers, "Thank you," without lifting her gaze.

"What aren't you telling me?" I ask, a crooked smile tugging at my lips.

She bursts out laughing and confesses, "I'm horrible at keeping secrets."

I chuckle, feeling my body relax as if whatever she's trying to hide appears to be for her enjoyment or to tease me. I'm not quite sure yet, but I'm okay with it either way. "I already figured that out, but that doesn't tell me what I'm missing."

She laughs harder and points down the pathway in front of us. I wait while she catches her breath and tugs lightly on my hand, urging, "Let's go see."

I turn down the path, willingly following anywhere she goes. We enter the next clearing, and I gasp, my mouth dropping open in awe. I no longer just smell the gingerbread, but I also taste it in the air. An entire mini gingerbread village is spread out over tables and platforms. "How do they keep the animals from getting in here and eating all the houses?" I ask, slightly stunned. "I can imagine this to be like Christmas morning for the animals in the neighborhood."

She laughs. "They don't always succeed in keeping them out, but they try. They cover them completely every night. There's also chicken wire set up around the outside to help protect it as well. Then they enhance the smell of gingerbread with fresh gingerbread cookies I made earlier today, but those get packed up every night."

"Did you do all of this?" I ask, my eyes wide.

She huffs a laugh and shakes her head, "No, there's no way I could do all this and the Christmas cookies for the Christmas train and get everything done at the bakery!" She laughs again. "There's a lot of us who actually work to put this together. The craft and baking clubs at the high school and a women's group all help, along with a few others in the community. It's definitely a group project, but it's a lot of fun. I like helping every year, but I usually don't come to see the final product."

"You help, but don't come to see the final masterpiece?" I question, surprised. She scrunches her nose up adorably as she shakes her head. I sigh as I step toward her. Reaching for her, I run my thumb over the corner of her mouth, putting all my nerve endings on alert. "Hot chocolate," I whisper in explanation, holding my hand up as proof. "Every time I learn something else about you, I'm more and more enamored by you. You're an incredible woman, Jessica."

She blushes and looks down at her hot chocolate. Then she takes a deep breath and looks back up at me with a smile, quietly admitting, "I think you're pretty great too, Jack."

My stomach flips, and my body warms from the inside out. I lean toward her, drawn to her, wanting to kiss her more than anything. My heart begins pounding so hard it feels as if it might burst out of my chest as she tips her head toward me.

"Hey!" a small voice yells as a snowball flies right past my head, barely missing the gingerbread display. We both turn just in time to see a little boy running after an older one making us laugh.

Jessica takes another step back, which serves as a reminder to me that I should tell her the truth before I kiss her. It's the right thing to do. I just hope I'll get my chance after she knows the truth.

I sigh in defeat as we turn to continue down the path. We pass decorations and lights of dancing elves, a candy canes forest, kids opening presents, a nativity scene, and a large family dinner. The very last scene reminds me a little of home. It's a scene of Santa Claus in his workshop, making my chest feel tight for a different reason. I pinch my lips tightly together at the sight. "You don't like this one?" Jessica asks, her eyebrows drawn down in confusion. I don't blame her.

I shake my head in denial. "It's fine, I just," I begin nervously. Pausing, I take a deep breath and try again, "I just have something I've been wanting to tell you."

Her body stiffens, and her eyes narrow as I see the hesitation return with a ferocity to her eyes, leaving me feeling cold, vulnerable, and on edge. "What do you need to tell me, Jack?" she probes accusingly, making me wince.

"It's something about my family," I admit releasing a heavy sigh. "Can we maybe go back to your house and talk?" I ask nervously, rubbing the back of my neck.

She crosses her arms protectively over her chest, closing herself off from me as she agrees, "Fine." Then she spins on her heel and starts striding away without another word. I don't have any choice but to follow and hope for the best. Not if I want this to work, as I know without a doubt, she is exactly what I want. I can picture her in my life for the long haul, being with my family as well as hers and standing right beside me as the future of Christmas. My stomach twists, a blizzard beginning to brew on my insides; just hoping she feels the same way about me.

CHAPTER 20
Jessica

Ibegin fidgeting with my hands as I walk around my living room, searching for something to do besides sit down with Jack on my couch. I don't know if I'm ready to have whatever conversation we're about to have. I know it's serious by the look in his eyes and the tone of his voice when he said he had something to tell me, making my stomach twist into knots. That's never a good sign. It feels as if I'm already losing him before our conversation even begins.

"Jessica," he says, calmly.

I gulp down the growing lump in my throat and look toward the kitchen. "Can I get you something to drink?" I offer, hoping to delay our conversation a little more.

He shakes his head. "No, thank you. I'm fine, but would you sit down and talk to me for a few minutes?" he says gently. "Please."

"I'm kind of thirsty," I tell him, not even sure if it's true, but I need a minute to pull myself together. "I'm going to get myself some water or something," I murmur, sounding unsure.

I turn and take a step toward the kitchen. But before I reach the door, he suddenly blurts out, "I have a present for you, Jess."

I freeze at the sound of my nickname, my heart beating erratically in my chest. No one except Holly calls me that since my parents died, but Jack does. Every time I hear Jack say it, it gives me chills and causes my heart to pound out of my chest. I slowly spin toward him, my eyebrows drawing together in confusion. I don't know what I expected him to say but telling me he has a gift for me definitely wasn't it. I thought he said it was about his family. I stride cautiously toward him and slowly lower myself to the couch a couple of feet from him, needing to keep my distance for just a little bit longer. "You bought me a present?" I ask, still unsure if I heard him right.

He nods, the corners of his lips twitching up. "Yes. I got you a little something to thank you for all your help with the Christmas train," he elaborates.

My eyes widen in surprise. "Oh! You didn't have to do that but thank you." I exhale slowly, feeling my body relax.

"You're welcome." He holds out a small box wrapped in red paper with Merry Christmas written in a white script all over it. "Here," he offers.

I hold out my hands, and he places the gift in my hands, his fingers brushing against mine, giving me goosebumps in the process. I stare at it for a moment before I mumble, "Thank you."

He nods in both acknowledgment and encouragement, a small grin on his lips. "Open it."

I smile at him and then focus on the box in my hand, quickly tearing off the paper and setting it aside. Carefully, I lift the lid off the box and pull out a small cream-colored oven hanging by a string about three inches wide and two inches tall. The door sits slightly ajar, prompting me to peek inside and see a plate of gingerbread cookies sitting on the rack. "Oh, wow," I murmur with wide eyes. "This ornament is beautiful."

"There's a scented pad in the back that even makes it smell like gingerbread," he informs me, excitement ringing in his voice. Enjoying his reaction, I giggle, causing him to shrug sheepishly in response. "It's not like you need that since your house usually smells like cookies anyway, but I thought that was pretty cool."

"Thank you, Jack," I murmur appreciatively.

He nods and smiles somewhat shyly, admitting, "It reminded me of you." He licks his lips and inhales deeply, hesitating before continuing, "I also thought about how you said your parents used to buy you a Christmas ornament every year and that you haven't done it since. I thought this might help you pick up the tradition again." He tilts his head, assessing me closely for my reaction.

My heart clenches at the gesture making it difficult to breathe. "Jack," I whisper, overwhelmed, and take a deep breath to calm myself down.

"Why don't you put it on your tree?" he suggests, nodding toward the tree.

I nod in agreement, needing something to do. On shaky legs, I stand and walk over to the tree, hanging it from one of the empty branches. I stare at it for a few moments, my chest tight as I remember a moment like this with my mom and dad. My eyes well as my emotions build, grateful for his thoughtful gift. Exhaling slowly, I attempt to steady my emotions and finally turn back toward Jack and smile. "Thank you," I repeat as I sit back down on the couch next to him, my heart feeling full.

"That was the first cookie of yours I tried, you know," he reminds me.

I laugh at the memory and scoot a little closer to him. "Yes, when you were on a date!" I exclaim, turning my body toward him.

He huffs a humorless laugh and shakes his head. "Yes, if that's what you want to call it. You know," he begins, catching my gaze, "even that day when I was at the bakery to meet another woman, I felt a connection with you."

I blush and look down at my lap, mumbling my denial, "No, you didn't."

"I mean it, Jessica, I did. I walked out of there wishing you had been my date."

"I was working. I was a complete mess," I insist, shaking my head.

He shrugs as he looks at me in admiration. "That's not what I saw. I thought you were beautiful." I gulp down the lump in my throat, not sure how to respond. "Jessica, my life can get a little crazy, especially this time of year," he informs me.

My stomach twists, and I bite my lip, realizing this is the part of the conversation I have been trying to avoid. "Mine can be hectic too. Between the bakery and Holly," I trail off, knowing he'll understand my meaning.

"Yes, but there's something else in my life that I haven't quite been able to show you the entire picture," he begins. I hold my breath as I feel my anxiety grow, desperately waiting for him to elaborate and also hoping he remains quiet, whichever path keeps him in my life. "It will get worse when I take over the family business, much worse," he emphasizes.

"Okay," I mumble dragging out the word. "What are you saying, Jack," I ask, suddenly feeling defensive. "Whatever you've been trying to say, I just need you to say it, please."

He reaches for my hand, but I quickly pull it back and wrap my arms around my stomach for comfort. As he drops his hand, he sighs heavily. "Jess, I just want to tell you a little more about my family business. I really like you, and I think it's something you should know before we take this any further. My family is a lot to handle," he admits sounding a little panicked.

My eyes narrow as I stare at him, trying to read his thoughts, but I'm afraid to ask. I take a deep breath and slowly exhale before nodding in encouragement, needing him to say more. "Okay. I met your mom. She was wonderful!"

"Yeah, but that's not what I mean. This...well, this is just...more," he stammers, not making any sense.

I try a different approach to make sense of what he's trying to say. "Okay, what do you want to tell me about your family business? Your family has a toys and tech business?" I prod, arching my eyebrows.

He laughs uncomfortably and rests his elbows on his knees, leaning down on them. Reaching behind his head, he rubs the back of his neck nervously and mumbles, "Well, sort of."

"You said that before. I don't understand what you're trying to tell me, Jack! What does sort of mean?" I ask impatiently, a whirlwind blowing through my insides.

He looks up at me before dropping his hands with a sudden look of determination in his eyes. "It means my family is in the business of Christmas, so that could be a lot of things. One of those things is definitely toys and tech, but that's not even close to all it entails."

"Okay, like how you coordinated the Christmas train event," I supply as an example, and he nods in agreement. Groaning in frustration, I mutter, "Jack, I don't understand where you're going with this! Please?" I beg. "What are you trying to say?"

He winces and grinds his jaw, blurting out, "It means my family is who everyone around the world thinks of when they think of Christmas.

It means I have a legendary legacy to live up to." I stare at him, still completely confounded. He watches me closely as he adds, "My last name is Claus." My eyes widen at his last statement. "My full name is Nicholas Jack Claus," he states slowly, pausing between each name. My mouth drops open in complete shock at his confession. He continues, sounding as if he's underwater as he speaks. "My father is known as Santa Claus, The Santa Claus," he emphasizes, "and I will be the one to take over for him one day."

"I...But...You...What?" I stammer, completely stunned. How am I supposed to believe anything that just came out of his mouth? "I don't understand. Why would you say that?"

Sighing, he reaches behind him, pulling his wallet out of his back pocket. He opens it and pinches his driver's license between his fingers, holding it out to me. "Here."

My shaky hands reach for the license, attempting to hold it steady between my fingertips as I glance at his name. My focus goes blurry as I read "Nicholas Jack Claus," barely registering the letters. I hand him back his license, staring into space. He swiftly tucks it back in his wallet and slips the wallet into his back pocket.

"Jess," he urges, prompting me to look at him. He reaches for my hand again, but I don't feel his touch. Instead, I suddenly feel numb; everything about his confession seems surreal. "For a very long time, I've been afraid I wouldn't be able to find a woman like you who would believe in me and fit into my life," he explains. "I think I've found exactly what I've been looking for with you, Jessica. I'm already falling for you, and I would give almost anything to know you feel the same way about me."

I gasp, all the air leaving my lungs. I'm not sure what to say or do. "Jack," I finally whimper, feeling as if a weight is lying heavily on my chest.

"I understand it's a lot to take in," he begins.

"A lot to take in?" I screech with incredulity, my breaths becoming heavy.

He freezes at my question. His whole body tenses as he murmurs my name with a touch of desperation, "Jessica?"

I shake my head in denial with tears in my eyes. "Why, Jack? Why would you do this to me?"

I barely notice as he drops my hand, his face falling in defeat as the light disappears from his eyes. "You don't believe me," he accuses, sounding hurt.

I huff a laugh of incredulity. "I don't understand," I cry, just as the tears I'd been fighting escape from the corners of my eyes.

"I can show you," he claims, attempting to reason with me. "Please, Jess," he begs desperately. "Let me show you."

I shake my head as his cell phone rings with the tune "Here Comes Santa Claus." I can't believe I never picked that up before. He takes a breath and reaches for me, but I flinch, backing away, increasing the pain in his eyes. "You better answer that," I insist, glancing at his phone.

He grimaces but stands and does as I ask after glancing at the screen. "Dad?" I watch his face as he talks. "Is everything okay?" he asks, his voice full of unease. He pauses, his expression morphing into one of concern as he listens to his father. "Yeah, of course. Whatever you need." He nods firmly and confirms, "I'll be home as soon as I can." My heart plummets from his simple statement, even though I know I have no right, especially now. He pauses again before adding, "I love you too, Dad."

He disconnects the call and looks at me, his eyebrows drawn down in apprehension. "Jess..."

"Go," I encourage, interrupting him. "It sounds like your dad really needs you. You should go."

He nods. "Yeah, he does. He fell and hurt his knee in the barn. He needs help for a few days getting ready for Christmas. He's not getting around too well right now."

My heart clenches. Pushing my own feelings aside, I focus on his dad. "I'm so sorry, Jack. Is he going to be okay?" I inquire, suddenly worried.

He nods in confirmation. "Yes, he'll be fine, but the doctor told him he needs to rest for a couple days. He should be back on his feet by Christmas, but he can't run the workshop and finalize all the plans for Christmas Eve when he's supposed to be resting," he explains. "He's not very good at asking for help, but my mom insisted he call me to come home to help; otherwise, he would be trying to do it all by himself."

I grimace, feeling slightly confused by his explanation. It feels like he's telling me a story instead of the truth. He suddenly reaches for my hands and pulls me up, holding them tight. His eyes light up with hope as he looks down into mine and pleads, "Come with me, Jess. Let me show you where I grew up."

I shake my head. "No, Jack. I'm sorry, but I can't go anywhere right now. Holly needs me here. I can't just leave her."

"We'll bring her with us. Please," he begs.

"We can't. She still has a few days left of school before she's off for Christmas break," I remind him, shaking my head in disbelief.

He nods and sighs heavily in defeat as he lowers our joined hands between us, still holding on. "Okay. I understand."

As I shrug my shoulders, I suggest, "Maybe it's a good thing."

He flinches as if I just hit him and drops my hands, nodding stiffly. "Maybe you're right," he murmurs dejectedly. "I have to go," he mutters suddenly, his voice hoarse.

"Jack," I murmur, a feeling of panic slamming into my chest, feeling as if it will consume me.

Pasting a smile on his face, he reaches out, squeezing my hand gently in support to help calm me down. "It's okay, Jessica, but I really need to go help my dad. I'm sorry I can't finish our conversation right now. Please tell Holly I said goodbye," he adds as he takes a step away.

My stomach twists, and my heart clenches tightly as my whole body begins to ache. "Jack," I rasp.

He steps toward me and wipes away a tear I didn't know had fallen. "I'll be back, but I really have to go," he reiterates apologetically. "You and Holly are both welcome to come up when she's done with school for the holidays. I would love the chance to show you around." When I don't respond right away, he quietly adds, "I probably won't be able to come back here until Christmas."

Gulping down the lump in my throat, I nod in understanding, forcing myself to respond, "Okay, thanks." My chest tightens painfully, and I bring my loose hand to my chest, attempting to rub away the stabbing pain. I can't help but feel like this is our final goodbye, the thought making me dizzy.

I can't comprehend what he told me tonight. I don't understand how he could tell me such a story. It feels like he's looking for a way to pull away from me, but why does he look so hurt by my reaction? It hurts to see that look on his face, and I don't know how to fix it without going along with his façade, and I don't know if I can do that. "Drive safe," I mumble and then pinch my lips tightly together.

He opens his mouth as if to argue but thinks better of it, shaking it off. He gives my hand a light squeeze and mumbles, "Thanks." I force a smile and nod in acknowledgment. He plasters a smile on his face as he declares, "I'll see you soon, Jessica."

"Okay." I nod stiffly, and he releases my hand. I lift the same hand to wave goodbye, suddenly feeling cold. Heaving a sigh, he turns, striding purposefully toward the front door.

As soon as the door shuts behind him, I close my eyes and take a deep breath as a few tears spill onto my cheeks. "It's for the best," I murmur to myself, feeling as if I may have just made the biggest mistake of my life. But he must be lying to me, and lying is something I can't deal with.

As I dry my tears, I shake my head, overwhelmed with disappointment. I need to focus on Holly, not on a relationship with Jack, especially now. I open my eyes and wander toward the kitchen, knowing exactly what I need to do to keep my brain occupied, bake. I just need to find out what ingredients I have left in my kitchen first, and I'll go from there.

CHAPTER 21
Jessica

Holly strides into the kitchen and drops her backpack down next to the stool at the end of the counter. "Hi, Jess! You're home early," she announces speculatively, looking at me out of the corner of her eyes. She steps up to the refrigerator and yanks it open, swiftly grabbing a bottle of water and instantly slamming it shut. She flops down onto the stool at the end of the counter with a heavy sigh.

I shrug and quietly admit, "Just a little bit. I wasn't feeling very well, so I came home early. Are you okay?" I ask, attempting to get her focus off me.

Holly ignores my question, and her eyes narrow as she carefully assesses me. "Are *you* okay?" she throws back at me, not fooled at all.

I sigh heavily. "I'm fine. Or I will be anyway," I answer flippantly. "How was school?" I prompt, trying again to pull her attention away from me.

She crosses her arms over her chest and tilts her head to the side. "School was fine. Mr. Simon loved our history project. My math test went well, too, and the rest of my tests are tomorrow or the day after," she rambles, finally answering me with narrowed eyes. "Now, what's wrong?" she demands, punctuating each word for emphasis.

I grimace, and avoiding her gaze, I declare, "Nothing."

She purses her lips, glaring at me as if I've just done something to her, making me feel bad for not just coming out and telling her about Jack. But how do I do that? "How was your date last night?" she probes, trying a different tactic.

I can't stop my visible flinch before I grumble, "It was fine."

Her expression instantly softens. "Did something happen with Jack?" she prods gently. My eyes fall to the cup of hot chocolate in my hands, avoiding her gaze. "It did," she observes, sounding surprised. "What happened?" she repeats, her voice soft.

My chest tightens, and I hold my breath, trying to tamp down my tears. She jumps off the stool and quickly strides over to me. I reach up, wiping away a tear as she sits at the table in the chair next to mine.

"Jess," she encourages softly, resting her hand on my forearm. "We're sisters," she reiterates. "We are always going to be here for one another. I will always have your back, no matter what. Tell me what's going on, so I can be here for you now," she gently prods.

Lifting my gaze, I look into her eyes, filled with concern, and exhale harshly. "Okay," I concede. "I'll tell you, but it is a little bit crazy," I grumble, not sure if that's the right word. I open my mouth and nervously begin while Holly attentively listens. "Everything was going so well at first. We had a really nice dinner at The Jingle House. Then we walked through the festival of lights in town." A soft smile tugs at my lips, enjoying the memory.

"You went to the festival of lights?" she asks, interrupting. I nod, twisting my hands together nervously, and she holds her hands up in apology. "Sorry. Keep going."

I take a deep breath and continue, "I kept getting in my head about how this could work for us long term, but I stopped thinking about that for a little while. Then we came back here to talk. He gave me an ornament of an oven with gingerbread cookies inside," I smile thoughtfully, remembering the look on his face as he gave it to me. "He wanted to bring back the tradition for our family."

"That's so sweet!" Holly smiles fondly.

I shake my head in an attempt to pull myself back on track. "Holly, that doesn't matter. None of that matters!" I insist, my breathing increasing as I feel my panic growing. "It doesn't matter how sweet he is or how generous, or kind, or handsome, or smart or perfect. It doesn't matter because he told me his name is Nicholas Jack Claus, as in the son of Santa Claus!" I mumble, my heart aching.

"What?" she questions, her eyes going wide with disbelief.

I nod. "He even showed me his driver's license, so I would believe him. At least I know he wasn't lying about his name. I can't believe I didn't know his last name until now. I was dating a man, and I didn't even know his last name. Who does that? Technically I didn't know his first name either," I mutter as the realization hits me.

"He showed you his license?"

I nod, overwhelmed. This doesn't seem real. "Yes, but even if that's his name, that doesn't have to mean anything. Right? But he believes his father is Santa Claus, The Santa Claus. Why would he tell me a story like that? He even invited us to go home with him so he could show us around."

"He did?" Holly asks, and I nod in response, feeling her eyes on me, assessing me. After a few moments, she shrugs and arches her eyebrows, asking nonchalantly, "What if he's telling you the truth?" I gasp, opening my mouth to argue with her, but she shakes her head and holds her hand up to stop me, "Jess, just hear me out."

I heave a sigh in resignation, too tired to argue, and whisper, "Okay."

"First of all, he's so good with people, more so than anyone I've ever seen. Think about what it's been like since you met him! He helped us with all of our Christmas decorations inside, including our tree, and then afterward, he decorated the outside of our house while we were sleeping, and I don't remember it ever looking that good. Plus, he went into town and brought your car home, which means he would've had to walk back into town to get his truck, and that was just what he did in one night," she adds. "I've been trying to figure out how he got everything done by himself, let alone all in one night."

"Maybe he had help," I suggest.

Holly shrugs. "He could've, but he didn't say anything about help. I feel like he would've said something to you if he was going to invite people over here for any reason, inside or out, especially in the middle of the night. What if one of us woke up and saw a stranger working outside our window? Besides the fact that neither of us heard anything."

I nod in agreement. "True."

"Then you've told me how incredible he is with kids, like the little boy who was lost and then the kids that were doing crafts at the festival. Besides, we both saw how wonderful he was with kids and their parents on the Christmas train when he played Santa. You couldn't stop watching him," she reminds me, making me blush. "Then you guys went shopping for a bunch of presents for the Gift Tree, and he even bought a bunch of extra things so any names that aren't picked would still have something. And didn't you tell me you found out afterward that his company also donated thousands of dollars of toys and electronics as well as a bunch of other stuff for kids and families in need?"

"Yeah, but," I attempt to interrupt, but she continues.

"I really like him. He always tries to include me in everything. Plus, it doesn't feel like he's being nice to me because he feels like he has to for you, but it feels like he genuinely wants to get to know me," she emphasizes. "That means a lot to me," she confesses, giving me a pointed look causing my stomach to flip-flop.

She continues, "And his mom," she pauses, smiling to herself, "she was one of the nicest people I've ever met. We wouldn't have gotten everything done if it wasn't for her, Allie and Katie. I also told you after she left that she looked like someone we know," she reminds me. "It's Mrs. Claus; that's who she reminds me of!" she proclaims excitedly. "Plus, even you said how young Allie and Katie look for how old they claim to be.

I scrunch my nose up, doubt still eating at me. Suddenly, remembering the words his mother told me   when true love works together, there's magic all around you, as long as you keep believing in each other. I inhale quickly as the words register. Was this what she was trying to tell me without saying it? "Do you really think it could be true?" I ask skeptically. I attempt to sort through everything that has happened with Jack and contemplate everything I know, trying to match everything up.

Holly shrugs, the corners of her lips pulling upward. "Why not? He's the kind of man that is the epitome of Santa Claus. He's kind, generous, helpful, and caring. Plus, he has a kind of excitement for Christmas that's helped to bring your Christmas spirit back, which I was starting to think would never happen," she proclaims, only half joking. Then she raises her eyebrows and gives me a look, daring me to argue with her, but I can't because she's right.

Guilt floods me. "I'm so sorry, Holly. I always tried for you. I will be better. I promise. I'm sorry."

She nods. "I know. It's okay, Jess. I know you always did everything you could to make sure I still enjoyed Christmas, and I promise I did and still do. I love Christmas. Although, I couldn't help but notice, after mom and dad died, you started making everything about me, even Christmas. It always seemed like you did it more out of obligation and love, and that's okay, but I want you to enjoy Christmas and everything else again too. You deserve it, and it helps it feel more like we're doing something together. That's the way it should be."

I shake my head, disappointed in myself. "Thank you, Holly, but it's not okay. Of course, I love you, but I never wanted you to feel how much we lost, the impact of it anyway, and at Christmas time, I worked twice as hard to make it happen. I figured if I showered you with love and attention, it wouldn't hurt so much."

"I know, Jess. But I wasn't the only one who lost my mom and dad. You did too, but you didn't take the time you needed. Instead, you turned all your attention on making sure I was okay. It's okay that you didn't enjoy some things like Christmas anymore. I understand, and I never blamed you for it. How could I when everything you did was because you loved me, but all your attention was on me, all the time," she emphasizes. "I think that was your way of coping, but I'm really glad to finally see you enjoying Christmas again and life, for that matter," she adds with a smirk.

I laugh and playfully prod, "When did you become the big sister?"

She giggles. "I didn't, but I sure have learned a lot from mine."

My body heats, filling with pride and love for my sister. I wrap my arms around Holly as my eyes fill with tears. "I love you, Holly."

Her arms wrap around my back and squeeze tightly, savoring the moment. "I love you, too."

Releasing her, I lean back and wipe my cheeks, laughing as Holly does the same. "You know I always enjoyed doing anything I could for you because I love you, and I want you to be happy," I insist.

She nods and smiles appreciatively at me. "I know, but you deserve the same." She pauses and circles the conversation back to where we started. "You know that's one of the reasons I wanted to sign you up on the dating website in the first place. Then when I found Jack, it's why I wanted you to go on a date with him for the first time. And yes, I'm making sure to take credit for being the one to set you up with Jack," she adds cheekily.

I laugh through my tears. "Of course you do."

She continues smiling. "I want to see you do something for yourself, and I think I'm right. He's helping to turn you back into who you were before," she emphasizes. "I've missed *that*, Jess."

I wipe more tears off my cheeks laughing. "Enough! I'm never going to stop crying if you keep going!"

She laughs along with me. When we both catch our breaths, she prompts, "Can I say one more thing?"

I take a deep breath and exhale in fake exasperation, "Fine, go ahead."

"I don't know if everything he's saying is real. I also realize it's something that's really hard for *anyone* to believe, but either way, he's been showing us he's the kind of man we both want for you." She grins, making me chuckle. "How hard is it to really believe in him? To believe that Jack could truly be Santa's son?" She pauses, and I can't help but feel overwhelmed by her words. "He offered to bring you home and show you around. What harm can it be to let him?" she suggests arching her eyebrows in challenge.

I scrunch my nose up, my nerves turning my stomach. "I don't know."

"Well, my gut tells me you should give him a chance," she insists. She shrugs with a small smile on her face and suggests, "Mom and Dad were always obsessed with Christmas. Maybe they have a little something to do with bringing Jack into our lives."

My chest clenches warmly at the thought. I giggle, thinking about our parents meeting Jack. "Mom and Dad would absolutely adore him." Holly nods, smiling softly. "Jack's Dad is Santa Claus?" I ask aloud, the question increasing my nerves.

Her head falls back as she laughs and shrugs at my question. "Maybe. Don't you want to know for sure? I definitely do. I also know you would regret it if you didn't."

I take a deep breath as I think about everything. Can I really put my heart on the line for Jack after all of this? Then again, my heart is already deeply invested. "How about this," I contemplate, "if there's any truth to what he said, he's going to be very busy the rest of the week, and

I need some time to think." Holly grins, her eyes filling with hope as I continue, "So what if I say if he comes back..."

Holly interrupts, "No. He said he would be back. He seems to always follow through with what he says he's going to do. It's not if he comes back; it's when."

My phone beeps, and I glance at the screen to find another text from Jack. I sigh and nod in agreement, "I think you're right."

She smirks. "Is that him?" I nod my head in acknowledgment. Her look turns smug, and she asks, "You think I'm right?"

I ignore her comment and his message, trying to continue my train of thought. "So *when* he comes back, I'll give him a chance to show me what his life is like, without judgment, but that probably won't be until after Christmas. So, in the meantime, I'm going to take the time to process all of this."

She nods in acceptance, "Okay, fine. That's fair." She pauses and adds, "You know, if you wait until then, I could always go with you if you let me since I'll be done with school for the semester and all." She smirks. "I've always wondered what the North Pole was really like." She grins wide.

I shake my head and laugh at the absurdness of it all. "I really can't believe this," I mumble under my breath. "This is crazy! I could actually be dating Santa's son."

She laughs again, then suddenly, her eyes widen in excitement. "Think about it, Jess! If everything works out with you two and you marry Jack, you will eventually be *The* Mrs. Claus! That is so cool!" she exclaims, her eyes wide.

My jaw drops to my chest in shock. "Oh my gosh! I didn't even think about that," I mumble in disbelief.

Holly stares sternly at me, not wanting me to panic. "No going back on your word! You promised you would give him a chance without judgment," she reminds me.

I nod, feeling a little lightheaded. "I know," I murmur. I drop my head onto my arms, crossed on top of the table. "I'll keep my promise," I grumble.

"I'll make sure of it!" she proclaims. "So, if my sister marries Santa's son, what would that make me?" Holly contemplates.

Groaning in exasperation, I ignore her question. I have more than enough on my mind. I can't worry about possible logistics too. I've been completely overwhelmed over the last twenty-four hours. I ask myself a question I know I'll be asking until I know for sure. "Could Jack really be Santa's son?" Which leads me to a second question, "If he is, what am I going to do?"

CHAPTER 22
Jack

"Will you at least let me sit and relax in the workshop?" I hear my dad ask my mom for the hundredth time as I walk into our living room. My dad sits on the dark green couch with his right leg propped up on a red pillow while my mom sits on a matching armchair next to him, narrowing her eyes in warning. There's no way my mom will let him even go near the workshop since he's hurt.

Inhaling deeply, I savor the scent of pine, wood, cinnamon, and chocolate strong in the air, scents I always associate with home. Jessica would love that smell. My stomach twists, and I stutter a step, realizing Jessica has already embedded herself in my home and my heart without even stepping onto our grounds. I can only hope she gives me a chance to share my world with her.

I glance around the room, decorated with a ten-foot Christmas tree in the corner near the stone fireplace, with our own red and green Christmas stockings hanging from the mantle. The tree is covered in colorful ornaments from around the world, just like I remember when I was growing up. A train continuously circles the tree on the outside of the red and green velvet tree skirt bringing a smile to my face. The tables and armoire are made of heavy barn wood resting on red and green braided rugs atop wide wooden floor planks with a similar look. Christmas decorations of snowmen, snow globes, angels, elves, and candles, tastefully cover the flat surfaces in the room. I exhale slowly, taking in the feeling of being home again, needing the familiar comfort.

"No! We all know you won't sit still in there! Besides, it's chaotic in the workshop, not relaxing," my mom reiterates like she's telling him something he doesn't already know. I can't help but smirk as she continues with her demands. "You are not setting one foot into *any* part of your workshop until the doctor says you can be back on your feet. I don't care what day it is!"

"I wasn't even hurt that bad," he protests. "Everyone has been blowing this out of proportion. If it was as bad as all of you say, I would be having surgery," he argues, arching his eyebrows in challenge. My mom crosses her arms over her chest and glares at my father. "What if I *promise* to sit still?" he begs, with the corners of his lips twitching up underneath his beard, making me laugh out loud.

They both startle, directing their attention to me. My mom smiles as her eyes meet mine. "Hi, Jack," she greets me, ignoring my father's question. "How's it going in there?" she prompts.

I grin and take another deep breath of the scent I've always loved as I step further into the room. I lower myself, sitting on the couch near my dad's feet. "Everything is running smoothly," I announce to both of them. "I promise," I emphasize, looking directly at my father.

"Ugh," he grunts and nods grumpily, reminding me why I came in.

I lift the laptop in my hand and suggest, "Dad, why don't you finish up the naughty and nice list? You can do that without going anywhere near the workshop, and that needs to get done right away," I urge.

My mom breathes a sigh of relief while my dad huffs from his position on the couch with resignation. "Fine!" he relents. "I do need to finish this list so I can finalize my route with Charlie anyway."

"I'll send Charlie up to talk to you when you're done," I inform him. He grimaces and takes the laptop from my hands without comment, setting it on his legs.

My mother stands and walks over to me, giving me a gentle hug. Pushing up onto her tiptoes, she whispers in my ear, "Thank you, Nicholas." She releases me, and I smile before she turns and strides toward the kitchen. "I'm going to work on the cookies for the elves' thank you gifts," she calls over her shoulder. "Call if you need me," she reminds my father pointedly.

I watch as my dad slips his wire-rimmed glasses on and swiftly opens the laptop. He logs in, quickly pulling up the naughty and nice list. He grins widely at the screen and informs me, "Jessica and Holly are both on the nice list again this year."

I smile at the thought of them. "I had no doubt that's where we'd find them."

He looks at me over the rim of his glasses. "Have you talked to Jessica since you've been back home?" he asks curiously.

Heaving a sigh, I slowly shake my head. "No, I've sent her a few texts every day since I had to leave, though." I grimace and admit, "Unfortunately, I haven't heard anything back from her yet."

He firmly closes his laptop and sets it on the coffee table next to the couch. "You have to do more than send a few texts, Nicholas," he insists, shaking his head.

I wince, hearing his disappointment in my creativity by just the sound of my first name. I nod in agreement and sigh heavily, my shoulders sagging. "I know, Dad, but I'm just trying to give her some time to process. I just unloaded a lot of information on her. I'm sure it's overwhelming. It isn't every day that you find out the guy you've been dating is Santa's son."

He chuckles softly, "Ho, ho, ho." Lost in thought, he strokes his gray beard and fondly confesses, "I remember that conversation with your mother. It sure didn't go very well for me the first time."

"Really?" I prompt, arching my eyebrows in surprise. "I don't remember ever hearing that."

"That's probably because I was too proud to admit it to my son."

"What did you do, Dad?" I plead, desperate for a way to solve this. "I don't want to lose her. I don't know how it happened so fast, but she's everything I've ever wanted in my life. I think I lost my heart to her the first time I saw her at her bakery. She's not just any girl; I know she's the one for me," I insist, my heart squeezing. "Her sister Holly is like a bonus. She's really a good kid and a lot of fun to be around. She's smart too." I smile thoughtfully.

He nods in agreement. "I know, son. I can tell how much you care about both of them and when you talk about Jessica, your eyes light up like a Christmas tree. Honestly, when it came to your mom, I just put my heart and soul into doing everything I could say and do to win her over," he admits, not giving me any specifics.

I laugh in exasperation. "Dad, that doesn't tell me anything. Please, you have to give me something," I beg, wide-eyed.

He purses his lips in thought for a moment with his finger pressed to his lips. "I think you need to be the one to come up with the idea, Nicholas. This is something between you and her."

Sighing, I nod in understanding. "Okay, but how?"

His blue eyes light up as he suggests, "Give her a grand gesture."

My eyebrows draw together in confusion, and I ask for clarification, "What do you mean by a grand gesture? How big?"

He arches his eyebrows in surprise. "I thought you always do everything big. I'm surprised you're asking me that."

I grimace and try to explain what I'm thinking. "I know, but she's just... more!" I blurt out for lack of a better word.

He grins and continues, "You're a smart man, Nicky, and like you just said yourself, you're my son! You've got this," he encourages, reaching for me and patting me on the back.

"Yes..." I say, dragging out, prompting him for more. "And..."

He chuckles and shakes his head but still gives me a little more. "You may not have all my powers yet, but hearing you talk about her, you know her. You know what she likes. You know what means the most to her," he emphasizes with a pointed look. "Be creative. Figure out a way to do something for her or give her something truly personal. What does she love?"

"Holly, her family, baking," I list.

My dad nods in acknowledgment and prods, "So, thinking about those things, what would mean the world to her?"

My eyes widen, and I can't help but smile as I declare, "That's it, Dad! Thank you! I've got the best idea! I know she'll love it!"

He chuckles and nods approvingly. "Good!"

"Now I just have to figure out a way she can't say no." I shrug like it's no big deal.

"Ho, ho, ho," my dad laughs harder, and I join in with him, feeling better about Jessica already.

"When will this plan of yours be complete so I can finally meet her as your girlfriend?" he taunts playfully.

I grimace as I think about everything I have to get done here before Christmas, plus everything I would have to do to make this happen for Jessica. "Maybe not until Christmas morning," I admit with a heavy sigh, wishing I could make it happen today. I miss her. My heart clenches as if to make my point. "If I work hard and have a lot of luck on my side, it will be Christmas morning."

My dad nods in acknowledgment and informs me, "I may just have to stop on my way back home that morning, then."

"I'll let you know." I grin. I place my hands on my knees and push, standing quickly. "Thanks, Dad!" I smile. I take a step toward the workshop when suddenly I pause as I finally process what my dad said a few moments ago. I slowly spin back toward him. "Dad?"

He looks up at me patiently. "Yes?"

"What do you mean to meet her as my girlfriend?" I ask curiously.

He just laughs and reminds me, "Do I need to tell you again that I'm the one and only Santa Claus?"

I take a step toward him with an overwhelming feeling of awe as a blush creeps into my cheeks. "I guess I haven't thought about it that way since I was a kid," I admit sheepishly, shrugging. "So, you've always known Jessica? And Holly?" I add curiously, wanting to know more. I slowly lower myself back to the couch, not taking my eyes off my father.

He nods. "Yes, of course, in the way I know all the children of the world. They were both wonderful little girls too." A smile tugs at my lips, just thinking about Jessica as a little girl. "As you already know, they had a rough few years, but Holly never lost her Christmas spirit, and Jessica did everything she could to make sure it stayed that way for Holly. From the looks of it, you've helped Jessica bring Christmas back into her heart for real, which is a beautiful sight to see."

Sighing, I regretfully concede, "You know, Dad, I didn't even realize she didn't have the true Christmas spirit in her heart at first, not really." I wince, my admission feeling like a failure. "Shouldn't that be something I should be able to tell?"

He shakes his head. "Not necessarily. That takes a lot of practice and time, Jack. Besides, Jessica is a special case because she never completely lost her Christmas Spirit because of Holly. It's more like it was hidden deep inside her and you helped pull it out of her to give it life again," he explains, making my heart pound faster knowing I was the one to help her. "Plus, the circumstances were different when you met Jessica. She was happy to meet and spend time with you, but I think you knew more than you realized at the time. Really think about it," he encourages.

I pause and think back to the time when I first met her in the bakery. She was beautiful with flour on her cheek and frosting in her hair, offering me her amazing smile, but it didn't quite reach her eyes. Then, on our first date at the Christmas festival, her anxiety was obvious, but I thought it was nerves for a first date. She did admit she hadn't been to the Christmas festival in a long time, but she said it was because she was busy. I don't really think I believed her then, though. I could feel her sadness, but I didn't want to push her for more until she was ready to share that part of herself with me. I shrug and hesitantly admit, "Maybe, but I wasn't sure it was about Christmas."

"You should have more confidence in yourself, Nicky. You're stronger and smarter than you give yourself credit for. I have all the confidence in the world in you. Some things will just take some time."

I smile warmly at my dad, my chest puffing up with the pride I see reflected in his eyes. My phone beeps with a text, and I quickly reach for it, hoping it's Jessica. I grimace, my shoulders sagging at the sight of Allie's name, causing my dad to burst out laughing, "Ho, ho, ho."

I lift my head and look at him with confusion. He smirks and nods toward my phone, pondering, "I'm guessing the message isn't from Jessica."

Flushing, I grin and shake my head. "It's Allie about work. I'm really that predictable, huh?"

"Maybe a little bit." He grins.

Taking a deep breath, I stand again and emphasize, "Thank you, Dad!"

"Anytime, Nicky, and good luck," he encourages. "You've got this."

"Thanks," I repeat appreciatively. "I'm going to call Allie back, and then I have some work to do to get this idea for Jessica rolling if I want it done by Christmas morning," I inform him. "I promise I'll get everything done in the workshop, too, so don't worry about a thing."

"I have no doubt you'll get it all done, but if you need any help at all, I can always come down to the workshop and take over for you in there," he adds, holding his breath.

I laugh and shake my head. "Sorry, Dad, but I have it. You have strict instructions to remain where you are and work on the list. There's no way I'm doing anything to go against mom."

He sighs heavily. "Well, I tried. Get out of here and get some work done then!" he demands, waving me away. He pulls his laptop back onto his lap, opening it up as I turn.

"Bye, Mom! I'll see you later," I call over my shoulder.

"Bye, Nicholas," she yells just as I exit.

"This has to work," I mumble to myself, feeling my excitement and anticipation grow in the pit of my stomach. With a sigh, I lift my cell phone to my ear, returning Allie's call and ready to beg for her help.

CHAPTER 23
Jessica

"Merry Christmas!" Holly yells just before she pounces on my bed, making my whole body bounce.

I half laugh and half groan, not ready to get out of my warm bed. I feel the mattress settle, and I turn to look at Holly, now lying on her side next to me, with wide eyes and a huge grin. "Merry Christmas, Holly," I whisper in adoration, my voice still raspy with sleep. I clear my throat and add with a smile, "I love how excited you always are on Christmas morning!"

She giggles. "Of course! Everyone should be excited! It's Christmas!" I chuckle at her response. "So," she mumbles, dragging out the word, "does that mean you're ready to go to the living room and open Christmas presents?"

"Why aren't you a normal teenager who wants to sleep as long as possible?" I ask, my smile growing with each word.

She giggles, taunting, "I'm pretty sure I'm the normal one."

I groan again and stretch my arms above my head, trying to wake up the rest of me. "Okay, I'll go brush my teeth and meet you in the living room."

"Yay!" she yells as she jumps off the bed and runs out the door.

Chuckling, I push out of bed and step into my slippers before padding toward the bathroom. "Oh, my gosh, Jess! What did you do?" Holly shrieks in excitement from down the hall.

"I don't know what you're talking about, but I'll be there in a minute," I call back. I trudge across the hall into the bathroom, tired from staying up late to finish wrapping the last of Holly's presents. I like her to be surprised when she looks under the tree on Christmas morning. Reaching for my toothbrush, I squeeze a small amount of toothpaste on before I begin brushing.

"Hurry up, Jess!" Holly yells impatiently.

"I'm coming!" I grumble over my mouthful of toothpaste. I finish brushing my teeth, wipe my hands and mouth and wander toward the living room as I gently run my hand through my hair, hoping to smooth it out.

Holly jumps up and down excitedly when she sees me walk into the room. "What has gotten into you?" I ask, laughing. I look past her and gasp, my mouth dropping open in shock. There are at least twice as many presents under the tree than when I went to sleep last night and so many more than we've had under our tree since we lost our parents. I can never do this much. "Did you do all of this?" I ask, stunned, pointing at the heap.

She stops jumping and freezes, her own mouth falling open. "You didn't do this? I thought you did this," she rambles, wide-eyed.

Shaking my head, I confirm, "Not me."

I watch as she runs to the tree and glances at the tag for the one on top. "To Holly, From Santa," she reads. She grabs the next one and reads, "To Jessica, From Santa," and the next, her voice increasing an octave as she goes, "To Jessica from Mrs. Claus," then another, "To Holly, From Jack," and another "To Jessica, From Jack."

"He must've done all of this," I murmur, shaking my head as my heart begins pounding erratically against my ribcage. "I can't believe it."

"You think Jack did this?" she asks, arching her eyebrows.

I nod, feeling light-headed, and murmur, "He must've."

"When? How?"

"I...I don't know," I admit, puzzled. "I never gave him a key," I murmur, shaking my head.

"Jess, what if," she begins, a smile tugging at her lips.

My eyes snap to hers, and I plead desperately in warning, "Holly."

She steps closer to me with a red and green wrapped present still in her hand. "But like I said before, what if it's all true, Jess?" she repeats, staring at me with wide eyes. "You promised you would try to keep an open mind about all of this. I mean look at this," she mumbles in awe, gesturing behind her, "I believe he's telling the truth," she confesses, biting her bottom lip. Her eyes fill with hope and joy, clenching my heart.

I squeeze my eyes shut tightly and take a deep breath to calm my nerves before looking back at Holly. "I don't understand," I whimper as my eyes well with tears.

She shakes her head. "You don't have to understand. You just have to believe in him. Why don't you open this and see what's inside?" she proposes, holding the box out for me. I stare at the beautifully wrapped box, momentarily frozen. "Please," she begs.

Sighing, I rasp, "Okay," not sure what else to do. Cautiously, I lift my shaky hands toward the box and sit down on the couch, curling my feet underneath me.

"Open it," she encourages me impatiently.

Glancing briefly at Holly, I take one more deep breath before I tear into the paper, dropping it to the ground. Then I lift the top off the white box underneath and gasp at the beauty of the rose gold angel wings necklace adorned with two small diamond stones. Carefully, I lift it out of the box and hold it up for Holly to see. "Wow," she whispers, "That's beautiful." I'm not able to do anything except nod in agreement, tears flooding my vision.

I notice a handwritten note underneath and pull it out. Blinking away my tears, I take another deep breath and read. "Dear Jessica, I know this isn't the exact one you saw at the holiday craft fair, but after I saw your eyes light up on that piece, I had this one custom-made at our workshop. I added the two diamonds to represent your mom and dad. I know they are watching over you and Holly, and they are very proud of both of you. This way, you can have them not only in your thoughts but also sitting close to your heart. Love, Jack." My vision blurs as tears stream freely down my face, a small sob breaking free.

Holly rushes to my side and wraps her arms around me in support. "Oh, my goodness. I'm so sorry. Maybe I shouldn't have had you open that. I thought it would make you smile. He usually makes you smile. Are you okay?" She leans back to look into my eyes.

I nod and smile through my tears. "These are happy tears. I promise," I admit, holding the card out for her to see.

Keeping one arm around me in support, she gingerly sits next to me and begins reading. She gasps and then suddenly jumps up, leaping toward the tree. "Where is it?" she asks, looking frantically all around.

I wipe my tears away and attempt to clear my thoughts, focusing back on Holly. "Where is what?" I prod, my eyebrows drawn in confusion.

"The present for me. The P.S. said he left something a little different for me," she explains. "Didn't you read it?"

I shake my head and try to clear my tears away. "I guess I didn't see it," I murmur, glancing back down at the note, and seeing his P.S. on the bottom.

"I think this is it," she screeches, grabbing a medium-sized box and tearing into the paper. As I watch her, I clasp the necklace around my neck and briefly close my eyes. My chest tightens, feeling as if our parents are here with us, bringing a smile to my face. He couldn't have given me a more perfect gift. I take a deep breath and exhale slowly before I open them and return my gaze to Holly.

She lowers herself to the ground, folding her legs underneath herself as she sets the box on the ground. Then she lifts the lid off the box, her eyes widening in surprise. She carefully puts her hands inside the box and slowly pulls something out in various shades of brown.

"What is it?" I ask curiously.

She spins toward me with a small smile and tears in her eyes as she holds up what appears to be a wooden box. "It's a hand-carved box with the same angel wings and stones on the top," she explains, tilting it toward me. She slowly tilts the lid up and pulls out a card. She grins. "He says it's for my special keepsakes." I watch as she sucks in a quick breath and swallows hard, her emotions getting the best of her. She lifts her eyes to mine and whispers, "It's perfect."

"Good." I smile at her, my heart aching for Jack. I can't help but wish he were here sharing this moment with us. The amount of thought he put into gifts for me and Holly warms me from the inside out.

"Let's open more presents," she proposes. Scanning the colorful boxes, she reaches for one and hands it to me. "This is from Mrs. Claus."

I take the gift from her and watch as she grabs another one for herself. "Thank you," I tell her appreciatively, loving her excitement.

I open Carol's gift to find a variety of new baking tools I had on my wish list, while Holly opens a book and a movie, followed by a makeup palette. She opens the sweater from me, her face lighting up. "This is beautiful, Jess, and so soft. I love it! Thank you! Now open mine," she urges, grinning from ear to ear as she hands me a gift.

I rip into the paper, opening the flat, rectangular box. My eyes widen as I look down at a small, square, sterling silver frame with a snowflake on each corner and a light blue snowflake ribbon laced through the top with a picture from our last family Christmas inside. "Holly," I rasp, my voice full of emotion.

She murmurs softly, "I loved Jack's idea of restarting our Christmas tradition, and I thought mom and dad should be a part of it." She pauses, shrugging. "It's another way for them to be with us every Christmas."

I stand, swiftly wrapping Holly up in a hug and squeezing her tight. "This was a wonderful idea. Thank you, Holly!"

She blushes. "You're welcome."

"Let's put it on the tree," I urge, standing. We walk over to the tree together and hang it toward the top, where it will easily be seen as we walk past. I put my arm around my sister as we both stand, admiring the picture. "It's perfect, Holly."

"I think so too." She sighs and breaks away from me. "Let's open more presents!"

I laugh, wiping away a tear as we sit down and continue opening the rest of the presents. "It's your turn."

When we're finally done, Holly stands, stretching her arms above her head. "I'm so hungry!" she declares. "What are we having for breakfast anyway?"

I laugh and nod in agreement. "I'm hungry too. I have some pistachio bread to start with, and I can make an omelet for us if that sounds good."

"Yum, that sounds perfect! I love your pistachio bread," she proclaims as she bounds toward the kitchen.

I stand and stretch before turning to follow her into the kitchen, but a knock on the front door causes me to quickly change direction. I glance down at myself in my candy cane pajama pants and the red t-shirt with white lace trim and pull my robe a little tighter. Then, I quickly peek through the window to see who it is, hoping whoever is there doesn't see me looking.

My breath hitches at the sight of Jack standing on my front porch. His hands are stuffed into his black coat pockets while he appears to be bouncing nervously back and forth on his toes, causing my heart to skip a beat and my stomach to instantly twist into knots. I fall back on my heels, take a deep breath, and gather my courage. Then, reaching up, I quickly run my hand over my hair, hoping to smooth it out before I pull the door open and look into his blue eyes with a shy smile and my heart pounding against my ribcage. "Merry Christmas, Jack! What are you doing here?"

"Merry Christmas, Jessica," he grins cautiously.

CHAPTER 24
Jessica

"Merry Christmas, Jessica," he grins cautiously. "I hope it's okay that I just stopped by this morning. I know I didn't call..."

I step back and pull the door open with me, waving him inside. "I'm still in my pajamas, but you can come in. It's cold out there."

He smiles appreciatively. "Thank you." He steps into the house, and I close the door behind him. I stare at him for a moment, shocked but thrilled that he's here on Christmas. He remains quiet, assessing me as well. When he doesn't speak up, I step toward the kitchen. "Holly and I just finished opening presents, and we were just about to have some breakfast. Would you like to eat with us?"

He takes a step toward me to stop me from going anywhere, lightly placing his hand on my forearm. "Jess," he prods.

I gasp at his warm touch, sending a shock right through me. Gulping, I clear my throat before I prompt, "Yes, Jack?"

"I have something for you."

"I already opened your present," I inform him, a smile curving my lips. I lift my hand and gently touch the wings around my neck. "Thank you so much, Jack. It's perfect."

He smiles, admiring the necklace. "It looks beautiful on you."

My face heats, and I whisper, "Thank you."

"I'm glad you like it, but that's not what I meant. I have something else I want to give you," he adds sheepishly.

My eyes widen, and I shake my head in disbelief. "You didn't have to do that. This is already so much, and it means the world to me," I tell him honestly.

He grins, shrugging. "I didn't have to, but there's nothing that's too much for you."

My body heats from head to toe while butterflies go wild in my stomach as I process his words. "Thanks," I mumble awkwardly, not sure what else to say.

He takes a shaky breath, and I realize whatever it is, he's just as nervous as I am right now. I open my mouth to say something to calm him down but quickly snap it shut when I realize I'm still not sure what to say.

Holly's footsteps begin to approach as she calls, "Jess, I'm going to eat all of this without you if you don't get in here soon!" She gasps, freezing as she steps into the room and spots Jack, "Merry Christmas, Jack!" she exclaims and rushes over to him, throwing her arms around him and hugging him tightly. "Thank you so much for the memory box! I love it!"

He laughs as he wraps his arms around her, returning her gesture. "Merry Christmas, Holly. What are you eating without us?" he asks curiously, arching his eyebrows.

"Jess made Pistachio bread," she announces, grinning as she steps back. "It's green Christmas bread, and it's sooo good!" she raves. "Do you want some?"

He looks over at me with wide eyes and his lips curving up in a hopeful smile, making me laugh. I already know I want him to stay and repeat, "Would you like some?"

He chuckles, shrugging. "Do you really have to ask? Of course, I do!" We all step toward the kitchen when he pauses again and repeats, "Actually, I have something for Jess first. Could we have a minute?" he asks, looking at Holly.

Holly grins, nodding as she teases him, "Hopefully, you'll get to try some of the bread before I eat it all! I'll see you guys in a few minutes." She giggles as she walks away.

He pinches his lips tightly together and stares at the ground. I bite my lip anxiously before I finally ask, "Jack? Is everything okay? You're making me nervous."

He looks up at me and apologizes, "Yes, I'm sorry, Jess. Everything is fine. I guess I'm just a little nervous about giving this to you," he admits shrugging.

"Oh," I mumble, my eyes widening in surprise. "You shouldn't worry about that. I'll love anything you give me," I admit, instantly blushing.

A crooked smile plays on his lips, making my heart leap. He takes a step toward me and reaches for my hands, holding them in his. Tingles shoot up my arms, spreading the warmth of his touch throughout my body. He holds my gaze as he asks, "What's the most important thing in the world to you?"

"Holly, of course," I blurt without even thinking.

He grins, nodding. "Of course, and she should be."

My eyebrows draw together in confusion, and I ask, "Why?"

"I want to give you something that will help with her."

"I don't understand," I declare, shaking my head.

He nods. "I know. I promise I'm trying. I guess my nerves are taking over my communication skills," he jokes. I giggle in response. He takes a deep breath and asks me another question, "Did you know Betty is retiring?"

"My boss, Betty? She is?" I prod, and he nods in confirmation. "I guess I knew she would in the next few years, but she always planned on handing the bakery down within her family," I tell him, my stomach suddenly churning with my building anxiety.

"Well, plans changed." He smiles.

My eyes widen, and I question with a shaky voice, "What do you mean, plans changed?"

"Well, she's retiring and wants the business to go to you."

I gasp, floored by the news. "What?"

"Her family is willing to continue helping out there, and she would like to keep a six percent stake in the business, but they don't want it. They all have different dreams they want to pursue that don't include owning a bakery. Betty wants to sell it to you," he adds, carefully watching me for my reaction.

My mouth drops open, and my heart squeezes, filling with hope when suddenly I lose my breath as reality hits me in the face like an icy wind. I shake my head. "I can't afford to buy it yet. I don't have that kind of money. I've been saving, but with all my expenses with the house and Holly," I ramble, panic-stricken.

He squeezes my hands, attempting to soothe me, still smiling. "Jess, slow down. You just need investors, or maybe just one investor."

I continue to shake my head, feeling my chest tighten, constricting my breath. "I don't know anyone who would be able to invest in a bakery for me!"

"Jess," he says my name to get my attention, "What about me?"

I freeze, and my heart stops. I stare into his sparkling blue eyes and gasp, "What?"

"I want to invest in the bakery for you. I honestly can't think of anything I could want more," he proclaims. Then, he smirks and squeezes my hands again, "Well, that's not true. I can think of one thing I want more than anything."

I feel myself blush deeply, my heart skipping a beat. I open my mouth, but the only word I can get out is his name, "Jack."

He chuckles softly and insists, "I mean it, Jess. I want to do this. If you own the bakery, you'll have more money coming in to help with everything. You could hire people to make your recipes and spend more time with Holly," he pauses and adds, "and hopefully me." I huff a laugh but remain quiet, staring at him. "Besides, I think I need to do this. You have the best desserts I've ever tasted. Honestly, your desserts are a perfect fit with our family business," he reminds me. "I'd be a fool not to invest in you. Please let me," he begs desperately.

I stand quietly in shock for a moment before I gulp down the lump in my throat and squeeze his hands in return. I mumble almost inaudibly, "It's like you're really Santa Claus."

The admission causes him to flinch, making me wince. He straightens his shoulders, forcing a smile as he waits for my answer.

I sigh, feeling both relieved and anxious, not knowing what's in store for Holly and me, or Jack and me for that matter.

"If you really mean it," I mumble, and he nods emphatically, making me laugh, "then I guess I should say thank you, partner."

He laughs and pulls me toward him, wrapping me up in his arms. He picks me up and spins me around, making me squeal in surprise and delight. "Wonderful!" he exclaims as he returns me to my feet but keeps me close.

"Thank you," I whisper again.

He grins and prompts, "Let me bring you home to meet my family." My eyes widen, not expecting his request. I think he can see the hesitancy in my face, even though I promised Holly I would give him a chance without judgment, and that's what I want too. But wanting something doesn't make it easy. "Please, Jess, all I'm asking is for you to come home to meet my family. I know you already met my mom, but my dad is on vacation for a while after today and will have some free time."

A hard rap at the door gives me the reprieve I need to put off answering his question for a little longer, although my heart is pulling me directly in his path. I pull my hands away, holding up a finger, and spin around. Reaching for the handle, I pull the door open without even looking to see who's behind it. I can't do anything but smile at the tall man with white hair, a white beard, and sparkling blue eyes dressed in a beautiful red velvet Santa suit adorned with white fur. "Hi. Merry Christmas. May I help you?"

"Hi, Jessica," he begins, my eyes widening in surprise.

"Dad?" Jack asks, stepping up behind me. "What are you doing here?"

My eyes widen further, and I step back out of the way to watch the two men. "Nicky, I wasn't sure you'd be here," he states.

"Nicky?" I ask under my breath.

"Remember, my first name is Nicholas. My dad always calls me Nicky, but he's the only one," Jack explains. Then, he returns his focus to his dad and repeats, "Dad, what are you doing here?"

He looks at me and smiles. "I was on my way home from work, and I couldn't wait another minute to meet Jessica, all grown-up."

He holds his hand out, and I take it as I slowly process his words. "What?" I probe, feeling more and more confused by the minute.

He chuckles. "I just wanted to meet the beautiful woman who has stolen my son's heart."

My heart jumps up to my throat and my skin heats. I shake his hand and force the words from my lips. "It's nice to meet you too."

"Dad, you look exhausted. You should be home getting some sleep after last night. How did you get here?" Jack asks, glancing behind him.

"Dasher brought me as soon as we dropped the sleigh and the others." He shrugs. "He's our fastest reindeer and although we're both exhausted, he was just as determined as me. Honestly, I'll probably sleep through the next two days, but I didn't want to wait any longer to come. I can't stay long, though."

My eyes widen in shock. I feel a little bit dizzy attempting to process his words. Dasher? Reindeer?

"Easy there," Jack murmurs, grasping my arms and steadying me. "Are you okay?" he prompts, assessing me, his eyebrows drawn down in concern.

I open my mouth to answer, but no words come out, so I quickly snap it shut. Instead, I nod, hoping he understands. "Are you guys ever coming?" Holly asks, sounding exasperated as she strides into the room, followed instantly by her own gasp.

Jack turns toward Holly with a broad smile. "Holly, this is my dad," he introduces them.

"Santa?" she questions wide-eyed.

Jack and his dad both nod in confirmation, eliciting a loud squeal from Holly in response. "I knew it was true!" She throws her arms around me from the back in excitement, knocking the wind out of me. "I told Jess to give you a chance," she mumbles into my back.

I glance back and forth between the two men, and there's no doubt in my mind that they're related. Plus, Jack's dad really does look so much like the ornaments on my Christmas tree. How would that even be possible unless it were true? Holly's arms loosen from around me, and she stands next to me, grinning from ear to ear.

"Thank you for the cookies, Jessica," Jack's dad states with a nod. "I look forward to your cookies every year," he admits, rubbing his stomach in appreciation.

"What?" I ask my eyebrows drawn down in confusion.

"The chocolate cookie with the filling and the candy cane crunched topping was one of my favorites. Nicky is right; you're an excellent baker."

My eyes widen, and I look at Holly, demanding, "Did you leave cookies out for Santa last night?"

She nods and smiles sheepishly. "I left one of those and the candy cane twist sugar cookies, she admits with only a nonchalant shrug.

He winks and proclaims, "Those were good too, but the other one was new, if I'm not mistaken."

"Did Jack tell you?" I question.

He shakes his head. "I remember. I haven't tasted one of your new recipes in quite a while. In fact, it's probably been about five or six years since you've had a new recipe."

"Yes," I whisper, my heart flip-flopping in my chest. This is the first year since my parents died, and I was ready and inspired to finally try something new. I never told Jack that.

"I know why Jack would want you to have our new North Pole kitchen," he admits.

"Dad," Jack admonishes. His dad's gaze flickers to him before coming back to me. "I didn't tell her about that yet. We just talked about the bakery here."

"What are all of you talking about?" Holly asks, looking between Jack and me.

Heaving a sigh, I quickly explain what I know. "Betty is retiring, and her family doesn't want to run the bakery, so she wants to sell it to me. Jack wants to invest in the bakery."

"And you," he adds, making me smile.

"And me," I grin happily, my cheeks turning pink. "For us, and it's a good investment with their family business," I add, my stomach twisting at the reminder.

"That's fantastic!" Holly exclaims. "That's a dream come true!"

I nod and turn back toward Jack. "What is he talking about though, Jack? The North Pole kitchen?"

He cocks his head to the side and rubs the back of his neck nervously. "Well, I was kinda' hoping to ease you into that one."

I arch my eyebrow and sarcastically announce, "It's a little too late for that."

He sighs and concedes, dropping his hand to his side. "I guess you're right." He takes a deep breath and continues, "At home, we have two huge professional kitchens. One is geared toward meals, and the other is for baking, desserts, and snacks. My mom runs the bakery kitchen, and she's good at it, but she has things she enjoys more. Anyway, I thought you might want to take over in there someday."

Stunned, I open my mouth to respond. "Jack."

He rushes on, stopping me. "I don't mean anytime soon, that's why I made a deal with Betty, as long as you were in agreement," he adds, sheepishly. "I know you want to be here for a while because of Holly, and that's where I want to be too, with you, wherever you are. It's not like I'll be leaving and taking over the family business soon, so we have plenty of time. Holly will hopefully be done with college by the time I really take over, and when that happens, I want you with me, Jess. Right now, I'm just trying to do what's right for you and Holly," he rambles.

I step toward him with tears in my eyes and my heart full as I press my finger to his lips. He freezes, quickly assessing my expression. With so many thoughts running through my head, I'm overwhelmed, but I don't want him to have any more doubts. Taking a deep breath, I whisper, "Thank you, Jack."

He grins and exhales slowly, his shoulders sagging in relief as I let my finger fall slowly to my side. His dad clears his throat and stares at me as he states, "Well, I have to go before I'm too tired to even sit on a reindeer, but I will hopefully see all three of you soon."

"Can we go, Jess?" Holly prompts, making all of us chuckle as I shake my head. She huffs, crosses her arms over her chest, and sarcastically grumbles, "Maybe I will eat all the bread."

"Don't you want to stay on the Nice list?" Santa teases.

Her mouth drops open, and her eyes widen as she blushes a deep shade of red. "I'm so sorry, I didn't say thank you for my presents!" she announces, seemingly out of the blue. "I was kidding about the bread, though," she adds, her lips twitching upward.

My head falls back as I laugh, and Santa turns toward the door, chuckling lightly. "Merry Christmas, everyone!" he calls over his shoulder before he shuts the door behind him.

"Merry Christmas," I murmur under my breath.

I turn around and stare with awe into Jack's eyes. "I'll see you in the kitchen," Holly murmurs as she wanders away again.

"Do you believe me now?" he prods, his eyes full of hope.

I take a deep breath, admitting, "I didn't need Holly telling me to believe in you. My heart knew it all along. I do believe in you, Jack. It's Christmas itself that I've had trouble truly believing in again, but because of you, I do," I confess, looking into his eyes, hoping he sees the truth in mine.

He smiles wide, making my heart race and tingles prickle my skin. "Do you know how to tell if you're *my* Mrs. Claus?" he playfully prompts.

Instead of answering him, I place my hands on his shoulders and slide them behind his neck. Gathering my courage, I push up on my tiptoes and reiterate, "Thank you, Jack," before I press my lips to his, taking both of our breaths away.

He cradles my face in his hands and pulls away breathlessly. "Exactly like that. I love you, Jessica," he proclaims before his lips come crashing back down on mine, my whole body on fire from everything I feel for this man.

I fall back on my heels, overwhelmed with information and love, desperate to tell him how I feel. "I love you too, Jack." He smiles wide, causing my stomach to twist.

"I'm still waiting!" Holly calls impatiently from the kitchen.

We laugh, and he brushes his lips across mine one more time as he smiles down at me. Then, he slides his hand down into mine, giving it a light squeeze, sending chills down my spine. "We're coming Holly," he calls toward the kitchen. We turn our bodies, but I struggle to take my eyes away from his as we walk hand in hand toward the kitchen for our first Christmas breakfast together.

CHAPTER 25
Jack

Three months later...

I lean against the door frame in dark blue jeans and an evergreen long-sleeved shirt smiling as I watch Jessica work while Holly rambles animatedly to her and Allie about something she just saw in the workshop. Jessica has her hair pulled back in a high ponytail, a few strands falling out around her face, taking my breath away with her beauty. A small smile plays on her lips as she listens to her sister while stirring cookie dough in a large red mixing bowl.

The first time I brought her into our commercial baking kitchen, her eyes widened to the size of saucers. She wanted to try out the ovens and stove almost immediately, her excitement palpable, making me laugh, but I love every second of it. I could stand here and watch her all day. She looks right at home in here in her black leggings and ivory turtleneck sweater with a red and green striped Christmas apron draped over the top. I watch as she bounces around the room as if she's floating from one thing to the next with nothing but pure happiness, warming my heart. To me, it feels as if she's finally where she was always meant to be. I can't imagine life without her. I never want to let her go.

Taking a deep breath, I step further into the kitchen, all eyes instantly turning to me. "Hey, Holly. I'm so happy you're here! I hope it was okay we had to send Allie to come pick you up?"

"Of course. Thanks for sending her. She's the best!"

"Thanks," Allie replies, preening slightly. "I like hanging out with you too."

"And thank you, Allie," I add. She nods, giving me a smile. Turning to Holly, I proclaim, "I'm really glad you decided to spend your Spring Break here with us. Most kids would rather go somewhere warm," I tease, arching my eyebrows.

She smirks, rolling her eyes dramatically. "That's just because they're not lucky enough to have a sister who's dating Santa's son. Who wouldn't want to spend a week at the North Pole? I can't believe this is our life. You need to keep this man." She nods toward her sister as her lips twitch in amusement.

I chuckle softly, my heart squeezing, knowing Holly supports us being together. "Well, now that you're here, I have that surprise I want to give your sister."

Holly grins conspiratorially. "Oh! Sounds good."

"Surprise? What surprise?" Jessica questions, her eyebrows drawn down in puzzlement as she looks from me to her sister before settling her gaze back on me.

Holding my hand out for her, I give her a crooked smile and lightheartedly suggest, "Why don't you come with me and find out?"

Giving her sister one more side glance, with Holly barely containing her excitement, she shakes her head and looks back at me. She peers down at my hand and grins. Without another question, she sets her spatula down, leaving it in the bowl, and reaches behind her, untying her apron before lifting it over her head and hanging it on a hook next to the door, along with a few others. Then she steps toward me, placing her hand in mine with trust in her heart. "Okay, let's go."

Smiling brightly, I clasp her hand tightly as my chest constricts with nerves and hopeful anticipation. It feels as if my heart is overflowing with love for her, and I'm barely able to contain it as we walk toward the workshop near the kitchen with Holly and Allie trailing behind us, whispering back and forth.

We step into the front of the workshop, the main room a wide-open space with several work benches and stools, many elves working on something different, almost like a creative classroom, to come up with new ideas for the next Christmas. Doors spaced evenly throughout almost the entire perimeter lead to specialized rooms with a similar setup, depending on the project being worked on the inside, each labeled on the front of the door with a white plaque and red writing. Elves dressed in colorful outfits, each showing their personality with a touch of Christmas red and green, notice us almost instantly, elbowing one another as we walk past.

As we reach one of the greenhouse doors, I halt in front of it, realizing many of the elves are nonchalantly attempting to follow behind us, making it difficult to hide my amusement. Jessica glances behind us, startling as everyone quickly averts their gaze. She chuckles uncomfortably. "What's going on? Why is everyone following us?"

I laugh and shake my head. "A lot of them helped me build something in here, and I want to share it with you, but I thought I should wait until Holly arrived here. I'm sure they just want to see what you think of it, and like me, they're getting impatient."

"Hmm," she mumbles, not giving away if she believes me or not. I did tell her the truth, just not all of it. She'll find out everything in a few minutes.

"Come on," I urge, giving her hand a light tug. "Let's go inside." I reach for the door handle and push the door open. I step inside before her, not wanting to miss a single moment of her reaction as she takes it all in.

In front of us, several pine trees sit surrounding a massive Gingerbread house, the size of a child's playhouse, made to look like a bakery with a large sign above the doorway labeled Jessica's Christmas Treats. Trays of baked goods can be seen through the windows, the entire room smelling of gingerbread and pine. A peppermint cobblestone walkway leads to the front door, with a bench halfway up to sit and enjoy the view. It appears as if it's made of various pretzel shapes, large twists for the back, small twists for the handrail on the sides, thick rods for the bottom, and nuggets to hold it off the ground. A snowman family that looks as if it's made of marshmallows sits off to the side with a few Christmas trees looking as if they are made of an upside down ice cream cone, frosting, and sprinkles for the lights.

"Wow, Jack, this is absolutely incredible. Is it made of real gingerbread, frosting, and candy?" she rambles.

I chuckle, enjoying the look in her bright green eyes. "I wish! It wouldn't last very long around here if it were."

"True," she grins, giving me a look. "But how does it smell like it, then?"

"Remember the ornament I got you for Christmas?"

She nods. "Of course."

"It gave me the idea to have the scent piped in."

Around every window and along the roof line, trim made to look like white ribbon frosting decorates the edges, enhanced with red and green decorations, including a wreath on the front door with a thick red ribbon. "Unbelievable, the frosting looks so real," she mumbles under her breath. A small garden sits on both sides of the walkway with replicas of the Amaryllis flower flourishing. "And the flowers...it's our flower."

I grin, my heart skipping a beat at the memory. "We have a few talented builders that were able to help me out to get it all just how I imagined."

"It's unbelievable, Jack. Can I walk on the path?"

"Go ahead," I prompt, gesturing with my free hand.

She giggles as she drops my hand and moves closer, stepping onto the walkway and making her way toward the bench with me following right behind. As she reaches the bench, she spins around with a bright smile on her face just as I drop down to one knee holding out a small red ring box. She gasps, her hands flying to her mouth. "Jack!"

As I gulp down the lump in my throat, I flip the box open and grin up at the woman who holds my heart in her hands. Staring into her eyes, I open my heart and share with her everything I'm feeling, "Jessica, the first day I met you, I walked away regretting more than anything that I didn't even know your name, but at least I knew where to find you. Even that day, I felt drawn to you. You gave me the smile and encouragement I needed, along with one of your tasty treats," I smirk, and she giggles in response.

"Then the next day, when you stood in front of me with an Amaryllis in your hand, I was more than grateful for my luck, but as I got to know you, that's when I knew I didn't want to live my life without you by my side. You're beautiful on the inside and out, lighting up a room the moment you enter. You're full of Christmas spirit even when it's not easy. You're strong, brave, and resilient, giving me some of your strength when I need it most. The way you care for Holly, the type of bond I see between the two of you, as well as the compassion you show for others show me who you truly are, only making me want to be around you more. You make me laugh, bring me joy and enhance my life with so much love, hope, and faith that I know I can do anything when we're together, even become the legacy I was born into."

Ignoring the excited chatter behind me, I take a deep breath and continue, Jessica, holding all my attention. "I believe with everything inside me, we were meant to go down this path side by side. I want you to be my partner in love and life. I love you, Jessica, with all of me, my heart, my soul, and my Christmas spirit. Will you make me the happiest man in the world and become my Mrs. Claus? Jessica, will you marry me?"

She swiftly wipes away her tears as she nods her head emphatically, gasping, "Yes! Yes! Yes!" Cheers erupt around us as more elves begin sneaking inside, joining the celebration.

My heart leaps as I stand, exhaling in relief. I swiftly wrap her up in my arms and spin her around, reveling in the sound of her joyous laughter. As I carefully set her back on her feet, I release her just enough to bring her left hand between us. Quickly, I slip the ring out of the box, lifting it toward her hand and sliding it on her finger. "I better get this on before you change your mind," I tease, my smile as bright as my heart. "You're stuck with me now."

She giggles. "There's nowhere else I'd rather be." We stand in each other's arms, admiring the round cut diamond with a small ruby and emerald on each side, representing all the colors of Christmas and our family. "This is absolutely gorgeous, Jack."

"Fitting," I mumble.

She blushes a beautiful shade of red, giving me goosebumps. "Thank you."

Lifting my hand to her face, I gently tilt her chin up, bringing her gaze to mine. "I love you, Jessica," I proclaim with my heart full.

"I love you too, Jack." Before she has a chance to say anymore, I press my lips to hers, sealing our love and promise with a sweet kiss. The cheers behind us quickly fade into the background as I focus on the future, Mrs. Claus.

"Yes! We have a wedding to plan," I hear Allie exclaim.

"This is going to be so much fun!" Holly chimes in. "Wait, my sister is going to be Mrs. Claus! So, what will that make me?"

We laugh, both of us breaking our kiss. We look into each other's eyes, sparkling with pure happiness, magic, and excitement, anticipating what our future will hold, but knowing it doesn't matter as long as we are in it together.

The End...

ACKNOWLEDGMENTS

I have so many people I would like to thank for getting this book out there. Of course my family always comes first. Thank you to my mom and dad for always encouraging me to do what I love. I wouldn't be where I am if it wasn't for you. Dad I miss you every day and I hope you're enjoying my books from above. Thank you to my sister who is always supportive. I'm grateful you are my sister. Thank you to my husband, son and daughter. I'm thankful for your love and patience even when I get lost in my own world. I love all of you with all my heart.

One of the first things I think about with this book is the day Candy Cain had read something I wrote and asked me where to begin with this style. That question gave life to Dating Santa's Son. Thank you for asking, and I'm always going to be grateful for all the stories we worked on together; yours, mine and ours. I enjoyed it every single time, my friend.

Thank you to Kenney Myers, the man of many hats, for bringing me along with you and your wonderful wife, Jolene on this journey. I've enjoyed working with you in several capacities over the years and I'm grateful to have you as a friend.

Thank you to Pen It Publications and the incredible team. I've truly enjoyed going through this process here. Thank you Dina for all your help. Ashlee, thank you for your editing expertise, and enhancing my work by doing yours. Donna, thank you for your beautiful cover design. You helped portray the look of the story perfectly. Jmee, thank you so much for formatting the book and helping to get it out there. I'm truly grateful for all of you and for everything you have done for me and my book! And thank you to Korey for your illustrating expertise.

Thank you to all my beta and ARC readers. I'm so grateful for every single one of you! I hope you enjoyed reading Dating Santa's Son. I value all of you and all my readers. And no matter what time of year it is, Merry Christmas!

ABOUT THE AUTHOR

Nicole Mullaney has always had a passion for reading and writing, especially romance and sweet romance stories around the holidays are a great way to relax and get lost in a story. She grew up in Wisconsin with her sister, mom and dad. Reading romance books and watching romance movies with her dad was always something they enjoyed together.

After college she lived in Florida working for "The Happiest Place on Earth" for a few years before moving to New York. She now lives on Long Island in NY with her husband, two kids and two large dogs. Nicole spends her free time reading or hanging out with friends and family and believes the holidays can be enjoyed all year.

She started working with the small and big screen when she met writer/director Candy Cain through her daughter's acting. Nicole wrote the first draft of Dating Santa's Son and soon, she began collaborating with Candy Cain on film/book projects, Ivy & Mistletoe their first project together in this capacity.

Now, she freelances as a script advisor, script supervisor and sometimes writer with TV and film. She enjoys being able to watch the stories come to life in different ways and be a part of it from the beginning whether it's a commercial, a show, or full-length film. After so much time passed, she thought it was time to go back to the first Christmas romance she wrote and share it with the world.

CONNECT WITH THE AUTHOR

For more Sweet Contemporary Romance, Read more by Nicole Mullaney (or Ethan Dulane).

Connect with Nicole here:
Author Website
https://www.nicolemullaneyauthor.com/
On Social as @nicolemullaney or @nicolemullaneyauthor

For Adult Contemporary Romance, Read books by Nikki A Lamers.
Connect with her here:
https://linktr.ee/NikkiALamersauthor

Milton Keynes UK
Ingram Content Group UK Ltd.
UKHW020213191223
434575UK00010B/140